HARBOUR NO SECRETS

A Welsh murder mystery with a huge twist

CHERYL REES-PRICE

THE BOOK FOLKS

Published by The Book Folks

London, 2023

ISBN 978-1-80462-110-3

www.thebookfolks.com

Harbour No Secrets is the eighth title in a bestselling series of standalone mysteries set in the heart of Wales.

Prologue

The intruder closed the door so gently it barely made a sound. With a gloved hand they let go of the handle and remained still. Listening. There was always a chance the occupant would awake. The only sound came from the steady humming of the fridge and their own breathing. They moved across the kitchen and set down a backpack. Inch by inch they opened the zipper. They had done this so many times they had perfected the art of silent movement.

First out was a bunch of flowers. Red and white roses with a ribbon binding the stems. They put them on the table and added a card. A smile played on their lips. They wished they could see the recipient open it, watch the horror on their face as they read the words. A gloved finger stroked the rose petals before taking out the next items. They opened the fridge and placed the flowers on the rack, rearranged the food. Next came the final touch. This was the tricky bit. They couldn't risk leaving any traces on themselves. They kept their hand steady as they emptied the vial. Gleeful eyes watched as the grains sprinkled onto the food and bounced before landing on the clean white bottom of the fridge.

They had done it again. Each time was easier. They took a moment to calm their emotions. Everything had to be done slowly, great care taken not to make a mistake. The next act would be a step further than they had dared to go before. It would be a big risk but it was worth it, they thought. They took the remaining vials from the backpack and grabbed the last items.

Using a pencil torch, they made their way upstairs. On the landing a floorboard creaked making their stomach flip. They turned the torch off and waited in the darkness. Holding their breath. Expecting a light to come on in the bedroom. Nothing happened. Just the bathroom to do, they thought. They crept forwards and pushed the door open just enough to slide through. The shower cubicle opened easily with a small pop. They knelt and laid out three items over the drain, then tipped the vial.

Back on the landing, they were about to take a step onto the stairs when they paused. The urge was too strong. Just one peak. The bedroom door was ajar. It was as though they were meant to go in. The door moved silently when pushed. They stepped inside. There she was, sleeping peacefully. They watched the gentle rise and fall of her chest. Her lips were parted and one hand lay next to her head. There was a faint scent of perfume in the air. They felt anger ball their stomach into a tight fist. They could do it now. It would be easy. It was so tempting it took all their willpower not to spring forward. They crouched down and crawled to the side of the bed. They had one vial left in their pocket. It would be enough. When she placed her bare feet on the floor, she'd feel the gritty substance against her skin. She'd probably brush it off without giving it a thought. Then realisation would dawn. They smiled, satisfied with this thought. They crawled to the bottom of the bed and stood up. Watching. She stirred in her sleep. Turned over. Then settled. They wondered what she was dreaming about. It didn't matter. Tomorrow she would wake up and the nightmare would begin.

Chapter One

Christie felt a fizzle of excitement spread through her body as she looked around her sitting room. So far everything had gone to plan. She switched on the fairy lights that surrounded the photo booth. All the props were in a box, ready to make a lasting memory of the night. She adjusted the large golden balloons shaped to make the number twenty-five. Now they hovered above the centre of the table. She nodded to herself then moved in front of the full-length mirror near the door.

The burgundy dress I've chosen is perfect, she thought as she looked at herself. It covered her arms and flowed over her body ending just below the knees. It hid her figure well. She was ready. Now all she had to do was wait.

The two women were the first to arrive. Iona, looking flawless, trailed a waft of perfume. Sammy with bouncing corkscrew curls gave a warm smile.

'It looks great,' Sammy said. She put her gift on the table. 'Alys is going to love it.'

'I hope so,' Christie said. 'She doesn't like a fuss.'

'I wouldn't call this a fuss,' Iona said. 'When it's my turn we are having the full works. I was thinking we should all go to Amsterdam or Paris. Better still, New York.'

Sammy laughed. 'I don't think my budget will stretch that far.'

'You've got a couple of months to save up,' Iona said. She turned to Christie. 'You up for it?'

Christie could think of nothing worse than being stuck with Iona for a few days. 'Maybe.' She watched Sammy move across the room and start digging through the props.

'This is so cool,' Sammy said. She wrapped a feather boa around her neck.

'It was my idea,' Iona said.

Christie was tempted to say that Iona had a lot of ideas for the party but hadn't contributed to the cost. Instead, she smiled and kept her thoughts to herself.

'Let's take some photos,' Sammy said.

Iona quickly moved in front of the mirror to check her reflection. She smoothed down her slinky black dress and tossed her chestnut hair which cascaded down her back in soft curls.

'You look gorgeous,' Christie said.

Iona touched her hair. 'I got the extensions done yesterday. I love them. My hairdresser is brilliant. Maybe you should go. I'm sure they could do something with your hair.'

'Iona!' Sammy scolded.

'What? I'm just saying.'

'I'll get the drinks,' Christie said. She walked into the kitchen and grabbed a bottle of wine from the fridge. Iona can be a bitch sometimes, she thought. I won't let her ruin the evening with her snarky comments. She took a deep breath and carried the wine and two glasses into the sitting room. By the time she poured the drinks the other two were taking photos.

'Come on,' Sammy said.

Christie joined them and put a hat on her head before posing. There was a lot of shuffling and giggling as they changed accessories before the flash went off.

When they had gone through the props, Iona grabbed a glass of wine from the table and plonked down on the sofa. She patted the pillows next to her. 'Who's sleeping here?'

'You,' Christie said. 'I've put a blow-up mattress in the small room for Rhodri and Sammy. Macsen and Alys are in the other room.'

'If I'd known I'd be on the sofa I would've had the party at my place,' Iona said.

Sammy laughed. 'You've only got one bedroom.'

'At least I would've had a bed.'

'You can sleep in mine if you want,' Christie said. 'I'll take the sofa. It doesn't bother me.'

'You're such a sweetie,' Sammy said.

The door opened and Rhodri walked in. Despite it being mid-March, he wore only a tight-fitting T-shirt over jeans. His contoured chest was visible beneath the material.

Iona smiled sweetly. 'Hi Rhodri.'

He gave her an upward nod before moving to Sammy. 'All right, babe?' He kissed her.

Christie saw a momentary flash of jealously in Iona's eyes and smiled to herself. She knew Rhodri had no interest in Iona.

'Do you want a beer, Rhodri?' Christie asked.

'Go on then.'

Christie grabbed a beer from the fridge and handed it to Rhodri while Sammy topped up the wine glasses.

'Where's yours?' Rhodri asked.

'I'm driving,' Christie said. 'I'll have a couple later.'

'We can walk there in twenty minutes,' Rhodri said.

'Iona doesn't want to walk,' Christie said.

Rhodri laughed. 'Lazy bitch.'

‘Oi,’ Iona said. ‘It’s dark, cold, and it might rain. You can walk but us girls are going in the car.’

The conversation was interrupted by the arrival of Macsen. His presence instantly filled the room. This was not because of his size, although he was tall and broad. It was the confidence he radiated. He’d been blessed with good looks, quick wit, and people naturally gravitated towards him.

‘You got back all right then, mate,’ Macsen said.

Rhodri looked confused for a moment. ‘Oh yeah, the job. Bloody waste of time. I couldn’t find the place so I was driving around in circles. I gave up.’

‘You and me both,’ Macsen said. ‘You could’ve told me you’d got out.’

Rhodri frowned. ‘Got out? What are you on about?’

‘The ditch.’

‘What ditch?’

‘Are you off your face already?’ Macsen asked.

‘No, this is my first drink.’

Christie moved to the kitchen and grabbed another beer. She could hear the conversation continuing. Macsen was becoming irate and Rhodri just sounded confused. She walked back to the sitting room and handed Macsen a beer.

‘Thanks.’ Macsen pulled the cap off the bottle and took a swig. ‘I’m talking about the message you sent this morning.’

‘I didn’t send you any message,’ Rhodri said. ‘I was in the middle of nowhere this morning. Didn’t even have a signal.’

Macsen took his phone from his pocket and scrolled through his messages. ‘I’m sure it was on Messenger. You said you’d got the car stuck in a ditch and to bring the jeep.’

Rhodri shook his head. ‘I honestly didn’t send any message. I was in Ystrad Fflur.’

‘Yeah, so was I. Looking for you.’

'If you were out looking for Rhodri you could've let me know,' Sammy said. 'I wouldn't have bothered to come up to get the cake.'

'I told you I was bringing the cake,' Macsen said. 'It's in the car.'

'No,' Sammy said. She grabbed her phone. 'You asked me to come to the farm to pick up the cake. I had to get someone to cover for me at work so I could sneak out.' She held out the phone to Macsen.

'I didn't send that message,' Macsen said.

Christie took out her own phone and scrolled through Messenger. 'You were also supposed to be here before ten this morning.' She held out her phone to Macsen.

Macsen read the message. 'I don't believe this.'

'Yeah, and I didn't send the message you can't find on your phone,' Rhodri said. He slipped his arm around Sammy's waist.

The atmosphere crackled with tension.

'Looks like you've been hacked,' Sammy said. 'Happened to me once. They get all your contacts from Facebook. Send out messages to all your friends. Be thankful it wasn't something embarrassing.'

'I didn't get a message,' Iona said.

'That's because you're not on his friends list,' Rhodri said.

They all laughed and the tension evaporated.

Macsen downed his beer. 'I don't see the point of it. It's not like some practical joke everyone has a laugh at.'

'It messed up everyone's day,' Christie said. 'I guess they get a kick out of it.'

'How?' Iona asked. 'It's not like they get to watch.'

'Do you think they got into your email account?' Rhodri asked.

Macsen shrugged. 'It's just the address for the job I went to didn't exist. I haven't been able to contact the client.'

'Better change your password, Macsen,' Sammy said.

Iona got up off the sofa, grabbed the wine bottle and emptied it in her glass. 'What time is Alys getting here?'

'Any minute,' Christie said.

'Are we going to turn off the lights and hide?' Sammy asked.

Iona rolled her eyes. 'It's not a surprise. She knows we're all here.'

'Yeah, but she doesn't know about the decorations,' Sammy said.

'Looks great, Christie,' Macsen said. 'Thanks.'

'OK, let's get this party started,' Rhodri said. He put his hand into his pocket and pulled out a bag of white powder.

'I thought you were stopping that,' Sammy said.

'I said special occasions and this is a celebration,' Rhodri said. He moved to the table and pushed the gifts to one side before tipping the contents on the smooth surface.

Christie saw him take out his bank card so she left the room. She didn't want to watch. She had never tried any drugs and wasn't sure if the others would join in. She didn't want to be the odd one out. It would give Iona a chance to have another dig at her. She waited until she was sure they had finished then joined them again. Macsen put on some music and they all started glugging down their drinks and cheering. Christie was beginning to doubt the drinks would last the night. She wished now she hadn't agreed to drive. She could've done with a drink. Everyone else was in high spirits. Then Macsen started on one of his stories and Christie found herself laughing with the others.

When she next checked the time, she saw nearly an hour had passed. 'We've got to leave or we'll be late for the restaurant.'

'Where's Alys? She should've been here ages ago,' Sammy said.

'Probably still finishing her make-up,' Iona said.

'She's had all day to get ready,' Sammy said. 'She took the day off work.'

'She didn't tell me she wasn't working today,' Macsen said.

'She sent a message to me last night. She said she'd see me here,' Christie said. 'She's never late.'

Macsen took his phone from his pocket. 'I'll give her a call.'

The room fell silent as Macsen made the call. A voicemail message came on over the speaker. Macsen left a message and hung up.

'Maybe she's on her way to the restaurant,' Iona said.

Christie looked at her companions and felt a twinge of annoyance. None of them seemed concerned. In all the time she had known Alys, she had never let anyone down. Macsen, out of them all, should have known better than to carry on drinking as if nothing was amiss.

'Let's go,' Christie said. 'We can all fit into my car. We'll go to Alys' house, check everything is OK. It will only take a few minutes.'

Rhodri called shotgun so Christie was stuck with him in the front. He turned up the music and drank from the bottle he had brought with him. It only took a few moments to reach Alys' house. Christie parked outside and Macsen jumped out.

'Car's not here,' he said. 'All the lights are out.'

'Told you,' Iona said. 'She's gone straight to the restaurant. Probably got one of Macsen's false messages telling her to meet us there.'

'Didn't think of that,' Christie said.

Macsen jumped back into the back seat and Christie pulled away. It didn't take long to drive into Ammanford. The small market town in South Wales was quiet. All the shops were closed and the pavements empty. The only sign of life was a few smokers lurking outside a pub. Christie drove through the square, passing the old Edwardian bank which had been empty for over a decade. The car speakers vibrated and she felt the beat of the music travelling through her body. It felt at odds with the peacefulness of the town. She would be glad to get to the car park.

'You can drop us off outside,' Iona shouted over the music.

Christie pulled over and they all got out leaving her to park and walk to the restaurant alone. They're all so bloody selfish, she thought as she opened the door. She was met with a wonderful aroma of spices. Her stomach rumbled. She had skipped lunch and hadn't realised how hungry she was. She could see the group seated at a table near the back. She moved among the tables. The clatter of cutlery, sizzling meat, and blended chatter swirled around her.

'She's not here,' Sammy said.

'Have you tried calling her again?' Christie asked.

Iona nodded. 'Just goes to voicemail. She might be on her way. Maybe she went to her parents' and just forgot the time.'

'Can we just order?' Rhodri asked. 'I'm bloody starving.'

Christie pulled out a chair and sat down. 'Have any of you talked to Alys today?'

'I sent her a message wishing her happy birthday this morning,' Sammy said.

'Me too,' Iona said.

Christie took out her phone and opened the group chat. 'All our messages are here but she didn't respond to any of them.'

Iona looked at her own phone. 'You didn't message her, Macsen?'

'I was going to call her before she went to work,' he said, 'but then I went on a mission to find Rhodri.'

'And you didn't bother when you got back?' Iona said. 'She's your girlfriend and you forgot to wish her happy birthday. No wonder she's not here. She's pissed at you.'

'She's not like that,' Christie said.

'She knows I go to bed early and get up at four. I have to take my turn with the milking,' Macsen said. 'I spoke to her at lunch time yesterday. I told her I had a surprise for her. She was all excited.'

'What surprise?' Iona asked.

'I'm not telling you. You can't keep your mouth shut.' Macsen pushed back his chair. 'I'm going outside to ring her mum.'

Christie watched Macsen leave the restaurant then appear again outside the window. After a while he began to pace. She knew what he was going to say before he came back in.

'She's not there. Her mum hasn't spoken to her today.'

Christie looked around the table. She knew what was going through her companions' minds. She saw it on their faces. It was the feeling that something wasn't right. A panic that you pushed down. Desperately trying to think of an explanation to quiet the dark thoughts.

'I think I should call the police,' Macsen said.

Chapter Two

DI Winter Meadows was sitting at his desk. The only sound in the office was the clacking of the keyboard. His fingers moved swiftly and his eyes were fixed to the screen. He wanted to finish his report before the rest of the team came in. He only had to get through another two days without a major incident, before he was free for the weekend.

He had made his plans. A ring was hidden in his sock drawer. His old friend, Iggy, had decorated his yurt at the commune and strung solar lights around the pergola. It would be a weekend away from work and any distractions. All he needed was his girlfriend, Daisy, to say yes.

'DI Meadows?'

Meadows looked up from his screen. A young man was approaching. He was slim and he guessed no more than five foot six. An inch or more of light brown hair stood up on top of his head. The sides were shaved leaving just a shadow. He wore a grey suit and held a padded coat in his hands. His small, upturned nose, and full cheeks, gave him a boyish look.

'DC Ben Harvard,' he said in a London accent.

'Hi.' Meadows stood up and extended his hand. 'I wasn't expecting you until later.'

'I'm keen to make a start, sir.'

Meadows smiled. 'No need to call me sir. You'll find we are quite laid back here.'

The aroma of coffee drifted into the office ahead of the team who came in with their usual morning banter. Meadows waited for them to settle before making the introductions.

'This is DC Ben Harvard. He is joining us on placement from DHEP.'

DS Rowena Paskin was the first to introduce herself.

'Paskin is our office manager and our go-to person for information,' Meadows said.

'DS Tristan Edris.' Edris held out his hand.

'AKA Golden Boy and that's not because of his hair. I'm DS Stefan Blackwell.' Blackwell, a heavyset man who rarely smiled, held out his hand.

'I'm DC Reena Valentine.' Valentine smiled and tucked a lock of black hair behind her ear. 'Welcome to the team.'

Harvard shook Valentine's hand. 'Thank you.'

'DHEP is the degree entry programme, isn't?' Valentine asked.

'Yeah.'

'How do you find it?'

'Really good. Most of the time it's been learning on the job.'

'Have you just started your training?' Blackwell asked.

'No, just three months left,' Harvard said.

Blackwell grunted something and went to his desk.

'Take no notice of Blackwell. His default mode is grumpy,' Valentine whispered.

Harvard smiled.

'You must've worked some big cases in the city,' Edris said.

Harvard shook his head. 'You get placed in a big team. A lot of the time I've been looking at hours of CCTV. I've attended some burglaries and domestics. Oh, I also had a placement with VICE. I want to get out of London. It's why I asked for a rural placement.'

'I worked a few years in the city,' Meadows said. 'I couldn't go back now.'

'I can't imagine you ever being there,' Edris said. 'You think Swansea is too crowded.'

Meadows laughed although there was some truth in Edris' comment. 'If you'll excuse me, I've got a report to finish. Grab yourself a coffee and settle in. You can take the desk next to Edris.'

'Great,' Harvard said.

'I'll show you the kitchen,' Valentine said.

Harvard put his coat down and followed Valentine.

'He doesn't look old enough to be out of school,' Blackwell said. 'How long have we got to babysit him for?'

'This is his last placement so three months,' Meadows said.

Blackwell huffed.

'You were young once. Granted it was long time ago,' Paskin said. 'You've forgotten what it's like to be a trainee. Be nice.'

'I remember well enough,' Blackwell said. 'I did three years' patrol.'

'I'm sure he will appreciate learning from your wealth of knowledge,' Meadows said. 'I think it's important he gets to work all aspects of a case and with each of us. We're thin on the ground at the best of times. This might be our opportunity to persuade the DCI to give us an extra pair of hands. Permanently.'

Valentine and Harvard came back into the office followed by Sergeant Dyfan Folland.

'I've got something for you,' Folland said. 'Body of a young woman found at Llyn y Fan. Hanes called it in.'

Meadows looked at Harvard. 'Grab your coat. You can come with me and Edris.'

* * *

Edris swivelled in the passenger seat to talk to Harvard as Meadows drove the mountain road.

'Why does Blackwell call you Golden Boy?' Harvard asked.

'Because I'm the favourite,' Edris said.

Meadows laughed. 'No, you're not. Edris and Blackwell had a personality clash. Edris had a hissy fit about partnering with Blackwell so he ended up with me. I wouldn't call that favouritism. I'm the one that had to suffer.'

'Thanks,' Edris said.

'What's wrong with Blackwell?' Harvard asked.

'Nothing,' Meadows said. 'He's a good detective.'

'He's just a miserable bugger,' Edris said.

Harvard looked out of the window. 'Wow, this is fantastic. Look at the view and not a car in sight.'

'Not so quiet in the summer,' Edris said. 'Worth coming up though. If you can get a parking spot at the top you can buy an ice cream from the van and sit looking down into the valley.'

'Can't wait to get a chance to explore,' Harvard said. 'I bought a pair of hiking boots.'

They reached the summit and started the descent on the other side. The road twisted downwards until they crossed the old stone bridge at the bottom. The road levelled and Meadows picked up speed until he took a right turning onto a single-track road.

'It's mostly farmland in this area,' Meadows said. 'Llyn y Fan is a glacial lake, popular with tourists. There's also the Usk Reservoir. You ever been fishing?'

'No,' Harvard said. 'I wouldn't mind giving it a try.'

'I wouldn't bother,' Edris said. 'It's dangerous. We had three bodies up here last year.'

'Drowning?'

'No, garrotted with a fishing line.'

'Nasty,' Harvard said.

'Just because it looks idyllic doesn't mean there isn't any crime,' Meadows said. 'We get our fair share. Still, I wouldn't want to live and work anywhere else.'

The road narrowed further with hedges blocking the view until they turned into a gravelled car park. Here the mountain peak, Picws Du, rose up before them.

Harvard opened the car door which was nearly ripped from the hinges by the wind. He pulled it closed again.

'Hope you've got a good hood on your coat,' Meadows said. 'The winds can be biting up here.'

'I've got my hat,' Harvard said. He pulled a brightly coloured striped bobble hat from his pocket. 'My mum took up knitting in the pandemic. Thought I should be prepared for country life.'

Edris laughed. 'Well, we won't have a problem with losing you.'

Harvard put his hands in the hat, stretched it, and placed it carefully over his hair. 'She even made it taller so it wouldn't flatten my hair.'

The three got out and walked to a police car parked along with three other vehicles. An officer greeted them.

'This is PC Abbey Taylor,' Edris said.

'Hi,' Harvard said. He turned his back to the wind.

'Please tell me we don't have to walk all the way up,' Edris said.

Taylor laughed. 'No, Welsh Water opened the gates at the trout farm. Forensics have already gone up. It's a bit of a bumpy ride. Hanes is up there keeping a lookout for hikers and sending them down. I've taken details from them all and been turning people away. Just waiting for the last lot to return then I'll move the car to the entrance.'

'Who found the body?' Meadows asked.

'A hiker. Mr Ludvig Berg. He's on a hiking holiday from Sweden. I've taken his statement and got the details of his accommodation and home address.'

'OK. Thanks, Taylor,' Meadows said. 'Right, let's go and take a look.'

The car rocked from side to side as Meadows drove the rutted track. To the left, the Afon Sawdde tumbled over rocks forming cascades and pools. They drove through the trout farm and continued up the steep incline. They passed a lone hiker and a couple with a dog heading to the car park.

'Strange to find a woman's body at the lake given the legend,' Edris said.

'What legend is that?' Harvard asked.

'The short version: a farmer was tending his sheep when a beautiful woman walked out of the lake and he instantly fell in love with her.'

'As you do,' Meadows said.

Edris laughed. 'She agreed to marry the farmer on condition he didn't strike her more than three times. Needless to say he didn't keep his promise. She returned to the lake never to be seen again.'

'It's not a very exciting legend,' Harvard said.

'I guess not,' Meadows said. 'The area does lay claim to the birthplace of Merlin.'

'And we've got a Welsh Robin Hood,' Edris said.

They reached the end of the track and Meadows pulled up next to the bothy. A forensic van was parked with the back door open, and a white-clad figure was leaning inside. At the sound of the car door closing, the figure straightened up and turned around.

'Mike Fielding, head of forensics,' Meadows said and introduced Harvard. 'What have you got for us?'

'I tell you what I haven't got. A point of entry,' Mike said. 'The body was in the water. Not that far in. Eight metres or so. She could've gone in at any point around the lake. My feeling is it wasn't far from where we found her. It's fairly sheltered here by the escarpment. The body wouldn't have moved far unless there was a high wind. Until we know the time of death it's impossible to tell. When we know more we can check the weather and wind direction. We've managed to erect a tent but it rained most of yesterday. Chances are any trace evidence would've been washed away.'

'I'm sure if there's anything to find you'll find it,' Meadows said.

'Grab some covers and I'll take you over,' Mike said. 'Hanes has climbed to the peak to see if he can find any more hikers. I think it was more to keep himself warm. Poor bugger.'

Meadows slipped on protective clothing and followed Mike to the tent that had been erected on the stony banks of the lake.

'We pulled her out a few metres in from here.' Mike pointed. 'As you can see the water is clear, with no vegetation, so she was easy to spot. I'll leave you to it.'

Meadows looked out over the glacial lake. It stretched to sandstone slopes that rose up to a peak topped by vertical crags. The peak cast a long shadow over the water, turning it a gunmetal grey. He had visited the lake in the summer when the water sparkled and invited hikers to take a dip. Now it just looked still and ominous.

'OK, let's take a look,' Meadows said and stepped inside the tent.

Daisy Moore, the pathologist, and his girlfriend, knelt, examining the body. Edris stepped in alongside him while Harvard hovered at the entrance.

Meadows looked down at the woman. She was fully clothed in jeans and a zipped-up pink coat. Ankle boots were secured to her feet. Her short blonde hair with dark roots was wet and clung to her head. Cloudy eyes stared lifeless. Her pale heart-shaped face was marbled with purplish veins.

Sadness washed over Meadows. 'She looks young.'

'I would say early to mid-twenties. At the most,' Daisy said.

'How long do you think she's been in the water?'

'There's maceration to the skin but no significant sloughing. The water temperature is low, which would slow down decomposition. All I can tell you is we are not talking weeks. Over twelve hours and up to a few days. She has sustained a trauma to the back of the head.' Daisy moved the woman's head gently to show the injury.

'Do you think that's what killed her?' Edris asked.

'I'm not going to commit myself to an answer,' Daisy said.

Meadows could see the smile in her eyes. 'Any other injuries?'

'Some damage to the fingertips and nails,' she said. 'I'll be able to tell you more when I have completed the post-mortem. I'll start as soon as I get her back to the hospital.'

'Thank you,' Meadows said. He gave her a smile. 'See you later.' He stepped out of the tent and looked across the lake. It had a serene quality which felt at odds with the tragic loss of life and the forensic activity. 'You OK, Harvard?'

Harvard nodded.

'Any thoughts?'

'It's very remote but open. I can't imagine someone would be out here preying on unsuspecting hikers. Accident? Although it's strange she would be out here alone.'

'Not really,' Edris said. 'Lots of women hike this area. It's generally safe.'

'Could be suicide,' Harvard said.

'Possibly,' Meadows said, 'but remember the golden rule.'

'Yeah, think murder,' Harvard said.

'Until we know for sure,' Meadows said.

'I'm guessing she must have died sometime yesterday evening, or early hours of this morning,' Harvard said. 'Otherwise she would've been found sooner. It looks like a popular spot.'

Meadows smiled to himself. 'Good point, but Mike already mentioned it rained yesterday. It was fine rain which can often make it misty on the mountain. It would've kept people away. What troubles me is the injury to the back of the head and her fingers.'

Edris nodded. 'That is odd. I suppose she could have fallen. Tried to scramble out.'

Meadows walked to the edge of the water. 'If she was sightseeing then this is about as close as she would've got. If she slipped at this point and fell backwards, she'd be on the bank and not in the water.'

'And who falls backwards like a plank?' Edris asked. 'It's the only way she'd get the injury at the back of her head.'

'Exactly,' Meadows said. 'You would expect one foot to slip and then go down at an angle. Still, it's not impossible.'

'What if she was walking away from the water?' Harvard asked. 'She falls backwards into the water. She hits her head and is dazed. Her wet clothes would've weighed her down. She turns and tries to pull herself out. Hence the injuries to her fingers.'

'She would have been closer to the water's edge. Unless like Mike said there was a strong wind. It would have to have been fierce to cause enough of a current to drag a body a few metres out,' Meadows said.

'She could've been in a high emotional state,' Edris said. 'She walks up here, falls as she rushes towards the lake, gets up and wades in as far as she can go.'

'What about the broken fingernails?' Harvard asked.

Edris shrugged. 'I don't know. She sinks to the bottom and grabs at stones and rocks to keep herself under. I've never tried to drown myself; I don't know how difficult it is. She could've changed her mind then been disoriented and scrambled around.'

'I think we are going to have to keep an open mind until we know more,' Meadows said. He could see Hanes making his way towards them. 'The next question is how did she get here?'

'Drive or someone drove her here,' Edris said.

'Can't see anyone else out walking,' PC Matt Hanes said as he joined the group. His nose and cheeks were red from the cold and he was breathless.

'Can you give Taylor a shout?' Meadows asked. 'Ask her if any vehicles are left in the car park. We saw a couple of walkers on the way up. If they owned two of the cars, that would leave one. If that's the case then ask her to get a check on the registration.'

Hanes nodded and pushed the button on his radio. He moved away as he spoke.

Meadows left Harvard and Edris discussing scenarios. He walked over to Mike who was collecting samples.

'Did you find a handbag or mobile phone?' Meadows asked.

'No, not yet. Nothing in her pockets. I've asked for divers to come and take a look.'

'You would've thought she'd be carrying something. Even if it was just car keys.'

Mike nodded. 'And nothing so far that would identify her.'

Hanes called out.

'Thanks, Mike,' Meadows said. He walked back to Hanes.

'Car is registered to a Miss Alys Pugh,' Hanes said. 'Reported missing on Tuesday evening.'

Chapter Three

Meadows listened as Edris talked on the phone. He was driving towards Llangadog, the home of Alys' parents.

Harvard leaned towards the front seat. 'Given her car was in the car park it seems more likely to be a suicide. Don't you think? If someone was with her and killed her they would need transport.'

'There's always the possibility it was a random attack,' Meadows said.

'But why would she not tell anyone where she was going? Why not have some sort of identification? A backpack or something. If someone intends to take their own life it's usually a case of just walking away. Leave everything behind,' Harvard said.

'Or someone took her things so she wouldn't be easily identified. Either case, her loved ones are going to want answers,' Meadows said.

'Description fits,' Edris said when he ended the call. 'They are sending the details. Apparently, she didn't turn up for a birthday dinner that had been organised by her friends. Her parents, Liz and Gareth Pugh, made the initial call. She wasn't considered high risk. Usual checks were made with the hospitals. It was thought she had most likely taken off for a few days. She had taken the day off work Tuesday and wasn't expected in yesterday. A request had been put in for her phone records and enquires were continuing this morning.' His phone tinged and he looked at the screen. 'Photo has come through. Yeah, it's her.' Edris shook his head. 'Twenty-five years old, and the Pughes' only child.'

'Poor parents,' Harvard said. 'It must be hell not knowing and just waiting for news.'

'Have you had any experience of informing next of kin?' Meadows asked Harvard.

'We covered it in training. I haven't actually, you know, delivered bad news. I've been involved with bereaved families in the aftermath of violent crime.'

'I'm happy to stay in the car,' Edris said. 'No point in all three of us going in.'

Meadows nodded his agreement as he pulled up outside Alys' parents' house. He noticed a figure in the window. They still have hope, he thought. Now he was about to shatter their lives. 'Let's not keep them waiting any longer,' he said.

Meadows didn't have to knock on the door. It was opened as soon as they stepped through the gate. A man in his fifties watched their approach. He wore joggers and a navy sweatshirt. Stubble covered his chin and his eyes were heavy with fatigue.

'Gareth Pugh?' Meadows asked.

Gareth nodded and looked towards the car as if expecting Alys to get out. 'Have you found her?'

A woman was hovering behind Gareth. Meadows guessed her to be Liz Pugh. She too looked like she hadn't slept. He introduced himself and Harvard. 'May we come inside?'

They followed the Pughes into the sitting room. It was nicely decorated and neat. The television was switched off and a heavy atmosphere lingered. It felt like the anxiety of the occupants had seeped into the foundations of the house.

'I'm sorry to have to tell you the body of a young woman–'

'No!' Liz's scream cut off Meadows. 'Don't say it. Please don't say it.'

Gareth put his arms around is wife. She struggled against him but he held her tight. Meadows felt every scream pierce his heart. He glanced at Harvard and saw the same emotion he felt on his colleague's face before he quickly slipped on his professional mask.

'Kitchen through this way?' Harvard pointed to the door.

Gareth nodded as he battled against his own anguish to help his wife.

What little colour Liz had in her face drained away and she sagged against her husband. He moved her to the sofa and they sank down. Meadows took the seat opposite. He gave them a few moments to compose themselves.

'Are you sure it's her?' Gareth asked.

'There will need to be a formal identification,' Meadows said. 'At this point we are fairly certain it is Alys. The description you gave the police and the fact her car was found nearby. It leaves little room for doubt. I'm so very sorry.'

'No,' Liz wailed. 'Please no.' Her whole body shook.

Harvard came back into the room carrying two mugs. He set them down on the table in front of Liz and Gareth, then he took a throw from the back of the sofa and wrapped it around Liz.

The kind gesture touched Meadows. He waited for Harvard to sit and take out his notebook before he spoke.

'I appreciate how difficult this is for you both but I'm going to have to ask a few questions.'

'Where?' Gareth asked. 'Where did you find her?'

Meadows knew there was no easy way of conveying the information. What the Pughes needed now was honest answers. 'Llyn y Fan. She was in the water and her car was parked below the track.'

'You mean she fell in?' Gareth asked. 'Alys was a good swimmer.'

'We don't know the full circumstances,' Meadows said. 'There will be a full investigation. Was Llyn y Fan somewhere Alys frequently visited?'

'She likes to go out walking,' Gareth said. 'I think she's been up a few times.' He looked at Liz. She shook her head.

'When was the last time you saw Alys?'

'Sunday. She came for lunch,' Gareth said.

'She always comes on Sundays,' Liz added.

Meadows noticed Liz didn't look at him when she spoke. She had a faraway look in her eyes. He'd seen it before. The brain protecting itself, removing the person from reality.

'How did she seem?'

'Fine,' Liz said. 'Just her usual self.'

'Did she discuss her plans for the week?'

'She was looking forward to going out with her friends to celebrate her birthday. They were having a dinner out at some restaurant. We weren't expecting her until Wednesday evening.'

'You reported her missing on Tuesday evening.'

'Macsen called me. He was worried when she didn't turn up,' Liz said. 'Macsen Lloyd. He's Alys' boyfriend.'

'Who else was supposed to be meeting her for dinner?' Meadows asked.

'Erm, Iona Young. They've been friends since school. Rhodri Williams, Sammy, and Christie. I don't know their surnames.'

'That's OK. So just the six of them?'

Liz nodded.

'Did Alys mention she was taking a couple of days off work?'

'No,' Gareth said. 'That's why we didn't see her on Tuesday. She was supposed be in work and then she was meeting her friends. She did say she had the day off Wednesday.' He looked at Liz. 'Remember? She said she would come early. I think they were all going to have a few drinks. That's why she was taking the day off.'

'Did you have any contact at all with Alys on Tuesday?'

'I sent her a text message wishing her happy birthday,' Liz said. 'She didn't respond.'

'Was that unusual?'

Liz shrugged. 'I guess so. I was in work so didn't think anything of it until Macsen called. I knew then something was wrong. She wasn't the type to just go off without telling anyone.'

'Had Alys been depressed recently?'

'No,' Liz said.

'What about in the past? Has she ever suffered from depression?'

'No,' Gareth said.

Liz shook her head.

'Any financial problems?'

'No,' Gareth said. 'She knew if she was short of money she could always ask us for help.'

'Can you think of anything at all that may have been troubling her? An argument with her boyfriend or one of her friends? Problems at work?'

'No, nothing like that,' Gareth said. 'If you're suggesting she would… she'd take her own life, then no, she wouldn't.'

'She was happy,' Liz said. 'She was going on holiday with Macsen. It's all booked. She was looking forward to it.' Rivulets of tears ran down her face. Liz made no effort to wipe them away.

'Can you think of anything out of the ordinary that's happened in the last few weeks?' Meadows asked.

'No,' Gareth said.

Liz shook her head.

'We understand Alys has a house in Llandybie. Does she share it with Macsen?'

'No,' Liz said. 'She moved out of here a couple of years ago. She wanted her own space. Macsen has his own place. I don't think it would have been long before they moved in together.'

'We will need to collect some of Alys' belongings. Do you have a spare key?'

'I'll get it for you.' Gareth stood and left the room.

'Alys would never do this to us deliberately,' Liz said. 'She must have had an accident.'

Gareth returned and handed Meadows a set of keys.

'I'm going to arrange for a family liaison officer to visit you. They will be able to answer any questions you may have and talk you through what happens next.' Meadows stood up. 'I'm very sorry for your loss. We'll see ourselves out.'

* * *

Meadows felt like the Pughes' grief was sticking to his clothes. He couldn't switch off the empathy he felt for those who suffered a tragic loss like some officers managed to do. He glanced at Harvard and wondered how he was feeling. He would have been told in training about how the job can affect you. About not taking your work home. To try and detach yourself. Not so easy to put into practice, he thought.

'You did well in there,' Meadows said when they reached the car. 'Little acts of compassion go a long way.'

Harvard smiled. 'Thank you. I know we are not supposed to get too involved but I felt so sorry for them.'

'Allowing yourself to take on board people's suffering helps drive you to find answers. Just try not to dwell on it too much. It can get to you.' He opened the car door and climbed inside.

Harvard filled Edris in on the conversation with the Pughes as Meadows drove towards Alys' house. 'Doesn't sound like she was suicidal,' he said.

'People hide all sorts of things from their loved ones,' Edris said. 'Especially their parents.'

'Yeah, but if she was depressed, they would have noticed some change in her behaviour,' Harvard said. 'They were adamant she wouldn't take her own life.'

Meadows nodded. 'Still, I don't think we can rule it out completely. What we need to know is what secrets she was keeping. No one thought to look for her at Llyn y Fan. That means she didn't tell anyone she intended to go there. Why? It's the sort of thing you would mention. You'd say you're taking the day off work to go walking. Let's hope there's something in her home which will give us an idea of the type of person she was.'

'Wouldn't her house have been searched when she was reported missing?' Harvard asked.

'Uniform checked her house to make sure there wasn't a break-in,' Edris said. 'With the car missing, they had no reason to go inside.'

They arrived in Llandybie and Meadows turned off the main road. Alys' house was an old stone end of terrace. Meadows got out of the car and fished the keys from his pocket. The door opened onto a bunch of post. He moved it aside and stepped in. The hallway was narrow with hooks in the wall for coats. Directly ahead was the staircase.

'We'll take a look upstairs first.' Meadows put on a pair of latex gloves and walked up the stairs. There were three doors. He pushed the one in front of him. It opened into a small bathroom.

'Harvard, you can check in here. Look for any drugs, prescription medication, or anything that looks out of place.' He turned to Edris. 'We'll take a room each.'

Meadows guessed the room he walked into was Alys' bedroom. The bed was unmade and various items of clothing lay on top. A heap of clothes and a pile of shoes lay in the corner.

'The other room is a spare. Empty,' Edris said stepping in behind Meadows. 'Not enough room to fit a bed.' He glanced around. 'Not very tidy, was she?'

Meadows smiled. He was used to Edris' liking of order and cleanliness. 'Looks like she was picking an outfit for the restaurant,' he said indicating the clothes on the bed. 'They're not work clothes.'

'Which suggests she intended to come back,' Edris said.

Meadows moved to the dressing table. Make-up was strewn across the top along with jewellery. The drawers were partly open and filled with underwear and socks. In the bedside drawer he found a packet of condoms, a variety of sex toys, and a packet of paracetamol. He moved back onto the landing where Harvard was waiting.

'Did you find anything of interest?' Meadows asked.

Harvard shook his head. 'Only what you would expect in a bathroom. There's some shaving gear and two towels hung up. I imagine they belong to the boyfriend. Also sand and a few shells in the shower tray. Looks like she took a recent trip to the beach.'

'Why would you have shells in the shower?' Edris asked.

'Probably cleaning off the sand,' Harvard said.

Meadows made his way downstairs and the other two followed. A wood panelled door opened into a sitting room. He looked around. It was the same as the bedroom. Items left lying around. A mug and a plate with half-eaten toast on the coffee table, clothes on the back of the sofa, and laptop on the floor.

'Bag the laptop,' Meadows said. 'We'll get Chris Harley from tech to see what he can get off it.' He moved to a shelf on the far wall and picked up a birthday card. 'From her parents.' He picked up another. 'Granny.'

'Got up, made some breakfast, and opened her cards,' Harvard said. 'Pretty normal start to the day.'

Meadows nodded and picked up a framed photograph. It showed Alys smiling at the camera. A man was standing next to her with his arm wrapped around her shoulder. He was tall and broad with thick dark hair. Long lashes framed brooding eyes. He handed the photograph to Edris.

'I'm guessing Macsen Lloyd,' Edris said. 'Looks like he's perfected the art of the smoulder.'

'Look behind them,' Meadows said.

'Llyn y Fan,' Edris said. 'Interesting.'

'Maybe he broke her heart and that's why she went there. The place could have had a special meaning for the two of them,' Harvard said.

'If that was the case then he wouldn't have been meeting her for dinner on Tuesday evening,' Meadows said.

'I don't know,' Edris said. 'He might be a nice guy and wanted to remain friends. Then again it would be a bit dickish to break up on her birthday.'

'I'm sure her parents would have known if they had broken up,' Meadows said. 'Unless he came around in the morning and they had a bust-up. Only one mug on the coffee table though. He would have either stayed overnight or come around in the morning. You'd at least have a cuppa and break the news gently.'

'Unless he did it by text,' Edris said.

'You'd have to be a proper dick to do that,' Harvard said.

'Yeah, but you don't have to face the drama.'

Meadows shook his head. 'I can't believe that just came out of your mouth.'

Edris laughed. 'You've no idea what dating is like now. There are some crazy people out there.'

'Perhaps it wasn't a break-up,' Meadows said. 'What if she arranged to meet Macsen there to celebrate her birthday?'

Edris nodded. 'They argue and he pushes her in.'

'We'll talk to him but I want to wait for the post-mortem results first. See what we are dealing with. Either way, we still need to find out what she was doing up at Llyn y Fan. Let's take a look in the kitchen.'

The kitchen was small with just enough room for a table and two chairs against the wall. Edris opened a cupboard and peered inside. 'Plenty of food,' he said.

Meadows opened the fridge. 'No signs she had been drinking heavily.' He moved a gloved finger over the bottom shelf. 'Sand. Look, it's sprinkled over the food.'

Harvard moved to look. 'Odd.'

Meadows stepped back and looked around. His eyes fell on the black dustbin in the corner. Flower stems were sticking out the top. He pulled off the lid and plucked out the wilted roses. Underneath was a card.

Happy birthday, Alys.
I can't wait for us to be together again.
Love, J

'Now why would she put flowers that had been given for her birthday straight in the bin?' Meadows peered into the rubbish then put his hand in and plucked out a stick of seaside rock. He read the label. 'It's from Tenby, and there's more.' He pulled out another four.

'Looks like she might have been seeing someone else,' Edris said.

Meadows nodded. 'Maybe that someone didn't want to let her go.'

Chapter Four

Meadows could see Harvard waiting at the hospital doors as he approached.

'He's keen,' Edris said.

Meadows smiled. 'Can't fault his timekeeping.'

Edris yawned. 'Yeah, and considering it was a late night.'

'Have you been leading him astray already?'

'Nah, we went over to Valentine's place. Hanes and Taylor were there. We just got a takeaway and had a few drinks. He's just moved here and doesn't know anyone so we thought we'd make him welcome.'

'Nice,' Meadows said. 'Looks like he didn't have as much to drink as you.'

'I didn't drink much. I'm just tired,' Edris said. 'Can't keep up with these youngsters.'

Meadows laughed. 'He's not much younger than you.'

'He's twenty-three!'

'Morning,' Meadows greeted Harvard.

Harvard smiled and took his hat off.

'We better get inside,' Meadows said.

They took the lift to the basement and walked down the corridor. They kept their voices low as they talked.

More out of a sense of respect, than fear of being overhead.

'You ready for this?' Edris asked.

'Yeah,' Harvard said. 'I have attended one post-mortem. Had to walk out. Really embarrassing.'

'We won't be witnessing the actual procedure,' Meadows said. 'Daisy is just going talk us through the findings.'

'She hasn't already told you then?' Edris asked.

'No, she stayed at her place last night. Closer to work. Besides, it wouldn't be professional,' Meadows said.

'Daisy and Meadows are an item,' Edris explained to Harvard.

'Oh, nice,' Harvard said.

Meadows pushed open the double doors that led into the mortuary. The light instantly changed. Bright humming strip lights ran the length of the ceiling and illuminated the stainless-steel worktops. The smell of formaldehyde and death permeated the air. He always felt a wave of nausea no matter how many times he had been in this room. Daisy, dressed in green scrubs, was washing her hands at the sink. She turned and greeted them then walked to the gurney where Alys Pugh lay. Alys' hair had been cleaned and was slicked back. Her eyes were closed and her face had a waxen pallor.

'Her father came in to identify her last night,' Daisy said.

'Poor man,' Meadows said.

'Liz Pugh came with him but she stayed outside the viewing room. Gareth kept trying to push her to come in. He said it would help. She could barely stand up. I did tell him they would get another chance to see her.'

'I suppose seeing her would make it too real,' Harvard said.

'It's not for everyone. Some prefer it not to be the last image of their loved one,' Daisy said.

Harvard nodded and glanced at Alys.

Meadows noticed that Harvard was pale under the lighting. 'You don't have to stay. There is no shame in leaving.'

'I'm OK,' Harvard said.

'Breathe through your mouth. It helps,' Daisy said. 'Right, first thing to note is this was not an accident or suicide.' She tilted Alys' head to the side. 'This injury I showed you yesterday did not kill her. I would think she was hit with some force in order to stun her. Not a smooth-edged object. Possibly a rock. Official cause of death: drowning.' She pulled down the sheet. 'There are bruises to the shoulders which extend over her back. Consistent with being held down. Evidence of a struggle. Bruising and scrapes to the knees and legs. It also accounts for the damage to her fingers.'

'Can you tell what size hands from the bruising?' Harvard asked.

Daisy shook her head. 'The bruising is too extensive. I imagine the killer's hands moved as she struggled.'

An image of Alys struggling for breath flitted across Meadows' mind. He imagined her fear in those last moments. He chased the thoughts away.

'No signs of sexual assault,' Daisy said.

'At least she was spared that,' Harvard said.

'Time of death?' Meadows asked.

'Sometime Tuesday morning. Rough estimate between eight and ten. Could be either side. Tox screen came back clear and there is no evidence to suggest she was a user. One more thing to note. She was around ten weeks pregnant.'

* * *

The team gathered around the incident board. Harvard had filled in the information and was now sitting next to Valentine. His pen was poised over his notebook as he waited for Meadows to speak. Next to him Blackwell was sitting with his legs stretched out. Paskin was perched on the edge of a desk. Edris was standing drinking a cup of tea.

'Alys Pugh,' Meadows said. He pointed to her photo. 'Twenty-five years old, department store worker. Murdered at Llyn y Fan sometime Tuesday morning.' He talked them through the post-mortem results. 'Her car was found in the car park. It has now been towed and is with forensics. As far as we are aware, Alys told no one of her plans to go to Llyn y Fan on Tuesday. She had arranged to meet a group of friends Tuesday evening to celebrate her birthday.' He nodded to Harvard.

Harvard flipped through his notebook. 'Macsen Lloyd, Iona Young, Rhodri Williams, Christie Bailey, and Sammy Miller. Macsen was Alys' boyfriend. According to her parents, these were the people Alys spent time with.'

Meadows looked back at the board. 'The first thing to note is the location. It's remote but popular with hikers. It's a long walk from the car park to the lake. I think it unlikely the killer would have dragged Alys there. Either it's a random attack or Alys went there with someone she knew and trusted. Also, they would've had their own transport. So did she arrange to meet someone there?'

'Could be more than one killer,' Blackwell said. 'One drives her there under duress and the other one follows. They kill her and drive off.'

'It's possible,' Meadows said. 'Why this location? We know Alys visited it in the past with Macsen. There's one connection.'

'It's risky,' Edris said. 'Could have run into hikers. Or be seen by anyone walking the peaks.'

'Spur of the moment,' Valentine suggested. 'They meet, there is an argument, Macsen kills Alys.'

Meadows nodded. 'He's our obvious suspect. However, we found a birthday card with flowers in the bin in Alys' house. Only signed with the letter *J*. It suggests a meeting. She could've been seeing someone else. That would be motive for Macsen to kill her but it could also be that person didn't want to let her go. The act of discarding the flowers shows she no longer cared for this person.'

'Or she didn't want the boyfriend to see them,' Paskin said.

'She could have kept the flowers and chucked the card. She could've said they were from work, or family. That way she could have enjoyed the gesture,' Valentine said. 'Binning them is a clear message she wanted rid of him.'

'There were also five sticks of seaside rock from Tenby and sand in the fridge and shower,' Edris said.

'And seashells,' Harvard added.

'That is weird,' Valentine said. 'Sounds like he was trying to remind her of happy times.'

Edris laughed. 'By putting sand in the fridge.'

'Yeah, well… guys are a bit *twp*,' Valentine said.

Harvard looked at Valentine. '*Twp*?'

'Stupid.'

'It was sprinkled over the food which is a spiteful thing to do,' Meadows said. 'It's not the sort of thing you would do in front of someone. Did they do it before or after she died? No keys were found with her. Did they go to her house after they killed her? I've asked forensics to check the birthday card for prints and to dust Alys' house. I want a complete background check on Alys and all of her friends. We need to build a picture of her life. Her routine, whom she met, where she went. Harvard, I'd like you to work on that with Paskin.'

Harvard nodded, his boyish face eager.

'We also need to put out an appeal to anyone walking the area on Tuesday morning,' Meadows continued.

'I'll get on to that,' Paskin said.

'Thank you. Uniform is carrying out house-to-house in the area. It's mostly farms but someone may have seen Alys' car and possibly a second vehicle in the vicinity. They will also speak to Alys' neighbours. Blackwell and Valentine, I'd like you to talk to Alys' family members and work colleagues. Edris and I will talk to Macsen Lloyd and this group of friends.' He pointed to the names on the board. 'Bear in mind we need to find out who *J* is and also the connection to Tenby. Alys was a young woman with plans for the future. Someone robbed her of that. They also took the life of the Pughes' only child, and grandchild – Alys was pregnant. Let's get them some answers.'

Chapter Five

The silence in the cottage felt oppressive. Rhodri didn't know what to do with himself. He opened the fridge, looked at the beer, then closed it again. He was so tempted to have a drink. More tempting were the pills in his pocket. He just wanted to get off his face; take himself away from this situation and not feel anything. He felt like he had been stuck in Macsen's home for weeks. He had rushed over after the police had found Alys. The hours since had dragged by. He'd done his best for his friend but he didn't know what to say.

He walked back into the sitting room. Macsen was still sitting in the same place. Unwashed and unshaven.

'Do you want a coffee?'

Macsen shook his head.

Rhodri bounced on the balls of his feet. 'Something stronger then?'

'I don't want anything.'

'You haven't eaten nor drunk anything since yesterday. You have to try. Maybe have a shower. It will make you feel better.'

Macsen looked at him. 'I can't. I just… This doesn't feel real. It's like it's happening to someone else. You see this shit on the news. It happens to other people. I don't know what to do. Nobody I know has died before. Well, no one close to me.'

Rhodri's mind wandered and took him to a dark place. He thought about the look in someone's eyes when they knew they were about to die. Just a fleeting moment but there was so much in that expression. Maybe your life really does flash before your eyes. Maybe that's what that look is, he thought.

'The police will be here soon,' Macsen said.

Rhodri snapped back. 'What?'

'The police. They want to talk to me.'

'Yeah, right. I need a drink.'

Rhodri went back into the kitchen and took a bottle of vodka from the cupboard. He didn't bother with a glass. He unscrewed the top and glugged down the clear liquid. It didn't take long for him to feel the effects. It was just enough to take the edge off his nerves. He splashed some cold water on his face then made two cups of coffee. He gave one to Macsen then sat down and took a gulp. He'd made it strong. He didn't want the police to smell alcohol.

'What do you think they are going to ask?' Macsen asked.

'Probably want to know where you were when she died.'

'Why? She fell in the lake. That's what her dad said. I don't even want to think about what I was doing at the time. What was she doing up there alone?'

Rhodri saw the tears in Macsen's eyes. He didn't know what to say. He felt so uncomfortable. He took his phone from his pocket.

'I'm going message your brother. See if he can come over.'

Macsen shook his head.

'Your mum, then?'

'I don't want to see anyone. All they did was sit there yesterday.'

'It's all I'm doing,' Rhodri said. 'What about Iona?'

'Maybe later.'

Rhodri sent a message to Sammy. She could round up the girls and come over. They could make a fuss. Take the pressure off him. The door knocked and he leaped up from the chair.

'I'll get that,' he said.

Two men were standing on the doorstep. The one who introduced himself as DI Meadows was the taller of the two. He had thick dark curly hair and green eyes. Rhodri thought the other one, DS Edris, wouldn't be out of place on the catwalk. His dislike for the younger detective was instant.

'And you are?' Edris asked.

'Rhodri. I'm Macsen's friend. I can shove off somewhere when you talk to him.'

'No need. We will need to speak to you as well,' Meadows said.

It was not the answer he hoped for. Just as well, he thought. Better to get it over with. 'You better come in.'

By the time the detectives had seated themselves, Rhodri had forgotten their names. He just sat back and let them introduce themselves to Macsen. He watched Edris take out a notebook and pen.

Meadows leaned forward in his seat. 'I appreciate this is a difficult time for you, Macsen, but I do need to ask you some questions.'

Macsen nodded.

'Firstly, I have to tell you we are treating Alys' death as suspicious.'

'What? You mean someone killed her? I thought…' Macsen shook his head.

'What did you think?' Meadows asked.

'We thought it was an accident,' Rhodri said. 'Her dad said she had fallen in Llyn y Fan.'

Meadows glanced at Rhodri then turned his attention back to Macsen. 'How long had you and Alys been together?'

'Since we were in school.'

'So, about ten years,' Edris said.

Macsen nodded.

Rhodri saw Edris scribble something in his notebook.

'That's a long time to be together. Any problems between the two of you?' Meadows asked.

'No,' Macsen said. 'We had a break-up a couple of years ago but we got back together.'

'Was there any particular reason for the break?'

Macsen shrugged. 'She went off to university and I stayed here.'

Rhodri shifted in his seat. They were treading on dangerous ground. Macsen was a wreck and he didn't trust him not to blurt something out. 'It wasn't for long,' he said. 'You went to see her loads of times when she was there.'

Meadows turned to him. 'Did you get along with Alys?'

'Yeah, we all grew up together. She'd hang around with me and Macsen when we were kids. I didn't mind when they got together. She was tidy, got along with all my girlfriends. Introduced me to Sammy.'

'Who's Sammy?' Edris asked.

'My girlfriend.'

Meadows turned his attention back to Macsen. 'Any recent problems?'

'No,' he said, 'everything was good.'

'When was the last time you saw Alys?'

'Erm, she stayed over on the weekend. Went home Sunday evening. I had to get up early for work on Monday.'

'What is it you do?' Meadows asked.

'Work on my parents' farm. I take it in turns to do the earlies with my brother. It's why Alys had her own place. So we wouldn't disturb each other.'

'Did you talk to her on Monday or Tuesday morning?'

'I called her on Monday.'

Meadows turned to Rhodri. 'When was the last time you saw or spoke to Alys?'

'Dunno,' Rhodri said. He tried to think back. It wasn't easy with the two detectives looking at him. 'The weekend before last. I think. Yeah, we were all together.' He looked at Macsen. 'Didn't we go to that pub?'

'The Stag,' Macsen said. 'Yeah.'

'I also have to ask, where were you both on Tuesday morning between seven and midday? We will be asking everyone who knew Alys.'

'I was on the farm by five,' Macsen said. 'Brought the cows in with Dan and Ellis. Then I went to Ystrad Fflur to help out Rhodri. That was about seven-thirty. I got back about ten-thirty. Maybe eleven.'

Rhodri watched Edris scribbling in his notebook. His pen stopped and he looked at him.

'And you?' Edris asked.

'I left home around seven for a job in Ystrad Fflur.'

'Address?' Edris asked.

Rhodri flicked through his emails and gave the address.

'What was the client's name?' Edris asked.

'Mr Prosser.'

'How long were you with the client?' Edris asked.

Unease crept over Rhodri. His mouth felt dry and he had to put his hands on his knees to stop them jiggling. Edris was looking expectantly at him.

'Erm… I couldn't find the address,' he said. 'I drove around for a while then went to work. Oh, I went home first to grab something to eat. Got in to work around twelve.'

'You were both in Ystrad Fflur at the same time. Is that correct?' Edris asked.

'Yes,' Macsen said. 'No, it was a misunderstanding. Someone was messing with us. They sent a message asking me to meet Rhodri.'

'Who sent a message?' Edris asked.

'I don't know,' Macsen said.

'I see,' Edris said. 'So, did the two of you meet up in Ystrad Fflur?'

Rhodri wanted to jump up and smack him one. He could see the interest in the detective's eyes. He knew he wouldn't let it drop. Now we're going to sound like a pair of twats, he thought.

'No,' Macsen said. 'I couldn't find the address either.'

'Crap signal up there,' Rhodri said.

'Did either of you stop to ask directions?' Edris asked.

'No,' Rhodri said.

'I asked some farmer,' Macsen said, 'but he'd never heard of the place.'

'Where was this?'

'I dunno,' Macsen said. 'I was lost.'

'I understand you were all meeting at a restaurant in Ammanford on Tuesday evening,' Meadows said. 'What time did you arrive?'

'We met up at Christie's place first. I got there around half six.'

'I was there just before,' Rhodri said. 'We were supposed to go out to eat then go back for a few drinks and crash at Christie's.'

'When did you realise something was wrong?'

'I tried to call Alys when she didn't show up,' Macsen said. 'We checked her place. The car was gone. We thought she'd be waiting at the restaurant. But we went and she wasn't there. That's when I called her mum… I don't understand what she was doing up there.' He put his head in his hands.

'I noticed Alys kept a framed photo of the two of you at Llyn y Fan,' Meadows said. 'Did you go up there often?'

Macsen looked up. 'No. It was taken on one of our walks. We've been there maybe twice. It was just before she went off to uni. She took the photo with her.'

Meadows nodded. 'Have you been to Tenby recently with Alys?'

Rhodri felt his stomach flip. Why would they be asking that? he thought. Panic rose until it constricted his throat. He saw the same fear on Macsen's face. An uncomfortable silence fell on the room. He reached for the mug of coffee and took a sip. The movement seemed to stir Macsen.

'No,' Macsen finally said. 'Why?'

'We're just looking into all the places she visited and all her contacts,' Meadows said. 'Did she mention going on a trip there? Perhaps with her friends.'

'No,' Macsen said. 'She may have gone at some time.'

'What about the initial *J*? Do you know someone who would sign their name that way? Or someone whose name starts with *J* that Alys knew?'

Rhodri glanced at Macsen. He looked like he was about to throw up. The name screamed in his head. He started running through names in his mind, desperately trying to think of someone else whose name began with *J*.

'Macsen?' Meadows asked.

Macsen was just staring blankly at Meadows.

Rhodri could feel sweat gathering on the back of his neck. 'Jordan,' he blurted out.

Meadows turned his gaze upon Rhodri. 'Who is Jordan?'

'Erm… one of the boys. He works on the scaffolding with me. I was just trying to think of names starting with a *J*.'

'Surname?' Edris asked.

'I don't know,' Rhodri said.

'Would Alys have known Jordan?' Meadows asked.

'No, I don't think so,' Rhodri said.

'Macsen, is there anyone you can think of?'

Macsen shook his head.

Meadows paused, leaned forward, and spoke in a softer tone. 'One more thing. Did you know Alys was pregnant?'

'What?' Macsen looked like he had been punched in the stomach and couldn't get his breath.

'Fuck,' Rhodri said. He leapt out of the chair. 'I think he needs a drink.' He rushed into the kitchen, grabbed a bottle of Jäger and poured a generous shot. Macsen still wasn't talking when he got back into the sitting room.

'Here, knock this back.' Rhodri tried to hand the glass to Macsen.

'I can't... can't... breathe,' Macsen said.

Meadows got up from the chair and moved in front of Macsen. 'You're OK,' he said. 'It's just a panic attack. Look at me. I want you to concentrate on your breathing. Breathe in through your mouth and out through your nose.'

Macsen followed the instructions as Meadows counted a rhythm. Rhodri hovered close by, not knowing what to do.

'There you go,' Meadows said. He patted Macsen on the shoulder and returned to his seat.

Rhodri held out the glass to Macsen. He gulped the liquid, coughed, and drank down the rest. He appeared a little calmer so Rhodri sat down.

'Come as a bit of a shock?' Meadows said.

'I had no idea. Oh God.' Macsen put his head in his hands.

'About ten weeks so she would have known.'

Rhodri counted back the weeks and realisation dawned. He should say something but now wasn't the time.

'How were things between you the last time you spoke to Alys?' Meadows asked.

Macsen looked up. 'All right.'

'She didn't appear troubled?'

'No, she was fine.'

'It's a little odd, don't you think? She was pregnant. She must have been concerned. It's not easy to keep a secret like that.'

'Why would she be concerned?' Macsen asked. 'She would've known I'd stick by her.'

'But she didn't tell you.'

'I don't know why. Maybe she wanted to wait. Until she was sure. I was going to be a dad.' Macsen jammed his fist in his mouth. His shoulders heaved as he struggled to contain his emotions.

'I think he's had enough,' Rhodri said. 'Perhaps you could come back another time.'

Meadows nodded. 'Both of you will need to come into the station to give your fingerprints for elimination purposes. In the meantime, if you remember anything give us a call.' He stood up.

'I'll see you out,' Rhodri said.

He moved quickly to the door and opened it. He couldn't wait to get rid of them. He shut the door as soon as they stepped out. He let out a long breath but the relief he felt was short-lived. A crash came from the sitting room. He rushed in and saw Macsen had overturned the coffee table.

'What the fuck,' Macsen screamed as he hurled a coffee mug across the room.

'Calm down,' Rhodri said.

'Why didn't she tell me she was pregnant?'

'I don't know,' Rhodri said. 'I think you have more to worry about than that.'

Macsen's eyes flashed with anger. 'What's that supposed to mean?'

Rhodri held up his hand. 'Don't have a go at me, bro. You told her, didn't you? Why else would they be asking about Tenby?'

Macsen stepped towards Rhodri. 'Shut your mouth. They don't know anything.'

Rhodri could see a vein pulsing in Macsen temple. 'I'm not going to say anything. You just have to be careful. Is there anything the police could find?'

'Like what?'

‘I dunno. Did you talk about it on Messenger? Or text about it? They’ll be checking her phone.’

‘I’m not bloody stupid,’ Macsen said.

‘What if she discussed it with someone?’ Rhodri said. He saw a look of worry on Macsen’s face. Now he had him. If he could keep his mind occupied, he wouldn’t start asking awkward questions.

Chapter Six

'We should arrest the pair of them,' Edris said. 'Neither of them gave a decent alibi and Rhodri was giving me the evils.'

Meadows laughed. 'We can't arrest someone for giving you the evil eye. He probably took a dislike to you because you're a detective.'

'He didn't look at you like that.'

Meadows shrugged. 'I wouldn't worry about it. He'd probably be the same with Blackwell.'

'That doesn't make me feel any better.'

Meadows started the engine and pulled away from the cottage. 'They had an interesting reaction to some of our questions.'

'Yeah, and did you see their faces when you asked about Tenby?'

'Even stranger was the fact they didn't ask why we wanted to know about someone with the initial *J*. They're definitely hiding something.'

Meadows pulled onto the main road and followed the traffic through Llandeilo. A few people were walking around the shops. Others were sitting in a café, cups held in hands, as they gazed out of the window.

'Maybe they followed Alys to Tenby and saw her with some guy,' Edris said. 'Then Macsen asks Alys to Llyn y Fan. They argue and he kills her. He calls Rhodri to come and pick him up.'

'He did seem genuinely grief-stricken, but I suppose it could be tied up with guilt.' Meadows drove down the hill and over the stone bridge which crossed the river Towy.

It wasn't the type of place you'd expect a crime. Meadows often wondered why the peacefulness of the countryside didn't calm the souls of those who lived there. He'd learned from experience such places harboured secrets and the communities looked after their own. He guessed everyone had a breaking point. Was that what happened? he wondered. Macsen lost it for a few seconds.

'We'll need to check their alibis. First, I want to talk to Alys' other friends. See what they made of Alys and Macsen's relationship.'

Just over ten minutes later, Meadows parked the car outside a detached house. It looked like a newbuild with a garage to one side and a lawn at the front.

'Nice place,' Edris said. 'I wonder how she affords it.'

'Maybe she shares. A lot do now with the rent being so high.'

'Come on then,' Edris said. 'We got another two after this and it's Friday. It would be nice to get home at a reasonable time seeing as I'll be in the whole weekend.'

'We all will,' Meadows said and climbed out of the car.

They walked up the pathway and knocked on the door. A few moments later it opened. A woman in her mid-twenties looked from Meadows to Edris. She had long russet hair which lay on each shoulder in two fat braids. Freckles covered her face, which was devoid of make-up. Meadows thought she had a vulnerability about her.

'Christie Bailey?' Meadows asked.

She nodded.

He introduced himself and Edris.

'Come in,' she said. She turned and led them into a sitting room where two women were on the sofa.

Meadows noticed the two balloons shaped to make the number twenty-five. They hung above the table which held unwrapped gifts.

'We left the decorations up,' Christie said. 'We thought she would come back.' Her voice caught and she folded her arms around her body. 'This is Iona.' She pointed to the petite woman with long chestnut hair. 'And Sammy. Can I get you a tea or coffee?'

'No, thank you,' Meadows said. He sat down in the armchair and looked around.

The room was large with an open staircase running up the back wall. Modern prints hung against pale grey walls and the black leather sofa and chairs sat on a pale salmon carpet. Everything looked fresh but there was no warmth, no personal effects to make it feel homely.

Edris pulled a chair from under the table and turned it to face the women.

Christie took the second chair, keeping a distance between herself and Edris.

'I'm glad we caught you all together,' Edris said. 'Saves us speaking to you all individually.'

'We came over earlier,' Iona said. 'We wanted to be close by in case Macsen needed us.'

Meadows noticed the coy smile she gave Edris.

'Rhodri texted me to say Macsen wasn't doing so well,' Sammy said. Her large hazel eyes glistened. 'It's awful.' She shook her head and her black corkscrew curls bounced.

'My mum has been over to see Alys' mum,' Iona said, and sat forward. 'She said someone murdered Alys. Is that true?'

'We are treating her death as suspicious,' Meadows said.

Sammy's hand flew to her mouth, Christie wrapped her arms around her body, and Iona's eyes widened.

'I understand you were all good friends. How long have you known Alys?'

'I'm her oldest friend,' Iona said. She flicked her hair back over her shoulder. 'We went to school together.'

'We work together,' Sammy said. 'So, about three years.'

Meadows looked at Christie.

Christie rocked slightly in the chair. 'I met Alys when I worked with Rhodri. He introduced us a couple of years ago.'

'Who else was Alys friendly with?' Meadows asked.

'No one,' Iona said. 'She was either with us or Macsen. I don't know what I'm going to do without her.' She sniffled and her bottom lip wobbled.

'Can you think of anyone who may have wanted to harm Alys? Someone she argued with. An ex-boyfriend maybe.'

Iona shook her head and two fat tears tracked down her cheeks. 'She's only ever been with Macsen.'

'Everyone liked Alys in work,' Sammy said. Her voice was hoarse and her eyes puffy. Meadows imagined that she had been crying before they arrived.

'Did Alys talk to any of you about her relationship with Macsen?'

Iona was the first to answer. 'Alys told me everything.'

'Did they have any problems?'

Iona shook her head. 'He'd get on her nerves sometimes. Just stupid stuff.'

'They did break up a little while ago,' Christie said.

Meadows caught the look Iona shot Christie. Christie shrank back into the chair.

'When was this?'

Christie kept her eyes downcast.

'It was just before Christmas,' Sammy said.

'Do you know why?'

Sammy shrugged her shoulders.

'It was nothing,' Iona said. 'They were just taking a break. Macsen works all hours on the farm and he wasn't spending much time with her. He was sorting things out.

Getting some extra help. It was a few weeks apart, that's all.'

Meadows had the feeling that wasn't all there was to it. He looked at Christie. 'You were having the party for Alys here. Why not Macsen's or Alys' place?'

'I have a bit more space,' Christie said. She spoke softly.

'We wanted to surprise her,' Sammy said. 'She didn't want a fuss, you know, a big party. She didn't like that sort of thing.' She balled her fists together on her lap and Meadows could tell she was fighting to keep the tears back.

'We were going to the restaurant and all coming back here,' Christie said. 'Everyone was going to stay the night. We'd all booked the day off work on Wednesday.'

'I wanted it to be special for her,' Iona said. 'We had a photo booth and games set up.' She glanced over at the balloons then quickly looked away.

'How was Macsen when he arrived?' Meadows asked.

'Just Macsen,' Iona said. 'He had a few drinks and was telling stories and laughing. We put on some music and danced.'

'I can't believe we were enjoying ourselves when Alys was probably dead by that time.' Sammy's voice broke and she put her fist to her mouth.

'So as far as you know,' Meadows said, 'Alys was happy with Macsen. They hadn't had an argument in the days leading up to the party?'

'Yeah,' Iona said. 'They were good.'

Meadows looked at the other two women. Sammy nodded her head. Christie gave a small shrug of the shoulders and looked away. He got the impression that Christie didn't agree with the other two. He waited a few moments but she didn't offer any more information.

'Did Alys tell you she was pregnant?'

'Pregnant? No,' Iona said.

Meadows noticed that Iona didn't look surprised. Sammy looked stunned and all the colour had drained from Christie's face.

'She was ten weeks pregnant.'

'Oh God.' Christie put her hand to her mouth and leapt off the sofa. She dashed to the stairs and ran up. A few moments later Meadows heard retching.

'Christie's a bit of a snowflake,' Iona said.

Meadows thought the comment was unkind. He had never viewed compassion as weakness. 'I expect it's been a shock for her.'

'For all of us.' Iona bristled. 'Especially me. She was like a sister.'

'When was the last time you saw or spoke to Alys?' Meadows asked.

'Friday,' Iona said. 'She came over with Christie. She brought a dress I wanted for the party. She had discount at the store. I sent her a message on Tuesday morning but she didn't respond.'

'Sammy?' Edris asked.

'I saw her at work on Monday and I sent her a message Tuesday morning,' Sammy said. 'I thought I'd see her at work but she called in sick.'

'So, she hadn't planned to take the day off? Had she been unwell on Monday?' Meadows asked.

'No, she was fine,' Sammy said.

'When I found out she hadn't been to work I thought she'd just pulled a sickie so she could get ready for the party. We've all done it,' Iona said.

'Not Alys,' Sammy said.

Christie came back into the room and sat on the sofa in between Sammy and Iona.

'Are you OK?' Meadows asked.

'Yes, sorry. It's just so horrible.' She wrapped her arms around herself and leaned back.

'Christie, when was the last time you saw or spoke to Alys?' Edris asked.

'I saw her Monday after work. We'd take it in turns to drive to Llanelli as she worked close by. Then she sent a message later. It must have been around nine. She said she wasn't going into work and would see me at the party.'

'Did she say why?' Edris asked.

Christie shook her head.

'Had there been any changes in Alys' behaviour in the past few weeks?' Meadows asked.

The women looked at each other.

'No,' Iona said.

'She thought someone was watching her,' Christie said.

Iona rolled her eyes. 'They don't need to hear about that. There was nothing to it.'

'When was this?' Meadows asked.

'It started about a month or so ago,' Sammy said. 'She thought she'd seen someone out in her garden at night.'

'Did she report it?' Edris asked.

'Don't think so,' Sammy said.

'She thought someone had been in her house,' Christie said.

'She was imagining things,' Iona said. 'There was no break-in. The doors were locked and the windows shut.'

'Obviously she wasn't imagining it,' Sammy snapped.

Iona glared at Sammy.

Meadows could feel the tension growing between the women. It appeared that Iona wanted to control what information was given about Alys.

'Why did she think someone had been inside?' Meadows asked.

'She said things had been moved around,' Sammy said.

'And stuff left,' Christie said.

'Can you be more specific?' Edris asked.

Christie shrugged and shrank further into the sofa. 'I think she said a straw had been left on the table, and a bowl.'

'And a bottle of wine,' Sammy said.

'Gifts then,' Meadows said.

'I told her it was probably the landlord doing a check and leaving her some wine. She said she would ask.'

'Did she?'

'Dunno,' Iona said.

'Who had keys to Alys' house?'

'Macsen and me,' Iona said.

'I have one,' Christie said. 'Sometimes I picked her up early. I'd go in and make a cup of tea. She did the same here when she was picking me up.'

'We swapped keys,' Sammy said. 'We gave spares just in case we locked ourselves out. We're always in and out of each other's houses.'

A lot of keys floating around, Meadows thought. 'Anything else out of the ordinary? Can you think of anyone who paid Alys a lot of attention?' He looked at Sammy. 'Someone in work or a customer.'

'No, we all get on well at work. There was no flirting if that's what you mean.'

'There were the date nights,' Christie said.

Iona's head snapped towards Christie. Meadows was quick to catch the look that passed between them. Iona looked furious and colour rose in Christie's cheeks. He looked at Sammy. Her discomfort was evident in her poise.

'Sorry,' Christie said. 'I thought it might be important.'

'It was just a couple of nights out,' Iona said. 'There's nothing to tell.'

'Sometimes it's the small details that matter,' Meadows said. 'I understand these questions can seem intrusive and you may want to protect Alys.' He looked at each of the women in turn. 'She was your friend and you don't want to feel you're being disloyal. What's important now is we catch the person responsible for Alys' death.'

They all nodded.

'What happened at the date nights, Christie?' Meadows asked.

Christie fiddled with the cuff of her sleeve. 'Alys was a bit down after she broke up with Macsen so we thought we would go out to cheer her up.'

'When was this?'

'Just before Christmas.'

'Are you sure there wasn't more to it than them just taking a break?' asked Meadows.

'Yes,' Iona. 'I already told you.'

'Christie?'

'She said she'd found out something about Macsen.' Christie squirmed.

'She didn't say anything to me,' Iona said and folded her arms.

'Did she say what she had found out?' Meadows asked.

Christie shook her head.

'Sammy, did she say anything to you?'

'Not really. She was very upset,' Sammy said. 'She wouldn't speak to Macsen or Rhodri. It was a bit awkward.'

Meadows looked at Christie. 'Tell me about these date nights.'

'It was just a bit of fun,' she said. 'We–'

'Actually, it was my idea,' Iona cut in.

Meadows ignored her. 'Go on, Christie.'

Christie looked uncomfortable. 'Iona found this speed-dating site.'

'I heard of those,' Edris said. 'The company hires different venues and sells tickets. You pick your age range and go along.'

'Yeah, that's right,' Christie said.

'Have you been to one?' Iona asked.

'Erm, no,' Edris said. 'Can you tell me the site you used?'

'It was called The One,' Iona said.

'Which venue did you attend?'

'There were two. In Swansea. One just before Christmas and one in January.' Iona gave him the details.

Meadows looked at Christie. 'What happened there?'

'Nothing really,' Christie said. 'The women sit at tables and the men rotate. You get three minutes to talk then the next one comes along. Everyone has a number and you put down the number of the ones you like. You wait to see if you get a match.'

'Did Alys match with anyone?'

'You don't know straight away,' Sammy said. 'You have to log into the site.'

'It was a waste of time,' Iona said. 'They were all a bunch of losers. We only went for a laugh. You'd have to be desperate to match with the type of men who go there.'

'What type is that?' Meadows asked.

'Ones that can't pull. You know, the saddos.'

Meadows imagined some shy awkward twenty-something plucking up the courage to go and talk to women. Poor buggers, he thought.

'Was there anyone in particular who showed an interest in Alys?'

'A few at the bar,' Sammy said. 'She was so pretty. I think everyone there would have put her number down.'

'I had a lot of hits,' Iona said. 'You got one, didn't you, Christie.'

Christie blushed. 'Yeah.'

'Do you think Alys met up with someone?'

'I think she–' Christie began.

'No,' Iona cut in. 'She wasn't interested in anyone but Macsen.'

'Christie?' Meadows said.

Christie shook her head.

'Did Macsen know about these date nights?'

'No,' Iona said. 'We all promised Alys we would never mention it.'

Meadows paused and watched the three women. Sammy was swirling a lock of hair around her finger, Christie was pulling at her cuffs, and Iona was sat back stiffly with her arms folded. He didn't think he was going to get any more information about the date nights, not with Iona trying to control the answers. He was sure if Christie was alone she would say more. He decided to change the direction of questioning.

'Have any of you taken a recent trip to Tenby with Alys?' Meadows asked.

Iona shifted in her seat. 'No, we haven't been there for years.'

'Did she mention going to Tenby?'

They all shook their heads.

'Did she talk about someone who calls themselves Jay or has the initial *J*?'

'No.' Iona's answer was instant. Meadows caught a glimpse of something. He wasn't sure if it was guilt or fear.

'Are you sure?'

'Don't think there's anyone,' Sammy said. 'Why?'

'It's someone we think Alys was in contact with,' Meadows said.

'There's Jonathan in work,' Christie said. 'He's an old guy so I don't think he would have known Alys. He may have heard me mention her.' She looked at Sammy. 'Wasn't there a Julie who worked with you?'

'Oh yeah,' Sammy said. 'She retired last year. You could probably get her details from work. I don't think Alys kept in contact with her. They weren't close.'

Meadows didn't think any more information would be forthcoming, especially with the three of them together. He looked at Edris and gave him a nod to continue.

'We're looking at everyone's movements on the day Alys died,' Edris said. 'It's important, not only for elimination purposes but also to jog people's memories. Can you think of anything unusual that happened that day? If we could start with you, Sammy. Where were you on Tuesday morning between the hours of seven and twelve noon?'

Sammy thought for a moment. 'I got up at seven. I do every morning for work. I was in just before nine. Then I got a message from Macsen asking if I could pick up Alys' birthday cake from the farm. I had to get someone to cover for me so I could sneak out.'

'Why did he need you to pick up the cake?'

'He said he had to go and do something for Alys later that day and he wouldn't have time to go back to the farm to get it.'

'It's a bit of a trek from where you work,' Edris said.

'Yeah,' Sammy said. 'Over an hour. I wasn't happy about it.'

'What time did you get there?'

'About ten-thirty.'

'And you saw Macsen?'

'No, he wasn't there. No one on the farm knew anything about the cake so I went back to work. I got back around twelve-thirty. I worked my lunch hour to make up time. I was a bit pissed off if I'm honest.'

'What about you, Christie?' Edris asked.

Christie, who had been picking at her thumbnail, looked at Edris. 'I was here until just after ten. I did some work when I waited for Macsen. He didn't show so I went to work. I was there for the rest of the day.'

'Where do you work?' Edris asked.

'Elfan's Plumbing in Llanelli.'

'What time was Macsen supposed to come?' Meadows asked.

'He said he would be here before ten. He wanted to drop some things off for the party. I sent him a message but he didn't reply.'

'So, Macsen was supposed to be here *and* at the farm?' Meadows asked.

'Yeah,' Sammy said. 'But later he said he never sent a message to me or Christie.'

'Text message?' Edris asked.

'No, we mostly use Messenger,' Christie said. 'We thought perhaps his account had been hacked. Maybe one of his mates messing around. Macsen was really angry about it.'

'The messages sound specific,' Meadows said. 'The mention of a birthday cake and a party. Who else knew about the planned celebration?'

'No one,' Iona said. 'I guess Alys' mum and dad knew but why would they send messages? They were pointless. I think it was Macsen and then he went off doing something else and forgot.'

'I thought that too,' Sammy said.

'Did you get a message from him, Iona?' Meadows asked.

'No,' Iona said.

'Where were you on Tuesday morning?' Edris asked.

'In work,' Iona said.

'Where do you work?'

'I'm a technical assistant for Level Up, the gaming company. It's only temporary while I develop my modelling career.'

'What time did you get into work?' Edris asked.

'Erm… Tuesday, I overslept. My alarm didn't go off. I got in about midday.'

Edris finished writing and closed his notebook. 'That's all the information we need. Thank you.'

'One more thing,' Meadows said. 'We have a team of forensic officers in Alys' house. It would be helpful if you would come to the station to give your fingerprints. It will help to isolate any prints that shouldn't be there.'

'Of course,' Christie said.

The other two nodded.

Meadows stood up. 'Just go in to Ystrad Amman Station and ask for DC Harvard. In the meantime, if you remember anything else, please let us know.'

'I'll see you out,' Christie said. She led them to the door.

'That Iona is a bit full of herself,' Edris said as soon as they were back in the car.

Meadows nodded. 'There's something odd about the group dynamics. You wouldn't expect Christie to be friends with Iona or even Sammy.'

'Maybe she was Alys' friend and tagged along as part of the group,' Edris said.

'But it's Christie's house they are gathered in. I had a feeling she would have said more if the others weren't there.'

Edris nodded. 'Iona didn't look shocked by the news Alys was pregnant.'

'I'm sure she knew.'

'Then why not say?' Edris asked.

'Macsen and Alys split up before Christmas. They all went out on a date night. Alys was ten weeks pregnant. Maybe the baby wasn't Macsen's.'

Chapter Seven

Iona watched out of the window until the detectives had driven away. She turned to face Christie. 'Why did you have to tell them about the speed dating?'

'I hope Rhodri isn't going to find out,' Sammy said.

'I'm sorry,' Christie said. She sank down into the chair. 'I thought it best to tell them everything. It could have something to do with what happened to Alys.'

Christie looked like she was about to cry. So pathetic, Iona thought. She never understood why Alys was friends with Christie. Everything about her got on Iona's nerves. The clothes, the hair, and she didn't even bother with make-up. She had tried to be nice, even suggested she use her hairdresser. Now she was just blurting things out without a thought for the rest of them. At least she didn't say anything about *J*. Did that mean Alys hadn't told her? She couldn't be sure. She'd have to get Christie alone to find out. She'd also have to stay close and make sure she didn't say anything to the police. Ew, that would mean she'd have to be nice.

'Don't worry about it, Christie,' Iona said. 'It's just we have to think of Macsen. His heart must be breaking. Imagine what it would do to him if he found out.'

'Found out what?' Sammy asked.

Iona rolled her eyes. 'Speed dating.'

Christie nodded. 'The police asked a lot of questions. What was all that about *J*?'

Iona felt her stomach flip. Christie was looking at her, her eyes searching. She knows, she thought. Panic tightened her chest when she thought about what Alys was going to do. She must have written something down. Why else would the police be asking questions about him? 'How would I know?' she snapped.

'When are you going to the police station?' Sammy asked.

'I'd rather we go together,' Christie said. 'I don't fancy going on my own.'

Just the thought made Iona nauseous. She tried not to think about the last time. The endless questions. The knowing look in their eyes. She had only just managed to get away with it.

'We'll go tomorrow,' she said. 'Don't worry about it, Christie. It's only fingerprints and we'll all be together.'

'Maybe we should go now,' Sammy suggested. 'Get it out the way.'

'We have things to do,' said Iona. 'First, we need to go and see Macsen. We should take him some food. That's what people do, isn't it?'

'I hope you're not expecting me to cook,' Sammy said.

'No. Christie, you're good at cooking.'

'Not really,' Christie said.

'Just something simple,' Iona said. 'Next, I think we should start planning the funeral.'

'Is it a bit soon for that?' Sammy asked.

'No. It's going to be huge. It can take weeks to plan. There are the flowers, the music, how she's going to travel, and the dress code. So much has to be done.'

'Won't her parents be planning the funeral?' Christie asked.

'They're not going to have a clue what Alys would want. When we've worked it out then I'll go and see them. I'm sure they'll be grateful. I expect they haven't even thought about it.'

'Her poor parents,' Christie said.

'I can't bear to think about what Alys went through,' Sammy said. 'She must have been terrified. Why would anyone want to hurt her? She was lovely and so kind.'

Christie moved to put her arm around Sammy. Sammy put her head against Christie and sobbed.

Iona turned her back on them. They have no idea what Alys was like, she thought. Now they are going to turn her into some sort of saint. Perfect Alys. It's all going to be about her now. What about me? She clenched her fists so tightly, her nails cut into the palms of her hands. No one knew what she had found the day after Alys went missing. There was no one she could tell now who would understand.

Chapter Eight

A part of Meadows wished he didn't have to go into work. He'd cancelled his plans for the weekend and all the excitement he had felt had drained away. He watched Daisy putting on her coat. Her long black hair was loose and fell over her shoulders. Her blue eyes crinkled at the corners as she smiled at him.

'I'm sorry about this weekend,' he said.

'Don't worry about it.' She reached up and kissed him. 'We can go to the commune another weekend. There's no point in going now. You'd only be thinking about the case.'

He laughed. 'You know me too well.' She had no idea what he had planned. Even if she did, she would never complain. He felt lucky. She made no demands on him.

'How's Harvard doing?' Daisy asked.

'Good. Fits in with the team. Even Blackwell.'

'I can't believe how young he looks. He's like a schoolchild.'

'He is young,' Meadows said. 'Very keen. Always smiling and gets on with the job.' He checked the time. 'I better get going.'

'Yeah, me too. I'll go and spend some time with Dad then pop in to see your mum. Go and solve your case then we'll have our break.'

'Thanks.' He kissed her and left his cottage.

As soon as he started the car, his thoughts turned to Alys Pugh.

* * *

Edris was the last one to walk into the office and was joined by Harvard.

'Bout time,' Blackwell said. 'Late night, was it?'

'My fault,' Harvard said. 'I kept him out.'

'Didn't expect you to be in today,' Valentine said.

'I thought we'd all be in this weekend, because of the investigation.'

'Let's see where we're at,' Meadows said. He walked up to the incident board. Alys Pugh smiled at him from the photograph. Her pixie-style blonde hair and large blue eyes tugged at Meadows' heart. This young woman who looked so full of life bore no resemblance to the still and waxen body he'd seen at the morgue. He turned to address the team.

'Forensics have retrieved Alys' handbag from the lake. It had been weighed down with stones. It looks like the contents were thrown into different parts of the lake. So far they have found her mobile phone and car keys. It's a large lake to search so it's going to take some time. Paskin, have we got her phone records?'

'Yes. Nothing of interest to note. Calls to her mum, Macsen, and friends. Last call was her work. At 6.31 a.m. on Tuesday. The call lasted less than a minute. I'm waiting for transcripts of text messages.'

'Her mobile phone has been sent to tech,' Meadows said. 'Hopefully we'll get more information if they managed to retrieve the data. Alys and her friends use Messenger to communicate. Chris Harley is looking at her laptop. Once he has access to her account, we'll be able to view Alys' messages. Anything from the appeal?'

'Not much,' Paskin said. 'No one walking the area at that time. There were a couple of hikers who walked to the lake Tuesday afternoon. We've talked to them. They said it was misty and they didn't see much. The only other thing of interest was a report of an argument between Alys and another woman. It took place at lunchtime outside a café in Llanelli. The other woman was a similar age to Alys. Long chestnut hair. The description matches Iona Young. The witness couldn't be certain of the exact date but it was around about a week before Alys was murdered. We're trying to pin that down and talk to the owner of the café.'

'Interesting,' Meadows said. 'What about her social media activity?'

'She had a lot of friends on Facebook. I'm keeping an eye on posts coming in. Lots of condolence messages. RIP, fly high, with the angels now – that sort of thing.'

'Why do people write that shit?' Blackwell asked. 'I hate RIP. It reminds me of cartoon gravestones. So disrespectful.'

'I guess people don't know what to say,' Valentine said.

'These posts are from people she's had no contact with for years.'

'Any of them have the initial *J*?' Meadows asked.

'I've flagged them to check out,' Paskin said. 'Alys was very active on Facebook and Instagram up until 2019. Lots of photos of partying. Posts about outfits, make-up, outings, and group photos. The usual stuff. Macsen features a lot. Then nothing. Iona tags her in a few posts but Alys doesn't comment.' She looked at Harvard. 'Your turn.'

Harvard glanced at his notes. 'Alys had no cautions or convictions. Good grades at school with no notable problems. She went to Bristol University in 2016. Studied Film and English. She didn't complete the course. Dropped out in the third year. Took a job in Weavers in

2019 where she's been since. Rents her house. She doesn't appear to have stayed in contact with anyone from university. She socialises with the group of friends we have listed on the board.'

'What about Macsen, and her friends?'

'Again, no convictions or cautions for Macsen. Poor performance at school. Left at sixteen and has worked on his parents' farm since. He owns the cottage in Llandeilo. It was left to him by his grandmother. Iona went through school with Alys and attended the same university course. She completed her degree with a third. Christie is originally from Bridgend. Studied Mathematics at Cambridge. She left with a first.'

'That's quite an achievement,' Blackwell said.

Harvard nodded and glanced at his notes. 'After university she worked for Rhodri before taking employment with Elfan's Plumbing. Sammy dropped out of college and has worked for Weavers since. She grew up in Llanelli where she still lives. Now, Rhodri does have a record. Possession. Class A. He also attended Bristol University at the same time as Alys, graduated with a 2.2 in Business Studies. His first company went under and he now owns the scaffolding business. None of them have a history of violence.'

Meadows added the information to the board. 'Blackwell?'

'No problems in work,' Blackwell said. 'Good timekeeping. Got on with all the staff and clients. She had booked Wednesday off but was expected in work on Tuesday. Phoned in sick, leaving a message on the answering machine. According to the manager, Alys rarely took sick leave.'

'Interesting,' Meadows said. 'Her decision not to go to work on Tuesday must have been a last-minute one. Otherwise she would have booked two days off. Christie and Alys shared the driving. She messaged Christie at around nine on Monday evening to say she didn't need a lift. If Christie dropped her off at about six on Monday evening then that leaves three hours. What happened in those three hours to make her decide to go to Llyn y Fan?'

'Someone must've come to the house or called her,' Valentine said.

'No incoming calls for that time in her phone records,' Paskin said.

'Could have been a call using Messenger or WhatsApp,' Harvard suggested.

'It would've been someone in her contacts,' Meadows said. 'Chris should have something for us by this afternoon. What about her family?'

'Two cousins on her mother's side and four on her father's side,' Valentine said. 'We've spoken to them all and the aunties, uncles, and grandparents. All tell the same story. Alys was a lovely girl. Lively as a child. No drug or drink problems. It was expected she would marry Macsen. Not one of them stood out as suspicious. Nothing in the background checks. Last time most of them saw Alys was at Christmas for a family gathering.'

'Uniform have reported back: the neighbours say she was friendly and quiet. Never had any problems or heard any arguments,' Meadows said. 'One neighbour stated her car was missing by the time he left for work at seven-thirty on Tuesday morning. He didn't see any other cars near the house that morning or the previous night. So far there are no sightings of her driving to Llyn y Fan.

'Alys had told her friends she was being watched and someone had been in her house. Then there's the flowers, card, and rock we found in the bin. That could have been done by Alys, but the sprinkling of sand over her food in the fridge is vindictive. Christie also mentioned Alys had been on a couple of speed-dating nights following a break-up with Macsen. It's interesting that Macsen didn't mention the recent break-up when we interviewed him. Could Alys have met someone there? Hence the flowers, rock, and birthday card. Then there's the fact she hid her pregnancy from Macsen. It all points to her seeing someone else. Theories?'

'Alys gets back with Macsen so she wants to end it with this *J* guy,' Edris said. 'She had given him a key and he was the one hanging around and leaving her gifts. That's why she didn't report it. She decides to meet him up Llyn y Fan so she can end it. It's isolated and if he causes a scene they won't be heard. He kills her. Then he goes back to the house. Bins the flowers and dumps sand over the food.'

'Where did he get the sand?' Valentine asked.

'Maybe it was some ornament he bought her to remind her of the time they spent together in Tenby. You know the type of thing. Sand and shells in a glass.'

'Don't think I've seen anything like that,' Valentine said. 'I suppose he could've made up some weird hamper with the rock.'

'It sounds more like she had a stalker,' Paskin said. 'He watches her, knows her routine, then he takes it further and picks the locks, starts leaving her things. She catches him. He takes her to Llyn y Fan and kills her.'

'Nah,' Blackwell said. 'He'd have to put her in the car, drive her there and drag her up to the lake. He certainly wouldn't be able to carry her up there. Then what does he do? Walk back to where? It's miles from anywhere. If it's some sicko he would have killed her in her house.'

'What makes you think it's a man?' Paskin said. 'It could be a woman. Jealousy or revenge.'

'I think it would have been someone she trusted,' Meadows said. 'She was somehow persuaded to take the day off sick and meet at the lake.'

'Llyn y Fan meant something to Macsen,' Edris said.

Harvard nodded. 'He finds out she is seeing someone else, maybe she tells him she's pregnant and it's not his, he meets her at the lake and kills her. A moment of madness. Alys has told him and her friends she's being watched so he goes back to the house to make it look like it's a stalker that's killed her.'

'All good theories,' Meadows said. 'But they leave a lot of questions unanswered. Other than Macsen we have these four.' Meadows pointed to the names on the board. 'Not one of them has a decent alibi for the time Alys was murdered. As Paskin said, it could be a woman. One of these three women?'

The room was silent as the team looked again at the faces of Alys' friends pinned to the incident board.

'I had the feeling they were withholding information,' Meadows continued. 'They were vague about why Alys and Macsen split up before Christmas. Christie said Alys had found something out about him. Whatever it was, she got over it as they got back together. Iona controlled the conversation. I think we'd get more out of them separately. They will be coming into the station at some point to provide fingerprints. Blackwell, Harvard, and Paskin, I'd like you to take one each. Get them to go over their accounts of Tuesday morning. Check out their alibis. See if you can get them to open up about Alys and Macsen's relationship and the possibility of Alys seeing someone else. That leaves Rhodri. Not an unusual occurrence to go off with your best mate's girlfriend. If he'd been in Alys' bedroom he would've left a trace. Chase him up to provide fingerprints. Valentine, I'd like you to look into the speed dating.'

Valentine nodded.

'We are now looking at two main lines of enquiry. One, Alys was seeing someone else, possibly a married man, given the secrecy. This turned sour, leading to harassment. She may have met him to try and end it for good. She could have told him about the pregnancy and he panicked. Someone must have seen them together. There is a connection to Tenby. We need to check all Alys' bank statements. Look for anything that would give an indication of when she was there. Petrol, shopping, or a meal.

'Second is Macsen Lloyd. He may have found out about the other guy. She tells him she's pregnant and he kills her in a fit of jealousy. Macsen claimed he was in Ystrad Fflur when Alys was murdered. We spoke to a number of people who work on the farm and his parents. They back up his claim that he left around seven-thirty Tuesday morning and returned just after midday. Edris, how long to get to Llyn y Fan from the farm?'

Edris called up the map on his phone. 'Thirty-six minutes.'

'An hour to walk to the lake at a decent pace. Even an hour and a half would give him plenty of time to kill Alys and get back to the farm,' Meadows said.

'Let's bring him in,' Blackwell said.

'We have nothing on him,' Meadows said. 'He claims he asked directions in Ystrad Fflur. I've asked uniform to check it out. We need to be able to place him near or at Llyn y Fan. Get tech to check his phone location for Tuesday morning. It's a long shot. We just need to prove he wasn't in Ystrad Fflur as he claims. When he comes in to give his fingerprints, ask him for a voluntary DNA sample. See what reaction you get. We also need to get a match on Alys' baby. It could well have been Macsen's. The timing is tight given the break-up. However, he's not out of the frame for being the father.'

'Perhaps she didn't know who the baby's daddy was herself,' Valentine said.

'If Macsen found out Alys was seeing someone else, why not just break up with her?' Paskin asked. 'They had already split up before Christmas. Killing her is a bit of an extreme reaction. There has to be more to it.'

'Spur of the moment,' Edris said. 'He could've just lost his temper.'

'What about the messages he sent to Christie and Sammy?' Harvard asked. 'He wanted them out of the way. Christie was at home waiting for Macsen. Otherwise she could have gone to Alys' house to see if she was OK.

Sammy might have tried to call her when she didn't come into work. Looks like he wanted to make sure no one knew Alys' plans. If it is Macsen then it's premeditated.'

'Good point,' Meadows said.

'It could all be about control,' Valentine said. 'She went off to university and left him behind. She comes back without finishing her course. Cuts herself off from all but a small group of joint friends. She even cut her hair short. It's like she had plans for a career and gave it all up to be with him. We've all seen it before. These types of men don't just break up with you. It's a case of if I can't have you then no one will.'

'I didn't get that impression,' Meadows said. 'If that was the case then they would be living together so he could watch her every move. It's still worth bearing in mind though. Edris and I will go and see her parents. I want to know what they thought of Alys' relationship with Macsen. They may also be able to shed some light on what made Alys change from an outgoing fun-loving girl to someone that lived a quiet life. I have the feeling we are missing something.'

* * *

The family liaison officer, DS Brianna Lloyd, opened the door to Meadows and Edris.

'Gareth and Liz are in the kitchen,' she said. 'I've been trying to get them to eat something.'

'Any visitors?' Meadows asked.

'Wyn and Anwen Lloyd – Macsen's parents. They came yesterday evening. Gareth's brother, Hywel, and Debbie Young.'

'Iona's mother?'

Brianna nodded. 'After that they asked me to keep everyone away.'

'How did you find the Lloyds?'

'They were very emotional. Wyn was openly crying. I got the impression they were genuinely fond of Alys. I'll take you through.'

It was silent in the house again and Meadows could feel the grief. It seemed to swirl in the air. Gareth and Liz were sitting at the kitchen table. Both had an untouched plate of food in front of them.

'I'm sorry to disturb you,' Meadows said. 'We would be happy to wait in the sitting room until you've finished eating.'

'It's fine,' Liz said. 'I can't face anything. Please sit down.'

'Have you got news for us?' Gareth asked.

'I'm afraid not.' Meadows pulled out a chair and sat down. 'We are following a number of lines of enquiry.' He knew how hollow that sounded. 'We need to ask you a few more questions.'

Edris took a seat next to Liz and opened his notebook.

'I understand from what Brianna has told us that you didn't know Alys was pregnant.'

Gareth shook his head.

'She didn't say anything to me,' Liz said. 'I guess she was waiting for the right time to tell us. We would have been happy.' She looked at Gareth. 'We're never going to have grandchildren. Never see our girl get married.' A tear tracked down the side of her face.

Brianna placed a mug of tea in front of Edris and Meadows. She turned to Liz. 'Can I get you anything?'

'No, thanks, love.' She turned to Meadows. 'She's been marvellous.'

Brianna grabbed another mug of tea and took her place on the other side of Liz.

'Alys and Macsen had been together a long time,' Meadows said.

'Yes, since they were young,' Liz said.

'I understand they had a break-up before Christmas.'

'Yeah, they had some falling out. Nothing serious.'

'Did you have any concerns about their relationship?' Meadows asked.

Liz shook her head.

'I thought they were a bit young when they first got together. Too young to be serious,' Gareth said.

'Yeah, but they broke up for a good while. Then they got back together. It's not like they never had any time apart.'

'When was this?' Edris asked.

Liz thought for a moment. 'Beginning of 2019. Yes, because she had come back from university.'

'Alys went to university in 2016, is that correct?' Meadows asked.

'Yes. Bristol.'

'Macsen didn't go with her.'

'No,' Gareth said. 'He had to work on his parents' farm. Don't think he had much choice.'

'Do you think he was unhappy about her going?'

'No,' Liz said. 'He encouraged her to go. He said he didn't want to hold her back. He went up to visit her a lot. She came home for the holidays. They seemed to be making it work.'

'She didn't complete her degree. Why was that?' Meadows asked.

'She struggled with the work in the third year. I think it all got too much for her. She came home for the Christmas holidays. She was her usual self, but then she became withdrawn when it was time to go back. Stayed in her room. We thought she'd be OK in a couple of weeks but she never went back.'

'Do you think Macsen had anything to do with her leaving university?'

'No, because they broke up after that. Must have been a year or more until they got back together,' Liz said.

'Wait, are you suggesting Macsen… that he… killed Alys?' Gareth said.

Meadows saw the instant change. From grief to rage. 'No, not at all. We have to look at everyone involved in Alys' life. Particularly those closest to her. We are just trying to build a picture of their relationship and of Alys' life, the people she met, places she visited, anything in her past that may be relevant. Not everyone we question is a suspect. We have to eliminate certain people and the only way we can do that is by asking questions.'

Gareth relaxed a little but Meadows guessed he'd be going through a list of Alys' acquaintances, mentally questioning everything about them.

'Do you know why they broke up?'

'No,' Liz said. 'She wasn't herself for a while. Didn't go out. Hardly spoke to us. I suppose it was depression.'

Meadows wondered why they hadn't mentioned Alys' depression the last time he spoke to them. He figured they must have been in shock at the time. 'Did Alys have any treatment for it?' he asked.

'No, nothing like that. Iona came back for the holidays and spent most of her time in Alys' room. Whatever Iona did, it worked. Alys snapped out of it. She cut her hair, got a job, and moved to her own place.'

'Have you any idea what caused her depression?'

'No,' Liz said. 'University was the first time she had been away from home. I've heard lots of young people struggle with the pressure of exams. Particularly in the third year. Although her grades had been good. She told us she was on track to get a first.'

'Would it be fair to say she changed after going to university?' Meadows asked.

'In what way?'

'From the photos we've seen on social media, Alys appeared to be like any other teenager at that time. Going out to parties with her friends, shopping trips, and posting updates every day. She was popular and interacted with lots of people. It's very different to what we are hearing now. She has been described as being quiet, someone who keeps to a small circle of friends. She also seemed to have removed herself from social media.'

Liz shook her head. 'No, she was no different. Other than that time she left university but she recovered from her depression. I don't think she changed, just grew up. Alys was eighteen when she went to university. That was seven years ago. All kids go a little wild when they reach their teenage years. She was no different. She just settled down.'

Alys would have only been around twenty-one when she changed, Meadows thought. 'Do you think Alys met someone while she was in university? And that could have caused the break-up with Macsen?'

'She didn't say anything to us,' Gareth said. 'It's possible, I guess. It was the first time she had been away from him.'

Liz shook her head. 'No, she wasn't like that. She wouldn't have cheated on him.'

'What about after they broke up. Did Alys date anyone else?'

'No.' Gareth said. 'If she did, it wasn't anyone important enough for her to mention.'

'Did Alys talk about a recent trip to Tenby?'

'No,' Liz said.

'Was it somewhere she liked to go?'

'I don't think she's been for years,' Liz said. 'Last time I remember her going was before university. A bunch of them from sixth form went for New Year's Eve. A last get-together before they went their separate ways. I was worried about her going because she was young. They all had a good time from what I remember.'

'Why are you asking about Tenby?' Gareth asked.

'We are looking at all the places Alys visited recently. We found some sticks of seaside rock in her house.'

'That will have been a gift from someone. Alys never liked rock,' Liz said.

'We also found a birthday card. It was signed only with the initial *J*. From the content, it appears it was from someone close to Alys. Does it mean anything to the two of you?'

'*J*?' Gareth shook his head.

'No one I can think of. Could be someone in work,' Liz said.

Edris' phone rang. He excused himself and left the room. Gareth's eyes trailed him.

'Did Alys keep any of her belongings here?' Meadows asked.

'Her room is just the same as the day she moved out,' Liz said. 'We haven't got round to changing it. There are some clothes, photos, and her books from school and university. Mainly bits that she collected over the years and didn't have room for.'

'I'd like to send an officer over to go through her things if that's OK. There may be something there that would give us an idea if she was seeing someone else.'

'Like what?' Liz asked.

'A photograph, a card. Something she wouldn't want Macsen to see.'

'I don't know if I want someone going through all her stuff.'

'How about we take a look together?' Brianna asked.

'OK,' Liz said.

Edris came back into the room and gave Meadows a nod.

Meadows pushed back his chair. 'Thank you for your time. I appreciate the questions are intrusive.'

Gareth looked at Edris. 'Has something happened?'

'No,' Edris said. 'Information we were waiting for has just come through.'

Meadows could see Gareth wasn't convinced. 'We will keep you updated on our progress,' he said. 'Right now we have a lot of information to process and interviews to conduct. We are doing all we can to find the person responsible for your daughter's death.'

'I'll see you out,' Brianna said.

When they reached the door, Brianna stepped outside. 'I hope you don't mind I suggested going though Alys' room with Liz.'

'Not at all,' Meadows said. 'It could be the case that someone she met at university came back into her life. It's worth looking into.'

Brianna nodded. 'I'll see if I can get Liz to open up more. There may be secrets that Alys shared only with her mother.'

Meadows turned to Edris. 'I take it that was Chris from tech.'

'Yeah, he's got something interesting for us.'

Chapter Nine

The digital forensic office was stifling. Computer fans whirred, fingers clacked on keyboards, and printers spat out sheets of paper.

'Don't they ever open the windows?' Edris asked as he took off his jacket.

'I think they're immune to the heat,' Meadows said.

Chris Harley was waiting at the far end of the office. He was one of the few people who were taller than Meadows. He had a mop of curly brown hair and his blue eyes were dancing with excitement.

'What have you got for us?' Meadows asked.

'I'm working on Alys' phone. Because it was submerged in water for a few days, a lot of damage has been done. I'm still hopeful. I did however manage to get into all her accounts on her laptop. The group of friends mostly use Messenger to communicate. It's where I found a message from Macsen Lloyd. He asked Alys to meet him at Llyn y Fan on Tuesday morning. I printed a transcript. Here.' He handed a sheet of paper to Meadows.

Meadows read through it. It was all the evidence they needed to arrest Macsen. He handed it to Edris.

'Looks like he was going to propose,' Edris said.

'Yeah, he talks about the surprise. Even tells her to phone in sick and not tell anyone where she's going. From this, it looks like he planned the whole thing. He must be a bit *twp*. We were obviously going to find the messages,' Chris said.

'Which makes me think it's not premeditated,' Meadows said. 'Anything else?'

'Just her friends wishing her happy birthday, and the message she sent to Christie saying she didn't need a lift into work the next morning. I've printed a list of her contacts. There's a group chat set up for Alys, Christie, Iona, and Sammy. Then one that included Macsen and Rhodri. Most of the messages are between Alys and Macsen. Some of them, well…' Chris pushed his glasses up his nose. 'They're a bit steamy.'

Edris laughed.

'It's not funny,' Chris said. 'Makes me feel like a voyeur. Lots of photos. I'll send the file to you. I recovered quite a few. Those ones are mostly of her time in university.'

'She had deleted them?' Meadows asked.

'Yeah, all of them.'

'It's got to be another man,' Edris said. 'She meets him at uni. Macsen finds out, so they split up. She comes home to get him back. Fast forward a few years and she meets up with the uni guy again, gets pregnant. Macsen takes her up Llyn y Fan and proposes. She has to tell him she's pregnant by someone else. He kills her.'

'It fits but we still don't know for sure the baby wasn't Macsen's,' Meadows said.

'Maybe Alys didn't know herself.'

'That's possible. All right, let's grab Harvard and bring him in.'

* * *

Harvard leaned forward from the back seat. 'I can't believe we've got him on day three.'

Meadows could feel the excitement radiating off him.

'Good start for you,' Edris said.

'We may have the messages but we've a long way to go,' Meadows said. 'No physical evidence and no witnesses.'

'Yeah, but motive and opportunity.'

'Not enough for a conviction,' Meadows said. 'You've also got to factor in the stalker. Defence will use that.'

'It was probably him. Making her suffer by leaving stuff,' Edris said.

'A few hours ago you thought it was spur of the moment,' Meadows said.

'So he planned it,' Edris said.

'And there lies our problem,' Meadows said. 'It's either premeditated and he overlooked the fact we'd see the messages, or it's loss of control and another person was harassing her.'

'He might just confess,' Harvard said.

'Yeah, there's always that,' Meadows said.

'Thanks for letting me tag along.'

'You're not here for the ride,' Meadows said. 'You're the one who's going to arrest him.'

Harvard smiled. 'Really?'

'Yes, you're part of the team. I want you to see the case through to its conclusion.'

'Thanks.'

'Uniform is going to meet us there for back-up. A full risk assessment has been carried out. Macsen's family are farmers. They'll have licensed firearms. An officer has visited the farm to make sure all guns are accounted for and secured. I don't anticipate any problems. However, you will need to wear a vest. We'll be with you the whole time. Any sign of confrontation, I want you out of there.'

'And take your hat off,' Edris said. 'He'll see you coming a mile off.'

'It's just so cold. It's supposed to be spring.' Harvard pulled his hat off and checked his hair in the rear-view mirror.

Edris laughed. 'It's Wales, what do you expect? It jumps from zero to heatwave for a week or so then you're back to rain and cold.'

A police car and van were parked at the end of Macsen's drive when they arrived, their presence hidden by large conifer trees. 'I wouldn't be surprised if he knows we are coming,' Meadows said. 'As soon as someone sees a police car, curtains twitch and the gossip starts.'

They jumped out of the car and were handed vests by Hanes.

'Let's go,' Meadows said.

Harvard led the way. The driveway was no more than a dirt track. It twisted past two large paddocks before opening into a courtyard. When they reached the door, Harvard gave it a loud knock. A moment later Macsen appeared. To Meadows, he looked to be wearing the same clothes as the previous day. His hair was awry and his face covered in stubble.

'Macsen Lloyd, I'm arresting you–'

'What the fuck?' Macsen's eyes were wide with shock.

'–on suspicion of…'

Before Harvard could say any more Macsen stepped back and tried to close the door.

Harvard pushed forward but the door wouldn't budge.

'Don't be stupid, Macsen,' Meadows said. He moved besides Harvard and shoved the door. It gave way.

'You can't do this,' Macsen shouted. 'I didn't do anything. I would never hurt Alys.'

Harvard took a breath and continued to read Macsen his rights.

'Shut it, you little prick.' Macsen took a swing at Harvard.

Harvard ducked and Edris, who was standing behind him, took the force of the punch.

Meadows caught hold of Macsen's arm and twisted it behind his back. 'Calm down.'

It took the help of Hanes to get the cuffs on Macsen. He continued to struggle and shout obscenities as Hanes led him away.

'You OK, Edris?' Meadows asked.

'Yeah.' Edris rubbed the side of his face. 'Got a fist like a brick.'

'He's all yours, Harvard,' Meadows said. 'Go with Hanes and book him in. Then he can sit in the cell to cool off.' He snapped on a pair of latex gloves. 'Let's take a look around. Forensics can get his phone, laptop, clothes, and shoes. Hopefully they can find some evidence to place him at Llyn y Fan.'

They walked through the cottage checking cupboards and drawers. There was plenty of alcohol and a bag of cannabis but nothing else of interest.

'It's surprisingly tidy for a guy living alone,' Edris commented.

'You can talk,' Meadows said. 'Your place sparkles like it's been covered in fairy dust.'

'Fair point, but he doesn't strike me as the orderly type.'

'You think he's been cleaning?'

'Maybe.'

'Let's take a look upstairs,' Meadows said.

The cottage only had two rooms upstairs. One was a bathroom with a cast-iron tub on brass feet. The other room was Macsen's bedroom. There were no dirty clothes lying around. The bed was made with a towelling robe draped across the bottom. Next to the window was a dressing table with two bottles of aftershave, a comb, and a mobile phone charger.

Meadows moved to the windowsill and peered inside a cardboard box. He could see face cream, a hairdryer, and some make-up.

'Looks like he's collected Alys' possessions and placed them in here.'

'Didn't hang around,' Edris said.

Meadows plucked a small velvet box from the top. He opened it and saw a gold band with a cluster of diamonds. 'It's an engagement ring.'

'I was right about that. He was going to propose. She must've told him about the baby.'

'We know now he has a temper,' Meadows said. He placed the ring back in the cardboard box.

Downstairs, Mike Fielding from forensics was bagging the laptop.

'I'll leave you to secure the place when you've finished,' Meadows said.

'Hope he's left his keys somewhere handy,' Mike said.

Meadows walked out into the hallway. Next to a mirror he saw a small rack of hooks with bunches of keys. One caught his attention. He plucked it off the hook and examined it. It was a car key with a keyring made of a heart-shaped piece of slate. White letters spelled out "Tenby".

Chapter Ten

It was evening by the time Meadows got a call to say Macsen's solicitor had arrived. The whole team was still in the office, eager to see if he would be charged.

'How's your face, golden boy?' Blackwell asked.

'Sore,' Edris said.

Blackwell laughed. 'Move quicker next time. Harvard was the arresting officer. Even he managed to walk away without damaging his hair.'

'You seen the size of the guy?' Edris asked. 'I'm lucky he didn't fracture my cheekbone.'

Meadows grabbed a file off the desk. 'Right, Harvard, let's go down.'

Harvard jumped up from his desk and followed Meadows down the stairs to the custody area. Sergeant Folland was sitting behind the desk.

'He's in interview room one,' Folland said. 'He's calmed down now but the bugger has given me a headache hollering all afternoon.'

'Who's his solicitor?' Meadows asked.

'Paul Gregson. He's OK by all accounts.'

'Yeah, I've had dealings with him before. Likes to settle things quickly. See you later.'

* * *

Meadows walked into the interview room. 'Sorry to have kept you.'

Macsen stared at him with barely contained contempt. Gregson acknowledged him with a curt nod. Meadows took a seat and waited for Harvard to settle. He made the introductions for the recording. Harvard called the time and date.

Gregson straightened his tie. 'Firstly, my client would like to apologise for his outburst during the arrest. He is grieving the loss of his long-term girlfriend and his emotions are running a little high.'

'An officer was assaulted,' Meadows said.

'It was an accident,' Macsen said. 'He got in the way. I wasn't trying to hurt him.'

'No, you were aiming for another officer.'

Macsen leaned forward. 'What do you expect? You're supposed to be out there finding Alys' killer. You turn up at my house, without warning. I had a shock. You're wasting time.'

Gregson put his hand on Macsen's arm. 'I'm sure my client is willing to answer any questions you have.'

Macsen sighed. 'I'm sorry I hit him. Can we just get this over with?'

'As part of our investigation we examined Alys' laptop. We now have a transcript of the messages sent to Alys, via Messenger, on Monday evening.' Meadows pulled a sheet of paper from the file and pushed it towards Macsen.

Macsen looked down and read. His brows furrowed in confusion.

'For the tape, we are showing Macsen a transcript of the messages between himself and Alys.' Meadows nodded to Harvard.

'The following conversation took place at 8.45 p.m. on Monday,' he said and proceeded to read from the paper.

Macsen: I can't wait to show you the surprise we talked about. Meet me at Llyn y Fan at 7.30 in the morning xx

Alys: I can't I have work.

Macsen: Pull a sickie. I've already asked my brother to cover for me but I'll have to show my face after lunch or Dad will pitch a fit.

Alys: OK then. Why does it have to be so early?

Macsen: Cause no one will be around. I want it to be just the two of us. Don't tell anyone.

Alys: I'm so excited.

'I never sent those messages,' Macsen said.

'The meet-up time was 7.30 a.m. Half an hour before the earliest estimated time of death,' Meadows said.

'I was in Ystrad Fflur,' Macsen said. 'Oh God, she thought she was meeting me.'

Meadows could see Macsen's eyes were weighted with tears. 'We will be checking your phone and any other devices you use.' He pointed to the paper. 'This is your Messenger account and your profile photo?'

'Yes, but I've never seen these messages before. Wait, there were others. Talk to Sammy and Christie. They both said they received messages I didn't send on Tuesday. I was going to change my password because I thought my account had been hacked.'

'Sammy and Christie did tell us about the messages,' Meadows said. 'Although they didn't seem convinced that your account had been hacked.'

'I got one from Rhodri. That's why I was in Ystrad Fflur. Rhodri said he never sent the message asking for help. Someone else is doing this.'

'You think some random hacker?' Harvard asked.

'It has to be whoever killed Alys.'

'There's a lot of details in those messages. The sender would have had to know it was Alys' birthday, know that you intended to surprise her. You did have a surprise for her, didn't you?' Harvard asked.

'I was going to ask her to marry me,' Macsen said.

'Who knew about it?'

'No one,' Macsen said.

Harvard sat back.

'You expect us to believe you bought the ring, were going to propose at Llyn y Fan, but someone beat you there and killed Alys?' Meadows said.

'No. I was going to propose at the dinner on Tuesday. I was going to put the ring on top of the cake. She would've seen it when she blew out the candles. Her friends would've been taking photos so they would capture the moment.' Macsen wiped his eyes.

He's not giving anything away, Meadows thought.

'What went wrong between you and Alys?' Harvard asked.

'Nothing.'

'Alys had a picture of the two of you taken at Llyn y Fan lake. It meant something to her. To the both of you.'

'Yes, but anyone could have seen that photo. I haven't been up there for ages.'

'So you say, but no one saw you in Ystrad Fflur,' Harvard said.

'I asked directions from a farmer.'

'Where?'

'I don't know. I was lost.'

'If we were to give you a map of the area, could you show us roughly where you were?' Meadows asked.

'I don't know. There's only so many farms around there. Surely you can check.'

'Did Alys tell you about the baby?' Meadows asked.

'No.'

'Was she seeing someone else?'

'No.'

'Alys was ten weeks pregnant. According to her friends, the two of you split up just before Christmas.'

'Yeah.'

'Why didn't you mention this before?'

Macsen shrugged.

'When did you get back together?'

'A few weeks later. In January.'

Meadows waited. He could see Macsen doing the math.

'Are you telling me the baby wasn't mine?'

'We won't know until we've carried out tests.'

'My client voluntarily gave a DNA sample and fingerprints,' Gregson said.

'Yes,' Meadows said. 'From that we will be able to determine paternity.'

'Who is *J*?' Harvard asked.

'I already told you I've no idea,' Macsen said.

'Yet you weren't curious as to why we asked you,' Meadows said. He took another sheet of paper from the file and pushed it towards Macsen. 'This is a copy of a birthday card we found in Alys' house. More precisely in her bin.'

Macsen looked at the paper and Meadows saw him stiffen.

'Did you find out that Alys was seeing someone else? Did you follow them?'

'No.'

'Did you see them in Tenby together?'

'What? No. Alys would never go to Tenby.'

'Why is that?' Meadows asked.

'She didn't like it there. Preferred Pendine. It's quieter.'

'So, as far as you know, Alys hasn't been to Tenby recently?'

'No, she hasn't.'

'Someone she knew visited there. Gave Alys sticks of rock. Only she threw them in the bin. Five of them. You know the type: pink with a white centre, the name of the seaside town running through the middle. These ones were from Tenby. We also found seashells and sand.'

Macsen was breathing heavily now.

'Would you like some water?' Meadows asked.

Macsen nodded. He pulled at his T-shirt collar as he tried to suck in air.

Harvard got up and left the interview room.

'I think my client needs medical attention,' Gregson said.

'It's a panic attack,' Meadows said. 'Macsen, take a slow breath. Count. Remember: in through your nose, and out through your mouth.'

Harvard came back into the room and placed a plastic cup of water in front of Macsen.

'Drink it slowly,' Meadows instructed.

He could see Macsen's hand shaking as he held the cup. Macsen's breathing returned to normal and he set the cup down.

'Are you OK to continue?' Meadows asked.

Macsen nodded.

Meadows noticed that he still looked pale and clammy. Why this reaction to the mention of Tenby? he thought. He knows something.

'Did you put those rocks in Alys' house? Maybe to punish her. Let her know she had been found out. Was it a romantic getaway? Did you see her on the beach with someone else?'

'No,' Macsen said. 'I don't know anything about bloody rocks. Someone must've given them to her and she binned them. Probably didn't like them. What does it matter?'

'When was the last time you were in Tenby?'

'Years ago. Alys went in the last year of school. I tagged along.'

Meadows reached inside the file, took out the car keys, and laid them on the desk.'

'Can you confirm these are your car keys?'

Macsen looked at them. 'Looks like them. The sheep keyring is one Alys gave me but I didn't put that heart one on there.'

Meadows flipped the heart over and heard Macsen gasp. 'Tenby,' he said. 'This doesn't look years old. The writing isn't worn. Come on, Macsen, the keyring is relatively new.'

'What is this?' Macsen jumped up and swiped the keys off the desk.

'Sit down,' Meadows said.

Macsen jigged from foot to foot. 'You're messing with me. Trying to get into my head. *You* put that on there.'

'Why would we do that? What is it about Tenby that's upsetting you?'

'Some sicko has killed my girlfriend,' Macsen said. 'Now you're saying he took her to Tenby, bought gifts for her. Yeah, I'm upset. You keep asking the same stupid questions. I didn't kill her!'

'I think my client has answered all your questions,' Gregson said. 'Are you intending to charge him?'

Good question, Meadows thought. 'We have the messages sent to Alys, the photograph of Macsen and Alys at Llyn y Fan, and no alibi. It doesn't look good.'

'You also have no evidence to place him at the scene of crime,' Gregson said.

'Would you like to take a break, Macsen?' Meadows asked.

Macsen huffed and plonked down in the chair.

Harvard retrieved the keys from the floor and placed them on the desk.

'I didn't put that keyring on there,' Macsen said.

'When was the last time you used the keys?' Meadows asked.

'When I was out looking for Alys. I haven't left the cottage since.'

'Are you telling us someone came into your cottage while you were there? Put the keyring on then left? Without you noticing?' Harvard asked.

'Yes,' Macsen said. 'Because I didn't put it on there. I've never seen that keyring before.'

'Tell me about your relationship with Alys,' Meadows said.

'What do you want to know?'

'Would you say it was equal or did one of you take control? Make all the decisions?'

'We discussed things. Alys was easy-going so there was not a lot of disagreements.'

'You must've had arguments?'

'Yeah. Everyone does.'

'What did you argue about?' Meadows asked.

'Is this going somewhere?' Gregson asked.

'It's important to understand if Alys was happy.' Meadows looked at Macsen. 'It's better to get these things out in the open. If there were problems between the two of you then we will find out.'

'There were no problems. We just argued sometimes. Stupid things. Alys was messy. She'd leave all her things laying around. I did stuff that got on her nerves. The only thing we couldn't agree on was the farm. I'll take it over one day. Alys didn't want to live there. We were talking about it.'

'You broke up with Alys when she left university. Why was that?'

Macsen shrugged. 'I don't remember.'

'It was serious enough for you to stay apart for over a year.'

'We just wanted different things at the time.'

'Were you unhappy about her going to university?'

'No. I wanted her to go. To follow her dreams.'

'Why didn't she complete her degree?' Meadows asked.

'I don't know. She wanted to come home.'

'Was she seeing someone else when she was in university?'

'No. Well, not that I know about. We were still together then. I went up to visit her. What does it matter now? I don't care if she saw someone else at that time. I don't care if she fucked half the uni. I just want her back.' Macsen put his hands to his head. He gripped his hair so tight it looked like he was trying to yank it out.

'My client has answered all your questions. He has given you an explanation for the messages, his whereabouts on Tuesday, and voluntary DNA. He's happy to make himself available for further questioning. Can we agree my client is free to go?' Gregson asked.

'We will be holding your client until we have examined his phone and other electrical devices,' Meadows said. 'If we find those messages were sent from his IP address then we will be charging him.'

'Fine,' Macsen said. 'Then I'll expect an apology for your cock-up.'

Macsen was escorted back to his cell. This time without a fuss.

'I hope he is going to behave himself,' Sergeant Folland said.

'I don't think he'll be a problem,' Meadows said. 'See you later.'

* * *

'Not what we hoped for,' Harvard said as they walked back upstairs.

'No,' Meadows agreed. 'I have my doubts.'

'Did he fess up?' Blackwell asked as soon Meadows walked through the door.

'Nah,' Harvard said.

'He claims he didn't send the messages,' Meadows said. 'We have to wait for digital forensics. In the meantime, the clock is ticking. If he is guilty we have to produce more evidence to charge him.' He looked at the team. 'Go home and get some rest. I'll see you all early in the morning.'

Meadows walked up to the incident board and looked at the photos and notes. The more he looked, the less it made sense. Macsen wasn't stupid. If he did plan to kill Alys then why send the messages? He wasn't troubled that his devices were going to be checked, he thought. The rocks and mention of Tenby caused a reaction. A panic attack. Then, Meadows realised what he'd just witnessed in the interview room. Among the grief was something else. Fear. Macsen Lloyd was frightened.

Chapter Eleven

Sammy woke up and it took her a moment to remember what day it was. Monday, she thought. Usually she would be rushing about getting ready for work. Alys would always be in before her and they would have a chat before the doors to the store opened. She rubbed at her chest. She couldn't get rid of the hollow feeling. She was thankful work had been understanding and given her compassionate leave. She didn't think she would be able to manage a smile for customers.

Next to her, Rhodri slept. He'd turned up after hearing Macsen had been arrested. He'd been wasted and continued to drink until he'd collapsed into bed. Sammy was sure he'd also taken something.

'Rhodri, wake up.'

Rhodri opened his eyes, groaned, and went back to sleep.

'I thought you were going into work today,' Sammy said.

'Yeah. Make us a coffee, babe.'

Sammy jumped out of bed and slipped on a dressing gown. She'd make him the coffee but only because she wanted him out of the house. She didn't have the patience to put up with his drinking today. She walked down the stairs and through the sitting room and kitchen. Her thoughts were far away and she took little notice of her surroundings. She pushed open the bathroom door and the cold air shocked her awake. The bathroom window was open and the curtains billowed in the breeze.

'Bloody men,' Sammy said. She shut the window then lowered the seat on the toilet. It was when she turned around that she noticed the seashells lined up along the rim of the bath. A coldness crept over her.

'Rhodri!' Sammy ran from the bathroom. 'Rhodri!' She stopped in the kitchen and her breath caught in her throat. A clear plastic bowl was sitting on the table. It was filled with liquid and three straws were leaning against the side. Next to the bowl was a card with a white rose on top.

Rhodri came thumping down the stairs. 'What are you screaming about?'

'Look.' Sammy pointed to the table. 'Did you do this?' She knew the answer before he shook his head. She stepped closer to the table and sniffed the bowl. 'It's alcohol. What's going on?'

Rhodri didn't say anything. His eyes were fixed on the bowl.

'The card is addressed to me,' Sammy said. 'Should I open it? Rhodri?'

'Yeah. Maybe one of the girls dropped it over.'

Sammy looked at him. He sounded as convinced as she felt. She moved the rose and picked up the card. The envelope wasn't sealed. She plucked out the contents with the tips of her fingers. It was a simple drawing of a suspension bridge sitting between two cliffs. Below, a winding river had been coloured a deep blue. She flipped it over and read the words out loud.

Sammy, you can do better than this. Jxx.

She tried to hand the card to Rhodri but he shook his head. He looked to her as if he was about to be sick.

'What's going on?' she asked.

'I don't know,' Rhodri said.

'The bathroom window was open and there are shells on the bath. The police were asking about someone with the initial *J*. This is what happened to Alys. Someone left her stuff then they killed her.'

Sammy could hear her voice getting higher. Panic snaked its way through her stomach and up to her chest. Every muscle in her body was tensed and poised for action, but there was no outlet. 'What if they're still here?'

Rhodri moved quickly and grabbed a carving knife from a wooden block.

'I'm calling the police,' Sammy said.

'Yeah, you do that and I'll look around.'

'Don't leave me on my own,' Sammy said.

She grabbed her mobile. While she made the call Rhodri kept close, his eyes moving from the bathroom door to the sitting room.

'They are sending someone,' she said.

'OK, let's look around,' Rhodri said.

They moved from room to room checking behind furniture and in the wardrobe. Sammy could feel her heart thudding in her chest. Any moment she expected a figure to jump out at them.

Rhodri let out a sigh. 'There's no one here.'

Sammy started to cry. She couldn't help it.

'Hey.' Rhodri put his arms around her. 'It's OK. Come on, let's get dressed. I've got to get going.'

'What? You can't just leave me.'

'You'll be fine. Lock the door behind me.'

'No,' Sammy said. 'I don't feel safe.'

'The police will be here soon,' Rhodri said.

'Yeah, and they will want to talk to you as well.'

'Fine. I'm going for a smoke.'

Sammy went upstairs to get dressed. She would have liked a shower first but she didn't like the idea of being in the bathroom alone. Knowing a stranger had been in there made her feel vulnerable. Then there were the seashells. The police will check for fingerprints, she thought. The violation of her home while she slept made everything look contaminated. She wondered if the intruder had crept upstairs and watched them sleeping. She realised she was trembling and she couldn't stop the tears. She slipped a warm jumper over her head and wrapped her arms around her body. Another thought struck her: this is how Alys must have felt when she kept finding things. None of us took her seriously. A wave of guilt washed over her. She moved swiftly down the stairs hoping to leave the feelings behind.

'All right now?' Rhodri asked as he handed her a mug of coffee.

Sammy nodded and moved to the sitting room. She didn't want to be in the kitchen where she could see the items on the table. She sat down on the sofa and had just taken a sip of her coffee when the door knocked.

'That was quick. I'll let them in,' Rhodri said.

Sammy expected uniformed officers but it was Meadows and Edris. She was glad it was them, at least she wouldn't have to explain about Alys.

'I understand you've had an intruder,' Meadows said.

'Yeah,' Rhodri said. 'He's left stuff in the kitchen and bathroom.'

Meadows looked at Rhodri. 'He?'

'He or she. What does it matter? Someone has been in here.'

'Do you know how they got in?'

'Bathroom window,' Sammy said.

'Can you show me?'

Sammy set her mug down and got up from the sofa. She led Meadows into the bathroom.

Meadows stepped up to the window and looked at the catch. 'It doesn't look forced. Are you sure it was closed?'

'Yeah. I sometimes open it if it gets too steamy. Just to clear the mirror. I always close it afterwards. I guess with everything going on I could've forgotten, but it was freezing in here this morning. I would've noticed the cold air when I brushed my teeth last night. Then there's these…' She pointed to the seashells on the bath rim.

She could tell by the expression on Meadows' face that this was serious. 'This is the same as what happened to Alys. Isn't it?'

'Yes, we did find similar items. What else was left?'

'I'll show you.'

Rhodri was standing in the kitchen talking to Edris who was writing in his notebook. Sammy knew the only reason he looked so calm was because he had smoked a joint before they arrived.

'Did you touch anything?' Meadows asked.

'I opened the card,' Sammy said.

She had left it with the writing facing upwards. As Meadows leaned over to read, the front door opened. They all turned to look. Iona came rushing into the kitchen.

'I came as soon as I could,' she said.

'What?' Sammy asked.

'Rhodri sent me a message. He said you had a break-in.'

'You were upset,' Rhodri said. 'I thought Iona could come and stay with you.'

Sammy tried to hide her annoyance. The last person she wanted to see right now was Iona. 'There was no need for you to rush over.'

'I don't mind,' Iona said. She gave Edris a smile. 'Did they take anything?'

'They left that.' Sammy pointed at the table.

Iona looked and gave a startled cry as she jumped back.

'What's the matter?' Meadows asked.

'It's… It's a fishbowl,' Iona said.

'Fishbowl?'

'You fill them with alcohol and share them at parties.'

'Why has it upset you?' Meadows asked.

'Erm… we used to have them at university. Remember, Rhodri?'

Rhodri nodded.

'Is it something you all did together?' Meadows asked. 'With Alys?'

'Yeah,' Iona said, 'me, Alys, and Rhodri. Don't think we've shared one, have we, Sammy?'

'No,' Sammy said. Now she was going to have to listen to the stories of their time spent together. Iona always brought up stories from the past that excluded her.

'I think we might have drunk from one of those at that club in Swansea,' Rhodri said. 'You remember? We all got wasted and Macsen was sick in the taxi?'

'I don't remember that,' Sammy said.

'I do.' Iona looked at Rhodri. 'Why is this happening to us?'

'The note was addressed to me,' Sammy said.

'Signed by *J*,' Meadows said. 'Are you sure you don't know who that is?'

Sammy shook her head but she noticed Meadows was watching Iona's reaction. She had paled.

'Iona, if you know who this is you should tell us,' Edris said.

Iona glanced at Rhodri. 'I don't know. It's obvious whoever killed Alys has turned their attention on us. They could be watching me. I live alone. There's no one to protect me.'

'Why has it always got to be about you?' The words came out of Sammy's mouth before she could stop them. She saw the look of shock on Iona's face. 'Sorry, it's just been a bad morning. Can we go to the sitting room? I don't want to stare at those things. They give me the creeps.'

She left the kitchen and the others followed. Rhodri sat on the sofa and Iona plonked herself down next to him.

'I'll get a chair from the kitchen,' Edris said.

Sammy sat in an armchair and Meadows took the other one.

'I don't think any of you are in immediate danger,' Meadows said. 'The window has not been forced. You will all need to be extra vigilant with security. I will send an officer over to advise you. We'll also ask them to call on Christie. Is she at home?'

'No. She went to work,' Iona said. 'I'm surprised but then she wasn't as close to Alys as me.'

'It does look like someone is trying to frighten you, Sammy. Is there anywhere you could stay for a few days?' Meadows asked.

'You could stay with your parents,' Rhodri said.

'Or I could just stay at your place,' Sammy said.

'Yeah, I suppose,' Rhodri said.

Edris put the chair down next to Sammy and sat.

'Could this be someone who works with you, Sammy?' Meadows asked. 'Given that you and Alys worked together.'

'I don't think so.'

'Did you go to any work parties? Somewhere they might have been serving these fishbowls?'

'No, nothing like that. We had a Christmas dinner. Some went on for drinks after but not me and Alys.' She ran through all her work colleagues in her mind. 'No, there's no one. It's mostly women who work there. The few men either have girlfriends or are married. I can't remember anyone coming on to Alys.'

'What about the date nights?' Iona asked. 'Did you and Alys match with the same men?'

'What date nights?' Rhodri asked.

Sammy felt her cheeks burn. She looked at Iona who had a smug smile on her lips. 'It was nothing.' She turned to face Rhodri. He was glaring at her. 'We all went to one of these speed-dating things. I only went to make up the numbers. It was really for Iona and Christie. I didn't put anyone's number down. I wasn't interested and neither was Alys.'

'No one there that stood out as odd?' Edris asked.

'No,' Sammy said.

'Was there anyone in university who Alys was friendly with?' Meadows asked. 'First time away from home, lots of parties and new people. It's easy to make a mistake.'

Sammy saw a look pass between Iona and Rhodri. It was just a fleeting glance but enough to make her think there was an unspoken communication.

'Alys had lots of friends,' Iona said. 'We did party a lot but that's all there was. Drinking and having fun.'

'Rhodri?' Meadows asked.

'I didn't see much of her in uni,' he said. 'I was on a different course.'

'Why did Alys leave in the third year?' Meadows asked.

Both of them shrugged their shoulders.

They know something, Sammy thought.

Meadows looked at Iona. 'Alys' parents said you came to stay in the holidays that year. That you were the one to help Alys. You two must have talked about her reasons for leaving.'

'Not really,' Iona said. 'I went to cheer her up. She'd got into a state. Not leaving the house. If I'm honest I think uni was too much for her. It's not like school. You have to take care of yourself. Cooking, washing, and cleaning. Alys wasn't good at all that stuff. Her mum and dad spoilt her. She was never short of money. The rest of us had to make do on student loans. I know she wanted a first. She wouldn't have been happy with less. I think that's why she quit. She thought she was a failure. I talked her around. We did some girly things together. I suggested she cut her hair and have a fresh start. It worked.'

'Why did Macsen split up with her at that time?'

'I dunno,' Iona said. 'You'd have to ask him. Probably couldn't cope with her being moody.'

'Rhodri?'

Rhodri shrugged. 'He didn't say much about it. He's not into all that "share your feelings" crap. We went out for a few drinks. He just said he wanted to move on.'

'Did he move on?'

'No, just worked longer hours.'

'What about this recent break-up?' Meadows asked.

'They just wanted some time apart. Nothing serious. They argued like most. They weren't this perfect couple,' Iona said.

'Did these arguments get violent?'

'No,' Rhodri said. 'He never laid a hand on her.'

Meadows turned to Sammy.

'No,' she said. 'She never told me anything like that.'

'Macsen would never hurt Alys. Why have you arrested him?' Iona asked.

'He's helping us with our enquiries. That's all I can tell you.' Meadows turned to Rhodri. 'Macsen is still insisting you asked him to meet you in Ystrad Fflur.'

'I didn't ask him,' he said. 'He was pissed off about it on Tuesday evening. I told him I didn't send the message.'

'Did you manage to track down the client you were supposed to see?' Edris asked.

'No. There was no response to the emails I sent. The phone number doesn't work. Someone was messing about.'

'Iona, I got the impression you knew about Alys being pregnant,' Meadows said.

Iona nodded. 'She didn't want anyone to know.'

'It's not like it matters now,' Sammy said. 'Why did you lie about it?'

Everyone turned to look at Sammy. She shifted in her chair. Great, now everyone thinks I'm a bitch, she thought. It was just that Iona liked to feel special. Keep secrets. Sammy didn't feel like playing along.

'Iona, why didn't you tell us you knew?' Meadows asked.

'I don't know,' Iona said. Tears filled her eyes.

Sammy wasn't moved. She knew Iona could cry at will when she wanted her own way. She'd seen it often enough.

Iona sniffed. 'It would have felt like I was betraying her trust.'

'Was Alys afraid to tell Macsen about being pregnant?' Meadows asked.

'No. She just wanted time to go through her options.' Iona unzipped her handbag and started to rummage around.

'Was she considering a termination?'

Iona kept her head down as she searched her bag. 'She talked about it. She felt like she was too young to be having a baby. She didn't want to be trapped.'

'Is that how she saw it? Being trapped?'

'Not like that. It's a big commitment.' She turned to look at Sammy. 'I need a tissue.'

'There's some in the kitchen,' Sammy said.

'Go and get some, Rhodri,' Iona said.

'Get it yourself,' Rhodri said.

Iona gave him a dirty look but didn't move.

Meadows thought for a second. 'Did she tell you the baby wasn't Macsen's?'

'No, because the baby was Macsen's.' She rooted around in her pockets, seemingly getting more agitated.

'She was ten weeks pregnant. Alys and Macsen had split up.'

'Yeah, but they were together for New Year's Eve. She slept with him. She told me. She thought that's when she got pregnant. They hadn't been careful.'

'Is that what you argued with Alys about?'

'What?' Iona stopped fidgeting. 'I didn't argue with Alys.'

Sammy saw the flush creep up Iona's neck. She's lying, she thought.

'There was that time Alys came over here,' Sammy said. 'Christie came too but she didn't want you to come.'

'I don't know anything about that.' Iona's eyes were wide. 'We hadn't argued.'

'You were seen outside Kay's Café,' said Meadows.

'You met Alys a few times there for lunch,' Sammy said.

Iona snapped her head towards Sammy. 'So did you.'

'Maybe someone thought you were arguing. You do get snappy,' Sammy said.

'Could that be the case?' Meadows asked. 'A disagreement?'

Iona jumped up off the sofa and left the room. She could be heard blowing her nose. She came back, sat down, and folded her arms. 'When was this supposed to have happened?' she asked.

'About a week before Alys died,' Meadows said.

'Can't think what we would have disagreed about,' Iona said. 'Probably what we were wearing to the party. Oh yeah.' She smiled. 'Alys couldn't get hold of the dress that I wanted so I had to choose another one. I had my heart set on the first one. I expect I looked disappointed. Maybe someone took that as me being upset.'

'OK,' Meadows said. 'Forensic officers will be here shortly. They'll take away the items for testing and check for prints in the bathroom.' He stood up.

'Are you going to let Macsen go?' Rhodri asked. 'He's not the one breaking in and leaving stuff, is he?'

'That will depend on the outcome of our enquiries,' Meadows said. 'If you really want to help your friend, I suggest you start telling the truth.'

Sammy noticed Meadows looked at Iona when he said this.

'We have,' Iona said.

Lying bitch, Sammy thought.

The minute the detectives left, Rhodri turned on Sammy. 'You made me look like a right div.'

'What?' Sammy asked.

'Going out speed dating.'

'I think you've got more to worry about than that,' Iona said.

'What's that supposed to mean?' Rhodri asked.

Iona scowled at him. 'I had a Bristol University prospectus through the post this morning.'

'Yeah, well you went there. You'll be on their mailing list.'

'Are you really that stupid? I was living with my parents when I was at uni. They wouldn't have my address. Bristol Uni, Tenby, and the initial *J*. It has to be him.'

'Don't be ridiculous. He's dead.'

'Who's dead?' Sammy asked.

'No one. Just someone we used to know. We didn't get on with him,' Rhodri said.

'What's he got to do with Alys?' Sammy asked. 'Why are things being left in my house? If you know something, you have to tell the police.'

'He's got nothing to do with it,' Rhodri snapped. 'Stop being a drama queen.'

'You and Macsen better sort it out,' Iona said.

Sammy looked at the two of them. She was sick of their secrets and lies. They thought she didn't hear the whispers each time she left the room. It had been the same with Alys and Iona. Alys had been scared. Sammy knew more than they realised and was certain she couldn't trust any of them.

Chapter Twelve

There was silence in the car as Meadows drove towards Christie's workplace. He knew Edris would be thinking the same as him. If the murderer and the person breaking into houses and leaving gifts was one and the same then they had the wrong man in custody. It wasn't a good feeling.

'Macsen could still be involved,' Edris said, interrupting Meadows' thoughts.

Meadows nodded. 'Two of them working together? I think Iona was lying about the argument with Alys.'

'I wouldn't trust that one's radio.'

Meadows laughed. 'I don't think any of them have been totally honest with us. Now it looks like Sammy is a target.'

'Are we going to let Macsen go?'

'Yes, unless we find something else to link him to Alys' murder. We'll wait and see if Chris turns up anything from his phone and laptop. Just to be sure.'

They arrived at the plumbing unit where Christie worked. Two vans were parked outside. One with the back door open and a man in blue overalls loading a toolbox.

Meadows got out of the car and introduced himself and Edris. 'We're looking for Christie Bailey.'

'I'm Elfan,' the man said. He was in his fifties with a bald head and a round, friendly face. 'Christie is in the office. Terrible business with her friend. I told her she could take as much time as she needed. She insisted on coming in. Said she preferred to keep busy.'

'What exactly does Christie do?' Edris asked.

'Handles all the office work,' Elfan said. 'Appointments, accounts, stock, and wages. Couldn't manage without her.'

'Does she get along with everyone?' Edris asked.

'Yes, lovely girl. Nothing is too much trouble for her.'

'She sounds very reliable,' Meadows said.

'She is.'

'I have to ask, for elimination purposes. Did you see Christie last Tuesday?'

'Yes, she came in late, not sure what time as I was on a job. I wasn't expecting her in. She'd left a message to say she had to wait at home for something to be dropped off. To do with the party she was having. She did some work from home. She had booked Wednesday off as a holiday.'

'How was she when you saw her on Tuesday?' Meadows asked.

'Fine. She was excited about the party. I don't think she goes out that much or has a lot of friends. It was nice to see her have some fun. Then this happens. Poor kid.'

'Thanks for your time,' Meadows said. 'We just need to ask Christie a couple of questions.'

'Yeah, no problem. Just go through.'

Christie was tapping away at the computer keyboard. Her hair was pulled back and dark-rimmed glassed were perched on her nose. She wore cargo trousers and a baggy jumper. Although she appeared to be working, she had a faraway look in her eyes.

'Hi, Christie. Sorry to disturb you at work,' Meadows said.

Christie jumped. 'Oh, I didn't hear you come in. I've been trying to concentrate on work but my mind keeps wandering.' She peered at the screen. 'Probably been typing rubbish again.'

'We won't keep you long,' Meadows said.

'It's OK. I was going to take a break. Do you want a cup of tea?'

'Yes, please,' Edris said.

'That would be nice, thank you,' Meadows said.

They followed her to the kitchen where two large flasks were sitting on a worktop.

'I keep these on the go as the boys always want a cuppa when they get back from a job.' She took a cup and placed it under the flask.

'I had the feeling you wanted to say more last time we talked,' Meadows said.

Christie kept her back to them as she continued to fill the cups. 'I don't suppose it matters now Macsen has been arrested,' she said. 'Iona didn't want me to say anything because he had already been through enough.' She handed Meadows a cup and gave one to Edris. 'Help yourself to milk and sugar.' She poured milk into her own cup. 'I was only trying to help. I just don't think sometimes.'

Meadows could sense her discomfort. 'I understand Alys was your friend and you may feel like you are betraying her. Think of it this way: anything you tell us could help catch her killer. That's something you could do for her now.'

'But I thought Macsen… well, that he killed her?'

'Why do you think that?'

'Because you've arrested him. It was a bit of a shock.'

Meadows poured some milk into his tea. 'We haven't charged Macsen. We are just questioning him. If you do know something then you really need to tell us.'

Christie nodded. 'I'm sure Alys was seeing someone else.'

'Who?' Edris asked.

'I don't know. We took it in turns to drive to work. The last couple of months there were occasions she would drive in alone. She said she was working late. I offered to wait for her but she said she wanted to take her time. One time I went shopping after work and Alys' car wasn't there. I thought it was odd. I asked Sammy about all the overtime and she said Alys never worked late, none of them did.'

'Did you ask her about it?' Meadows asked.

Christie shook her head. 'Not really my business. Then one time she asked me to cover for her. If Macsen was to ask, I had to say she spent the night at my house. We had a few drinks so she couldn't drive home. She said she didn't feel like seeing him and needed an excuse. And there were other times when she cancelled plans.'

'Do you think Macsen knew or suspected?'

Christie blew on her tea. 'I don't know. When she said she thought someone was watching her I thought it might be Macsen.'

'Do you think she would have told Sammy or Iona if she was seeing someone else?' Edris asked.

'I didn't get the impression they knew anything, but Iona… well, she likes to feel special. She'd hint at knowing things but not tell you. I guess she might have known and felt she had one up on me and Sammy.'

'You don't get on with Iona?'

'She's OK. She was more Alys' friend than mine.'

'What was their relationship like?' Meadows asked.

Christie took a sip of her tea. 'I don't want to be bitchy.'

Meadows smiled. 'How about you just be honest.'

'Alys was beautiful and far kinder than Iona. Everyone loved Alys. Like when we went speed dating, all the men there wanted to talk to her at the bar.'

'Anyone in particular stand out?' Edris asked.

'No, they just sort of gathered around. Offered to buy her drinks. I think Iona was jealous of Alys.'

'Of her looks?' Edris asked.

'Yes, and of her relationship with Macsen.'

'Was there ever anything between Macsen and Iona?' Edris asked.

'I don't think so. Alys and Macsen were together in school. They've all known each other a long time.' Christie bit her bottom lip. 'Iona does act differently with Macsen. I've seen the way she looks at him sometimes. It's difficult to explain but I got the impression she was jealous whenever Macsen kissed or hugged Alys in front of her. She'll happily do anything for Macsen but no one else. I've seen her openly flirt with Rhodri but not Macsen. It's like she's trying to hide her feelings. From what I can tell neither Macsen nor Rhodri are interested in Iona in that way.'

'Does Iona have a regular boyfriend?' Meadows asked.

'No. She goes out on a lot of dates but they don't last long. She gets the ick and moves on to the next.'

'Do you think that may be because she is in love with Macsen?' Meadows asked.

Christie nodded.

Meadows could imagine the underlying friction it could cause between the women.

'Did Iona and Alys argue a lot?' he asked.

'I wouldn't say argue as much. Iona influenced Alys.'

'In what way?' Meadows asked.

Christie leant against the counter. 'I don't know… Little things, like she would make snide remarks, comment on what Alys was wearing. Alys would change to a different outfit. It was Iona who persuaded Alys to go to the speed-dating nights. She said it was time for her to move on.'

'What about the past few weeks? Was there any change between them?'

'There was some tension. They were friendly enough towards each other. I guess Iona was sort of passive aggressive. She wanted Alys to have a good birthday but didn't like her choice of location. Joked about it. She took credit for the decorations but didn't contribute anything. I just had a feeling something wasn't right between them.'

'Do you think Iona would tell Macsen if she knew Alys was cheating?' Meadows asked.

'I honestly don't know,' Christie said.

'What about Sammy? How did she and Alys get along?'

'Great. They worked together and it sounds like they had a laugh. Sammy is normally upbeat and you never hear her complain. She's taken Alys' death hard. I think Iona was a bit put out by their friendship.'

'Sammy's house was broken into last night,' Meadows said.

'On no.' Christie's eyes widened in shock. 'Is she OK?'

'Yes, she's fine,' Meadows said. 'Some items were left. Similar to the ones we found in Alys' house. Seashells, and a fishbowl filled with alcohol. Can you think of any reason why Sammy would be a target?'

Christie shook her head.

'There was a card left for her. Signed *J*. Does that mean anything to you?'

'No.' Christie's eyes filled with tears. 'What's going on? Poor Sammy must be terrified. I should go over.'

'Rhodri and Iona are with her and I got the feeling they are not telling me everything they know. Iona reacted badly when she saw the fishbowl. Macsen was also troubled by what was found in Alys' house. If you know anything about these items, or what they mean, then you need to tell us.'

'There is nothing more I can think of.' Christie wiped away a tear. 'Alys, Macsen, Rhodri, and Iona grew up together. They often talked about the past. They have their little in-jokes. Sammy and I were not a part of it. Iona would never confide in me. We all went over to see Macsen after we'd spoken to you. Rhodri was already there. Iona went into the kitchen with them and Sammy and I could hear them whispering. I couldn't make out what they were talking about but Macsen was angry.'

'Whatever it is, it looks like Sammy is a part of it,' Meadows said.

'Then it has to be something to do with work or the speed dating,' Christie said. 'There were some odd guys there.'

Meadows' phone pinged. He looked at the screen and saw a message from Chris.

'It would be helpful if you could remember any names from the speed-dating night,' Edris said.

'I'll try,' Christie said. 'Iona would've had more matches than me. I didn't contact anyone after the event. It's just numbers. They introduce themselves but you only talk for three minutes. With twenty men in one night you forget the names by the time you move to the next.'

'OK,' Meadows said. 'We won't take any more of your time. Thanks for your honesty. An officer will call with you to check the security in your home and see if you need any additional measures.'

'Oh.' Christie looked alarmed.

'It's just a precaution. Try not to worry.'

They left Christie and Meadows tossed the car keys to Edris. 'You can drive.'

'Good, that means I can choose the music.'

Meadows laughed. 'No, it doesn't. My selection of tracks is to help me think.'

'Old-school rock. I don't think that's gonna help.'

'Less of the old,' Meadows said and jumped in the car.

Edris started the engine. 'This case is getting more complicated. I'm sure Rhodri, Iona, and Macsen know something. If that's the case, why would Sammy be a target? Unless Rhodri is in on it and he put those things in Sammy's house to take the heat off Macsen.'

'Or it's one of the women,' Meadows said. 'Sounds like Iona would do anything for Macsen. Now with Alys out of the way she can make her move.'

'That would work,' Edris said. 'She spies on Alys and tries to spook her by leaving things in her house. She has a key. She tells Macsen that Alys is cheating. He kills her Alys and calls Iona. She goes to help. She didn't get into work until after twelve on Tuesday. Plenty of time to drive to Llyn y Fan and pick up Macsen. Iona was the only one not to get a message sending her someplace on Tuesday.'

'I don't know,' Meadows said. 'She was freaked out by the fishbowl.'

'Not freaked out enough to tell us what's going on,' Edris said.

'That's true. The question being, is it guilt or shame that stopped her from talking?' Meadows leaned forward and turned the radio up. 'I need to clear my mind.'

* * *

Meadows thought Chris looked worn out. There were dark circles under his eyes and his hair was wilder than usual.

'You look like you've been up all night,' Edris said.

'Yeah, when I start something I just keep going. I like a challenge.'

'I appreciate your enthusiasm but don't work yourself into the ground,' Meadows said.

'So, what good news have you got for us?' Edris asked.

'Don't get too excited,' Chris said. 'I've been working on tracking the IP address by–'

'Simple terms,' Edris said. 'I don't do tech.'

Chris laughed. 'You know what an IP address is?'

'Yeah, Internet Protocol address. It's a unique code that identifies devices on a network. You can trace it to a physical address, but that's as far as it goes.'

Chris smiled. 'Put simply, yeah. The messages that were sent to Alys did not come from any of the devices recovered from Macsen Lloyd's home.'

'Could he have another phone?' Meadows asked.

'He could but he would've been hacking his own account.' Chris scratched his head. 'This is where it gets complicated so stop me if I lose you. I can't track the IP address, which means the hacker's been clever. Could be they're using a VPN. A virtual private network hides your location, can make it look like you are in a different country. It's going to take me some time to work on it, and even then, if I can track them to a VPN host, they are not usually willing to give up the real IP addresses.'

'Yeah, that does sound complicated,' Edris said.

'Then there's the messages. They were sent to Alys then removed from Macsen's account. Hidden in chat but not very well. I also found the messages Macsen supposedly sent to Christie and Sammy. Again, hidden on Macsen's account. This is where it gets interesting. A message was received from Rhodri asking Macsen to meet him in Ystrad Fflur. After Macsen replied, the message was removed. The messages from Macsen to Alys, Christie, and Sammy, and the one he received from Rhodri are from the same IP address.'

'Are you saying both Rhodri and Macsen's accounts were hacked?' Meadows asked.

'It looks that way,' Chris said.

There was silence for a few moments as they processed the information.

'Yeah, but Macsen could've still done it from another device,' Edris said.

'The reply Macsen sent to Rhodri was from his own phone. Then it was hidden.'

'What's the problem with that?' Edris asked.

'Why bother to hide the reply he sent to Rhodri or get rid of the messages he sent himself from Rhodri's account? It was his alibi,' Meadows said.

Chris nodded.

'Now I'm getting confused,' Edris said.

'Basically, I don't think Macsen sent those messages to Alys or the others,' Chris said. 'He could have a hidden device but it wouldn't be easy. Also, if he was that clever there are better ways of getting rid of the messages. Why not hack Alys' account and remove the messages?'

'Why bother getting rid of some of them, why not all?' Edris asked.

'The killer wanted Alys at Llyn y Fan but didn't want Macsen to see the messages. Then they get Macsen out of the way by sending him to Ystrad Fflur with a message from Rhodri. They couldn't risk Rhodri seeing the message or replying to Macsen. So, they remove the message as soon as it is read. It would have to be fine timing,' Meadows said. 'How would the killer know when the message had been read and a reply sent?'

'Sophisticated hacking,' Chris said. 'Keylogging. Allows the hacker to snoop as you type, tap, or even talk.'

'Would they need access to your device?'

'No. If they get close enough they can use Bluetooth. Most people leave it on. Then there's phoney apps or phishing attacks.'

Edris pulled out his phone. 'I'm making sure my Bluetooth is off. Chris could be getting the dirty on me as we speak.'

Chris laughed. 'Pop down anytime and I'll check your security.'

'I think I'll do that,' Edris said.

Meadows' phone pinged. He looked at the screen. 'It's Daisy. The results are through on Alys' baby.'

Chapter Thirteen

Macsen got out of the car and looked at his cottage. He had never felt so relieved to see his front door.

'Are you sure you don't want me to come in with you?' his father asked.

'No, thanks, Dad. I just want to have a shower, drink a beer, and go to bed. I don't think I slept the whole time I was in that cell. It bloody stank and the noise went on all night.'

'OK, call if you need anything.'

'I'll see you in the morning,' Macsen said.

'Why don't you take a few days off? I've got it covered.'

'I want to get back to work,' Macsen said. 'I've had enough of staring at four walls.'

'Yeah, probably best. Take your mind off things. I'll pick you up at five.'

Macsen nodded. He didn't think anything could distract him from his thoughts. At least he could work himself to exhaustion. 'I'm hoping the police will let me have my jeep back soon. I don't know what they are hoping to find.'

'It's no problem for one of us to pick you up.'

'Thanks.' He shut the car door and took his house keys from his pocket.

He wasn't sure what he expected to find when he opened the door. The idea of the police going through his things irked him. He tried to shut down the anger he felt. At least they wouldn't have found anything, he thought. What he didn't want was a mess.

The door opened into a sitting room with an open fireplace. The first thing he noticed was upturned cushions.

'Bloody pigs,' he said as he straightened them out.

A tinkling noise caught his attention. He stood still and listened. He couldn't make out where it was coming from. He imagined the police had broken something and it was dangling from somewhere. If that was the case then he was going to put in a claim for compensation.

He walked into the kitchen and opened the fridge door. As he put his hand in to grab a beer he saw them. Five pink sticks of rock lying on the middle shelf. He froze. His heart drummed against his chest and his breath caught in his throat. He tried to take a deep breath but the room felt airless like all the oxygen had been sucked out. Panic gripped him. I'm going to die, he thought. His vision darkened and he could feel himself slipping away. Breathe and count, he told himself. In, two, three, four. He held his breath then let it out slowly. He kept repeating this until he felt his body relax. He slammed the fridge shut. Panic turned to anger.

'If you want me, come and chance it,' he shouted out. He was met with nothing more than the strange tinkling.

He went back to the sitting room then ran up the stairs trying to find the source of the noise. There was nothing in the bathroom. He moved quickly and flung open the bedroom door. The window was open but it wasn't the cold air that sent shivers through his body. Above his bed, a windchime moved in the breeze. The colourful shells tinkled as they knocked together.

Macsen watched them for a moment. He remembered the smell of the salty air. The waves crashing against the harbour wall. He shook away the memories. He couldn't go there. He grabbed at the windchime and yanked it down. With it in his hand he went through the cottage checking every cupboard and drawer to make sure there were no more surprises. Satisfied, he grabbed the rock from the fridge and dumped then in the bin with the windchime.

As he pulled out the black bag he thought about what the police had said. They had found rock in Alys' bin. Had she felt the same fear? Why didn't she just call? He knew the answer. She thought she was going to meet him. Emotion constricted his throat and he wiped at the tears that had escaped his eyes. He dumped the rubbish outside, locked the door and hung up the keys.

He tried to rest on the sofa but the coldness that had crept over him wouldn't go away. It felt as though he was chilled to the core and would never get warm again. He went back upstairs, stripped off, and jumped in the shower. He turned the temperature up to as high as he could stand and let the water run over his body. It chased away the chill and the smell of the police station but not the memories.

The longer he stood in the shower, the more he thought about the water. Alys struggling for breath. Her clothes soaked through. Cold and alone in the lake. He turned off the tap and got out. He heard a noise from downstairs as he was drying himself. It sounded like a door shutting. He looked around. There was nothing to use as a weapon. He wrapped the towel around his waist. Someone was messing with him. Someone had killed Alys. Anger spiked his veins. He wasn't going to wait until they came for him.

He ran out of the bathroom, down the stairs, and towards the kitchen. He charged through the kitchen door, saw a figure, and launched himself. There was a scream as they both crashed to the floor. Macsen rolled over and pulled back his fist. He only just managed to stop when he saw Iona's terrified eyes.

'What the fuck are you doing?' Iona shouted.

'What am I doing? You're the one creeping around my house.' Macsen grabbed the towel which had fallen off, and covered himself.

'You asked me to come.' Iona's eyes filled with tears. 'I thought you were going to kill me.'

'You're lucky I didn't, and I never asked you to come.'

'Yeah, you said bring beer.'

'Fuck's sake,' Macsen said. 'You know my account has been hacked. Why do you think the police arrested me?' He stood up and held out his hand to her.

'I didn't know.' Iona took his hand and pulled herself up. 'Why would they arrest you for that?'

Macsen explained about the messages found on Alys' account.

'Why didn't you change the password after Christie and Sammy said they had messages from you?'

'Because Alys went missing and I forgot about the stupid messages. I've only just had my phone back from the police.'

'You better change it now.' Iona smoothed down her dress. 'Anyway, I bought some beer for you and put it in the fridge. You may as well drink it. I'll join you.'

Macsen didn't feel like company. He was thinking of how to get rid of her quickly when he remembered he had locked the cottage. 'How did you get in?'

'Keys.'

'What keys?'

'The keys under the stone by the back door.'

'I don't keep spare keys outside.'

'That's what your message said.'

'The message I didn't send?'

'Oh,' Iona said.

'Where are they?' Macsen asked.

'On the table.'

Macsen pushed past her. He saw the keys and recognized the keyring.

Iona came to stand next to him. 'What's wrong?'

'They're Alys' keys.' He turned to face her. 'You're the only one not to have received a message that day. You were always telling her what to do. Followed her to university. Tried to control her. You killed her, didn't you?'

'I'm not listening to this.' Iona turned to leave.

Macsen grabbed her by the wrist and yanked her back. 'I'm sick of your games. Alys told me everything. She couldn't live with it any longer. She was going to come clean. She told you what she was going to do. Didn't she?'

'I don't know what you're talking about.'

'You want to hear me say it?' he said.

'You know nothing, otherwise you would've gone to the police.'

He hated Iona in that moment. He wanted to put his hands around her throat and squeeze. 'The only reason I didn't tell the police is because of Alys. I won't drag her name through the dirt. But I will if I find out you had anything to do with what happened to her.'

'You really think I'm capable of killing Alys?'

'Yeah.'

'Dick,' Iona said. 'This isn't just about Alys. While you were at the police station, Sammy had a break-in. Stuff was left.'

'What stuff?'

'A fishbowl filled with alcohol, a card, and shells in the bathroom.'

Macsen felt like he had been punched in the stomach. He let go of Iona's wrist.

'Are you listening to me?' she said. 'Seashells.'

'Why Sammy?'

'I don't know. You tell me. It's got to be–'

'Don't,' he said. 'He's got nothing to do with it.'

'He has everything to do with it. You want to blame someone for Alys' death? Maybe you should look at yourself.'

'What's that supposed to mean?' Macsen asked.

'Don't act thick,' Iona said. 'I know what you did.'

Chapter Fourteen

The team, all holding tea and coffee, gathered around the incident board.

'One week since Alys' murder,' Meadows said. 'I understand you are all disappointed we had to let Macsen go and we have no viable suspect. I appreciate all the extra hours you've put in. Now we need to take a step back and re-examine everything we've got. The DNA taken from the foetus is not a match to Macsen. Paskin, anything on who Alys was seeing?'

Paskin shook her head. 'No one saw her with anyone. The neighbours, family, and work colleagues have all been interviewed. I've checked all her messages and phone calls, nothing unusual. Same with her bank statements. No trips to Tenby or any seaside town. Whoever she was seeing, they were careful.'

'So far there is nothing from forensics with regards to Sammy's house,' Meadows said. 'No fingerprints on the items found. Sammy admits she hasn't cleaned the floors for a while, so getting any unidentified latent prints isn't going to be easy if she's had a lot of visitors. There were some entries in the calendar on Alys' phone. Times and I guess locations, or people she met up with. GS, MP, QCP.

Then there is one entry that just says Bristol. Alarm scheduled for six days after she died. A reminder is set three days before she died. The entry simply says, "book appointment Bristol". We need to find out what Alys planned on doing in Bristol.'

'Abortion clinic?' Paskin suggested.

'She went to university there. Maybe she was meeting up with someone. Could be her lover,' Harvard said.

'Possible, but she wouldn't have written "book appointment". She's more likely to have put "make arrangements" as a reminder,' Meadows said. 'Paskin, can I leave those dates with you? See if you can find out where she went and who she met.'

Paskin nodded.

'Anything on *J*?'

They all shook their heads.

'Harvard, how are you getting on with the timeline?'

'There is no change to her routine in the last two weeks leading up to the murder. She goes to work, sees Macsen or her girlfriends. Shopping on Saturday. Sunday lunch with the parents. I'm working on the period of time before that. I've also made a start on the photos taken off her phone and laptop. The last photo she took is interesting. It's of her at Llyn y Fan. From what I can tell it's not a selfie. She looks relaxed and happy.' Harvard passed the photo to Meadows.

'You're right. Someone took this photo of her. I'd say about halfway up. Who was she with?'

'It could've been some random hiker,' Valentine said.

'No one has come forward from the appeal,' Paskin said.

'Would you?' Valentine asked. 'Think about it. You're some guy walking alone. You've stopped and chatted to a woman and taken her photo. The next thing you see on the news, she's been murdered. You'd be afraid of becoming a suspect.'

'Good point,' Edris said.

'Keep going with the photos,' Meadows said. 'Especially those from university. Alys deleted them. There has to be a reason. See if you can identify the people that appear regularly. We now know Macsen's and Rhodri's Messenger accounts were hacked. We're looking for someone with the technical skills to do that.'

'Iona works for a gaming company and Christie has a degree in mathematics, bright girl,' Blackwell said.

'Rhodri has a degree in business. He probably knows his way around a computer,' Harvard added. 'Anyone could pick up those skills if they know who to ask.'

'OK, let's look again at the friends,' Meadows said.

'Macsen is the obvious one,' Blackwell said. 'Motive, opportunity, and it's possible he sent those messages himself. If he's clever, he makes himself a suspect and then gets us to prove he isn't guilty.'

'His motive being that he's not the baby's father?' Meadows asked.

'Yeah,' Blackwell said.

'What about the break-ins? The gifts? He was in a cell when Sammy's was broken into,' Meadows said.

'Rhodri,' Edris said. 'He could be the father of Alys' baby, and doesn't want his best mate to find out. He's got opportunity. We know they all went to Tenby before going to university. That could have been the start of it. He tries to remind Alys of their time together. Iona said they drank from fishbowls in uni. He puts that stuff at Sammy's to make us think it's some stranger and he gets Macsen off the hook at the same time.'

'Not a bad theory,' Meadows said.

'Yeah, but women are not that stupid,' Valentine said. 'Sammy would have noticed if something was going on between Rhodri and Alys. So would Iona. You can't hide a relationship for that long. They all spent time together. It would only take one look between them to give them away.'

'And why kill her?' Paskin asked. 'Alys wouldn't have wanted Macsen finding out. She would have wanted the affair kept secret. I can't see it.'

'What about Iona?' Blackwell said. 'Plenty of opportunity. She claims she slept in.'

'Motive?' Meadows asked.

'Jealousy,' Blackwell said. 'Alys had everything she wanted. She taunts Alys by leaving things in her house. Makes her insecure.'

'She looked shook up when she saw the items in Sammy's house,' Meadows said.

'And why would she start leaving things for Sammy?' Valentine added.

'That leaves Christie and Sammy,' Meadows said.

'Both have opportunity,' Edris said. 'Christie claims she was working from home. If she's the hacker then she could have scheduled emails, no problem. No one saw her that morning. Sammy claims she went to the farm. It's just under one and a half hours to get to Llyn y Fan. She's there to meet Alys. Drives to the farm which is only thirty-eight minutes away then on to work.'

'But a work colleague said they covered for her to leave that morning. She wouldn't have had time to go in and then leave again,' Valentine said.

'They're not going to change their story now to say she was never in,' Edris said. 'Did anyone actually see her arrive in the morning? She could've just sent a text.'

'Motive?' Meadows asked.

'Erm… well, opportunity is a start,' Edris said.

'What about traffic cameras or CCTV? Surely we can place one of them travelling. They would have had to set off early to get to Llyn y Fan in time to kill Alys,' Harvard said.

'That would work if we were in the city,' Meadows said. 'Not here. Llyn y Fan is remote and there are no cameras on the roads leading there. If you know the back roads you can travel to anywhere around here without a camera picking you up. Opportunity isn't the problem. We need some physical evidence and a motive.'

'Maybe there is no motive and it's just some sicko,' Blackwell said.

Meadows didn't like the idea that Alys was chosen at random. It meant the killer could be stalking their next victim. That would mean Sammy. 'If that's the case then it had to have started somewhere. Stalkers usually have some initial contact. Saw her in work or in a pub.'

'Speed dating,' Valentine said. 'Great opportunity to find girls to follow. I spoke to the organiser of the one Alys attended. There are no checks made on the attendants. You just book online with your name. They don't keep lists of previous attendants or payment details from bookings. There is, however, one running tonight and another tomorrow night. I can ask for us to be fitted into the group.'

'Undercover work. I'd be up for that,' Harvard said.

'What's the minimum age?' Blackwell asked.

'Under twenty-five tonight and over tomorrow.'

'Well, Harvard will be all right with a bunch of teenagers,' Blackwell said. 'But a spinster of your age might have some problems.'

'Fuck off,' Valentine said. 'I'll have you know I was asked for ID to buy alcohol last week. Anyway, I think it's worth a try. Check out the type of men that hang out there. It's the same company and venue as the one Alys attended. We might get some useful information.'

Meadows turned to look at the timeline on the board. 'It looks like Alys first mentioned being watched and things being moved in her house after the date nights. I think Valentine is right. If it is a stalker then that's a good place to start. The only problem with that theory is the gifts appear to be personal.'

'Maybe only to him,' Valentine said. 'He could have some hang-up. Maybe he met a girl on holiday. They had a romance, beach walks, drinks, that sort of thing. Then it ends. He tries to recreate it in his mind.'

Blackwell laughed. 'I think you've been watching too many creeper films. Can you imagine this great romance happening in Tenby, sitting on the beach and freezing?'

'It doesn't have to be Tenby,' Paskin said. 'It could just be a reference to the sea. Then there was the sand in the fridge and shells in the shower.'

'Yeah, and also a bottle of wine,' Valentine said.

'OK,' Meadows said. 'Harvard and Valentine, you can take part in the dating. Edris and I will sit at the bar. If this is where the killer saw Alys then we might get lucky.'

* * *

Meadows was sitting at the bar watching the tables that had been set up for the speed dating. As more people arrived, the noise level increased along with the heady smell of various aftershaves and perfumes. All of the attendees were dressed up in the hope of meeting their perfect partner. The women branched off into small groups while the men ordered drinks at the bar. He thought a few of them looked like they needed the alcohol. They only had three minutes to sell themselves. He was glad he didn't have to worry about dating anymore. He didn't think he could handle the pressure that was put on the younger generation now. Social media constantly showing you the unattainable. Perfect body, perfect partner, and perfect life. Shame they can't see the lie, he thought.

'Looks like fun,' Edris said and took a sip of his orange juice.

'Looks like my worst nightmare,' Meadows replied.

A hand touched his shoulder and Meadows turned his head.

'Would you like to buy a lady a drink?' Daisy asked.

Meadows smiled. 'What are you doing here?'

'Edris was concerned you'd look like a pair of old perverts sitting on your own,' Daisy said.

'Not me,' Edris said. 'He's the old one.'

'Move up,' Daisy said.

Edris moved to the next stool and Daisy settled in the middle. Meadows ordered her a glass of wine.

'So, what are we looking for?' Daisy asked.

'Anyone who gives you the creeps,' Edris said.

Daisy looked around. 'Valentine looks gorgeous.'

'Yeah, she does,' Edris said.

'Harvard looks a little too excited,' Meadows said.

'At least he's not wearing his bobble hat,' Edris said.

A bell rang and the women took their seats at the tables. The men sat on the opposite side. Both parties wore large numbers pinned at their shoulders. Every three minutes, a bell rang and the men moved to the next table.

Meadows watched Valentine interact with each man that took a seat opposite her. She smiled and looked interested. When the bell sounded she scribbled notes on a piece of paper. Halfway through, there was a break. Valentine approached the bar with a couple of women and took up position next to Meadows.

'First time?' one of the women asked.

'Yes,' Valentine said. 'It's fun.'

'We're regulars,' the other woman said. 'I'm Amy, and this is Jess.'

'I'm Reena,' Valentine said.

'Looks like we have some fresh meat tonight,' Jess said.

'Is it usually the same men?' Valentine asked.

'I've seen over half of them before,' Amy said. 'He's new, number fourteen.'

Valentine looked over towards Harvard.

'He's kinda cute,' Jess said.

'We could take him home and have ourselves a sandwich,' Amy said.

Meadows nearly choked on his orange juice. He saw Edris and Daisy giggling so much they had to turn their heads away.

'Do you get any odd ones here?' Valentine asked. 'I'm not sure how things work. I don't want to give my number and have someone harassing me.'

'There are some weirdos. Never make direct contact with them. Some try to give you their phone number. If you match with anyone then only contact them through the site,' Jess said.

'We usually arrange a double date,' Amy said, 'or one of us will be close by, just to be on the safe side. You have to be careful especially after what happened to that girl.'

'What girl?' Valentine asked.

'The one on the news. Alys Pugh. You must have seen it. She was found in the lake. Murdered,' Amy said.

'Oh yeah,' Valentine said. 'I haven't heard anything about her meeting up with someone for a date.'

'She could have,' Jess said. 'I've seen her here before. She came with two other girls. We had a chat and a bit of a laugh.'

'Do you think she could have met someone here?' Valentine asked.

'The freak in the corner was trying to talk to her,' Jess said.

'And the one who thinks he's a sex god was pestering her. Number seven,' Amy said.

'I'll stay away from those two then,' Valentine said. 'Have you spoken to the police?'

'No, do you think we should?' Amy asked.

'Oh yeah,' Valentine said. 'You could have vital information. Especially if you saw someone pay special interest in her. I'm sure I saw a contact number somewhere. They were asking for people with information to come forward. It will be on the police website.'

Meadows sneaked a glance at the two women. Both looked excited at the prospect of being involved.

'Drink up,' Jess said. 'It'll be starting again in a minute. I hope you're not going for number fourteen. We won't stand a chance.'

'All yours,' Valentine said.

'Looks like Harvard's in luck,' Edris said.

Daisy laughed. 'They'd eat him alive.'

Meadows glanced across and saw Harvard give one of the women a cheeky wink. 'I don't know about that. He looks like he can hold his own.'

The second half of the speed dating moved quickly. When the round was finished they all mingled. Valentine kept close by allowing Meadows to listen in on the conversation. He kept a watch on the room. One man with the number nineteen was sitting in the corner of the room. He was heavyset with thin blond hair and a round face. He held his phone in his hand and looked at the screen. Now and again, he would look up to see if anyone was approaching.

'Looks a bit shy,' Daisy said following his gaze.

'Yeah, but that doesn't mean he's harmless,' Meadows said. 'If he can't speak to women maybe he likes watching.'

'Hi,' one of the attendees said.

Meadows looked to the left and saw a man approach Valentine. He had a full beard and his long brown hair was tied back in a ponytail. The number thirteen was pinned to his chest.

'You had a good evening?' Valentine asked.

'Yeah, I really enjoyed talking to you.' He looked down at his feet.

'Thank you,' Valentine said. 'It's the first time I've been to one of these. It was better than I thought. Have you been before?'

He nodded and glanced at her quickly before looking away. 'It's nice to get out and talk to people instead of looking at a screen.'

'Yeah,' Valentine agreed. 'I gave Tinder a go but didn't like it much. Can't tell much from a photo.'

Colour crept up the man's neck. 'I better go,' he said. 'Early start tomorrow. It was nice to meet you.'

The man moved away.

'I've lost my pulling power,' Valentine whispered to Meadows.

'I don't think so,' he said. 'Another one approaching.'

This one had number seven pinned to his chest.

'Buy you drink?' number seven asked.

'I've got one, thanks,' Valentine said.

'That's OK. I'll buy you another.'

'I'm leaving after I've finished this one.'

'Great, we can move on to somewhere else.'

'I don't think so,' Valentine said.

Meadows swivelled in his chair. Seven put his hand in his pocket and pulled out a card.

'Take my number.' He handed the card to Valentine. 'Give me a call,' he said then walked off.

'What a dick,' Valentine said. 'Don't blame Amy and Jess for making a beeline for Harvard. I'm going to walk around. I'll talk to a few more, see what vibes I get.'

Meadows nodded.

Slowly the room began to empty. Bearded man and the shy one in the corner had left. A few women were talking to Harvard. Valentine moved between groups. Number seven was seated at the other end of the bar. Meadows noticed he didn't take his eyes off Valentine.

Chapter Fifteen

Meadows was standing in DCI Nathan Lester's office waiting for a decision. He wasn't at all unnerved facing his boss. Equality had been instilled in him throughout his childhood. He'd learned he was no better than anyone else and no one was better than him, just different personalities existing together. For this reason, he was never worried about speaking up.

'Are you sure about this?' Lester asked.

'Yes. I've sent you a risk assessment.'

'Which I read. That's not the issue. It's a lot of overtime and resources for us to use on what Valentine *thinks* she saw.'

'I trust Valentine's judgement. She said the car followed her after she had dropped Harvard off. She lives in a cul-de-sac so only got suspicious when she stopped outside her house. The car didn't drive past. It idled for a few moments and reversed.'

'She didn't get the plate?'

'No,' Meadows said, 'they put on full beams so she couldn't see. That in itself is a bit suspect. The organiser has provided us with a list of those who attended last night and who are attending again tonight. It's the only way we'll know for sure if someone is following these women home. We have no suspects in the Alys Pugh case. This could be the breakthrough we need.'

'OK, but I want regular updates.'

'Thank you,' Meadows said.

As he left the room he heard Lester mutter, 'Thank you, sir.'

Meadows smiled to himself. One day he'd call Lester "sir" just to shock him.

'Well?' Blackwell asked as soon as he walked into the office.

'We're on,' Meadows said.

'Excellent,' Valentine said.

Meadows gathered the team around. 'Paskin and Valentine, you will travel in separate cars. Same thing as last night. Keep it friendly at the tables then mix for an hour. Edris and Harvard, you'll be waiting in your own cars in the car park. Harvard, you follow Valentine home. Edris, you tail Paskin. Keep your distance. Allow one or two cars in front of you. We don't want to spook anyone. Valentine, I'll be waiting at your place. Blackwell, you can take Paskin's house.'

'What about your husband?' Blackwell asked.

'I've already told Aiden to go to his mother's house for the night,' Paskin said.

'Won't he mind me lurking about?'

'Nah. I did say he could spend the evening with you. He wasn't keen, I don't know why.'

Everyone laughed but Meadows detected some tension in the air. 'If any of you want to pull out, it's not a problem. I don't want anybody to feel unsafe.'

'We'll be fine,' Valentine said. 'Edris and Harvard will be in the car park. It's busy when everyone leaves. The only risk is getting from the car indoors. If one of these guys is Alys' killer, then his MO is to watch and leave gifts.'

‘Hanes and Roberts will be parked close to your homes keeping watch,’ Meadows said.

‘Then we’re all good,’ Paskin said.

‘I’m betting on number seven,’ Harvard said. ‘I don’t think he liked that you turned him down. Maybe Alys did the same.’

‘I didn’t like the look of number nineteen. He was just sitting in the corner not speaking to anyone,’ Edris said. ‘I reckon he’s the type to be creeping around.’

‘I hope whoever it is shows his face tonight,’ Valentine said. ‘Because if Alys’ killer is there and he’s not watching us then he’s already picked his next victim.’

‘That’s what worries me,’ Meadows said. ‘I don’t want any of you to take any chances. Walk together to your cars and if you feel at all unsafe, let us know and Edris and Harvard will come into the building.’

* * *

Regular updates came through all evening as Meadows waited in Valentine’s flat. Hanes had joined him and they played cards and drank tea to pass the time. Meadows’ phone pinged and he checked the messages.

‘Another man has left,’ Meadows said.

‘So that’s two out of the picture,’ Hanes said.

‘Unless one of them wants to get ahead of her,’ Meadows said.

‘I hope the bastard shows his face tonight,’ Hanes said. ‘He’s gonna get one hell of a shock.’

There was another ping from Meadows’ phone. ‘Harvard and Edris have got eyes on them. They are just getting into their cars.’

Hanes stood up and looked out of the window. ‘All quiet.’

He remained standing and Meadows picked up on his anxiety. He felt the same. Even though they had carried out the risk assessment and put safety measures in place, there was always the chance of the unexpected.

'Fifteen minutes away. You better get going,' Meadows said.

Hanes nodded and left the flat.

Meadows turned off the lights. In the darkness, he could watch through the window. He saw Hanes cross the road and get into the car. Dressed in black, he blended into the night. He kept his position until he saw Valentine pull up. She got out of her car and crossed the road. If she was nervous, she didn't show it. When she disappeared from sight, Meadows held his breath. She was in a blind spot. Hanes would have checked the stairwell on the way out but there was a back door. He had checked it was secure, he reminded himself. He heard the flat door open and stepped away from the window as Valentine turned the lights on.

'How did it go?' Meadows asked.

'Good. The same guys approached me, and a few new ones as the age category changed. I don't think anyone other than Harvard followed me home.'

'Harvard will drive by, circle back, and repeat every half an hour. He'll see if anyone is hanging around,' Meadows said as he put a call through to Blackwell. 'Anything?'

'Bugger all,' Blackwell said. 'I'm gonna stay the night, just in case.'

'OK, thanks. See you in the morning.'

'I hope you're not planning on sitting up all night,' Valentine said. 'I'm safe enough indoors and I'm more than capable of looking after myself.'

'I don't doubt it,' Meadows said. 'But the more eyes we have to keep watch the better. We can take it in turns.'

Valentine nodded. 'I'm going to grab a cuppa.'

They talked for a while and Meadows got up periodically to peek out of the window. 'Hanes is still out there.'

Valentine yawned. 'Poor bugger. You should send him home.'

'He won't go. Go and get some sleep.'

'Yeah, call me to sub you.' She turned off the lights.

Meadows plonked himself down on the sofa. In the background, he could hear the tap running in the bathroom. Then the click of a light switch and a door closing. A few moments later, Valentine called out.

Meadows moved swiftly to the bedroom. 'What is it?'

Valentine was standing by the window. 'We have company, in the garden.' She lifted her top over her head.

Meadows turned his back on her. 'Whoa. What are you doing?'

'Giving the little creep a peep show. That should hold his attention for a while. He'll wait to see more. Then we can catch him in the act.'

'I'm not sure that's a good idea,' Meadows said.

'Do you want to catch him?'

'Yeah.'

'Right then. Move away from the door.'

Meadows stepped back.

Valentine came through the door wearing only a sports bra, pyjama bottoms, and trainers. She took off towards the front door.

'Wait!' Meadows shouted. He called up Hanes as he chased after her. 'Around the back,' he shouted into the phone.

He flew down the stairs after Valentine. She hit the button on the wall and the back door began to swing open. She squeezed out and took off. She had the advantage of knowing where her prey was standing.

'Oi, you perv!' Valentine shouted.

Meadows caught a glimpse of a figure taking flight but they weren't fast enough. Valentine picked up speed and leapt at the figure, knocking her quarry to the ground.

'Like to watch, do you?' Valentine said. 'You picked the wrong one to spy on this time.'

Hanes came running towards them with his flashlight in hand. The figure struggled beneath Valentine.

'Sorry I couldn't get in. Had to jump the back wall,' Hanes said.

'I don't think she needs our help,' Meadows said.

Hanes moved forward and handed Valentine the cuffs. She locked them in place and turned the figure over. His face lit up in the torch beam. It was the man with the beard and ponytail.

'Number thirteen,' Valentine said.

Chapter Sixteen

Meadows pushed open the flat door and his nostrils were assaulted by the smell of sweaty socks, unemptied bins, and stale food.

Edris wrinkled his nose. 'So this is what the lair of a stalker looks like. I think we need hazmat suits.'

Meadows laughed. 'Forensics are on their way. You can wait to get a suit off them if you like.'

'I'll manage with gloves for now,' Edris said. 'Let's just get through it quickly.'

The sitting room was small with only enough room for the battered two-seat sofa and a flimsy coffee table. It was strewn with empty takeaway boxes, cans of lager, and mugs with mouldy liquid. There were no curtains, and a blanket had been thrown over the rail in an attempt to block out the light.

'How do people live like this?' Edris asked. 'I don't even know where to start.'

'Look for anything to do with the seaside. If Valentine's theory is correct, then he could have some mementos. We also need anything that could tie him to Alys. If he was in her house, he could have taken something. He lives on his own so pick anything that looks like it might belong to a woman.'

Meadows searched among the empty games and DVD cases then helped Edris sift through the litter on the floor. There was nothing that stood out.

'Laptop on the sofa,' Edris said.

'We'll leave that for forensics to take. Nothing much else here of interest. Let's check the other rooms. I imagine one is the bathroom and the other the bedroom. We'll take one each.'

'If we must,' Edris said.

Meadows moved across the room, opened the first door and stopped.

'Shit,' Edris said coming to stand next to him.

All the walls were covered from floor to ceiling with photographs. Meadows' eyes travelled around the room. The photos were of different women. Some were taken through windows, others while they shopped or were leaving their houses. All were shot seemingly without their knowledge.

'There's hundreds of them,' Edris said. 'He must've been doing this for years.'

'Now his obsession has crossed the line,' Meadows said. 'Look for Alys.'

Meadows and Edris took a wall each and moved along without talking. The women in the photos were all very different. There didn't seem to be a common pattern of any features.

'He must have used a zoom lens,' Edris said. 'You can get them to attach to your phone.'

'Here.' Meadows pointed. 'It's Alys leaving her house. This looks like it was taken at her work.'

'Got one,' Edris said. 'This looks like the date-night venue. It's taken at an awkward angle. Gives me the creeps.'

'I've seen enough,' Meadows said. 'Let's go and interview him.'

They met Mike Fielding and his team as they left.

'The bedroom is covered in photos,' Meadows said. 'I don't think he brought anyone back here but it would be good to find anything belonging to one of the women.'

'We'll turn this place upside down,' Mike said. 'We heard he went after Valentine. Let's get him put away.'

'Thanks, Mike.'

Meadows and Edris walked outside and back to the car. They paused before getting in, enjoying being free from the oppressive atmosphere of the flat.

'Do you want me to drive?' Edris asked.

'Go on then. It was a long night.'

'You can close your eyes for a few minutes. I'll wake you when we get back.'

Meadows settled in the passenger seat but the simmering anger he felt stopped him from resting.

'Poor Alys,' he said. 'She was frightened by this pervert watching her and leaving gifts. Then she goes to Llyn y Fan expecting her boyfriend to be there with a surprise and is met with a stranger. We need to check all the reports of stalking and break-ins. See if we can match the victims to the photos on the wall. The very least we can do is give them some piece of mind.'

'Yeah, starting with Sammy,' Edris said.

'I didn't see her photo on the walls. Did you?' Meadows asked.

'No, but there were so many.'

'Yeah.' Meadows put his head back, closed his eyes and let his mind wonder. There was something off. It seemed too simple, and there were aspects of the case that didn't fit. Maybe he was just tired, he thought. They had the photos for evidence. This man had been caught stalking Valentine. Perhaps Alys being pregnant had nothing to do with it. But why didn't she report it? If someone breaks into your house and leaves gifts, you'd be running to dial 999. He didn't voice these concerns. He'd find out soon enough when they spoke to the stalker.

There was a buzz in the office when they arrived. Despite everyone being tired, they were all busy collecting information on the stalker.

'One week since we found the body. Not bad,' Harvard said.

'Yeah, and it's Friday tomorrow,' Edris said. 'We may just get a weekend.'

'Still a long way to go,' Meadows said. 'Paskin, what have you got?'

'Cerith Ryan. Twenty-nine years old. Only child. He's been living at his current address for two years, previously lived with his mother. He works as a warehouse packer. Blackwell has gone to speak to the manager. No previous convictions and a clean driving licence.'

'Solicitor and appropriate adult have arrived,' Valentine said.

'Appropriate adult?' Edris asked. 'Don't tell me he's already claiming to have a biscuit missing from the tin.'

'I requested one,' Meadows said. 'I got the impression he didn't fully understand the trouble he was in last night. He's been assessed and deemed fit for the interview. If we want to talk to him before we have his medical records then we need to make sure all the necessary procedures are in place.'

'Yeah, we don't want him walking out on a technicality,' Valentine said.

Meadows nodded. 'Paskin and Edris, can you check CCTV and traffic? See if you can catch him travelling from his address on the morning of the murder. Also look at last Sunday night when Sammy's house was broken into. Harvard, look at any reported cases of stalking in the area. Start with a fifty-mile radius. Valentine, it was your catch so you can sit in on the interview. Let's go.'

Valentine grabbed a file from her desk and they walked downstairs to the interview room.

Cerith was sitting between a man and a woman. Meadows had met Steve Rees, the duty solicitor, on a previous occasion. The woman introduced herself as Sue and was acting as appropriate adult. Cerith's shoulders were hunched. His hair looked matted and his T-shirt was crumpled. He fingered his beard nervously as they took their seats. Valentine recorded the time and date together with those present. All the while Cerith watched her.

'Cerith, do you understand why you were arrested?' Valentine asked.

'Yeah, but I didn't kill anyone.' He looked at Valentine. 'You didn't say you were a police officer.'

'Would it have made a difference?' Valentine asked.

Rees put his hand on Cerith's arm warning him not to respond. 'As I understand it, you dated my client.'

'For three minutes, and it was a speed-dating evening,' Valentine responded.

'Even so. Entrapment. While not illegal it could be viewed as an abuse of process.'

'There was no entrapment. We were there conducting enquiries into the murder of Alys Pugh,' Meadows said. 'Detective Valentine was followed home. For her safety, we had officers keep watch. At no time did my colleague solicit attention from your client.'

'You did follow me home,' Valentine said.

Cerith stroked his beard. 'I only wanted to see where you lived.'

'That would be stalking,' Valentine said.

'We've been to your flat,' Meadows said. 'It's quite a collection of photos you have.'

Cerith reddened. 'I like pretty women. They never talk to me. I only take their photos.'

'That's not all you do, is it?' Meadows asked.

Cerith looked at him. 'I see where they live and work. Sometimes I watch, to see what they like to do. It's only to get information. If I meet them then I'll know what to talk about.'

'Do you approach these women?'

'No. I want to but I can never get up the courage.'

'Do you look at their social media?'

'Oh yeah. But everyone does. That's what it's there for. Gives you a chance to get to know someone.'

'Then you hack their accounts,' Meadows said.

Cerith looked confused. 'No. Someone hacked my account once. They posted bad stuff on my page. I would never do that to someone. I don't know how.'

Meadows nodded to Valentine.

Valentine took a photo of Alys from the file and placed it on the desk. 'Alys was very pretty. Wasn't she?'

Cerith nodded.

'Did you meet her at one of the speed-dating nights?'

'Yeah, she was nice.' Cerith wiped a large hand across his brow. 'Not like some. They look at you like shit and don't bother to talk to you. You have to sit there the whole time trying to talk, and they don't listen. Alys was like you.' He gave Valentine a shy smile. 'She talked to me the whole time. She was interested; asked all about me.'

'So, you followed her home,' Valentine said.

Sue, who had remained quiet up until that point, cleared her throat. 'That's suggestive,' she said.

'Cerith, did you follow Alys home?'

'Yeah. I wanted to see where she lived. I sent her a friend request but she didn't accept.'

'Did you watch her?' Valentine asked.

Cerith fidgeted in his seat and nodded. 'I wanted to talk to her. I tried once in the shop where she works. I watched her talking to another customer. They left but then I couldn't do it.'

'If you were watching her, you must've seen she already had a boyfriend,' Meadows said.

Cerith's eyes darkened. 'Yeah, I saw him.'

'Did that make you angry?' Meadows asked.

'No. I was happy to wait. I knew it wasn't a proper boyfriend. Why else would she be looking for someone new at the speed-dating nights?'

'Why did you leave her gifts?' Meadows asked.

'I didn't.'

'We know you went into her house. You left things there.'

Cerith's eyes widened and he sat up straight. 'I never went inside. I stayed in the garden or across the road. I'm not like that. I wouldn't want to frighten her.' He looked at Sue. 'I didn't go inside. I didn't.' He stood up. 'I want to go home now.'

'It's OK, Cerith,' Sue said in a soothing voice. 'They just need to know, and you've answered their question. Isn't that right, Detective Meadows?'

Meadows sat back, folded his hands, and gave Cerith what he hoped was a reassuring smile. 'Yes, that's right. Please sit down, Cerith.'

Cerith looked at Sue who nodded. He sat on the edge of the chair and picked up one of the plastic cups of water that had been set out.

'OK, Cerith?' Meadows asked.

Cerith took a sip from the cup then set it down. 'Yeah.'

'Good. We still need to ask you a few more questions. Can you tell us, where were you Sunday night? March 19.'

'Erm… when was that?'

'Last Sunday,' Meadows said.

'At home.'

'Come on, Cerith. We know you like to go out late at night to watch women. We can easily check CCTV to see if you left the house.'

Colour spread up Cerith's neck. 'OK, there's this girl who works in payroll. Lauren. She's new. I wanted to see if she had a boyfriend.'

'Where does Lauren live?' Meadows asked.

'Morriston.'

'I think you might have got your days mixed up. I think you were in Llanelli,' Meadows said.

Sue cleared her throat again and Meadows held up his hand. 'Is there someone you like to watch in Llanelli?'

Cerith shook his head. 'I don't think so. No. There might have been, a couple of years ago.'

'What about Tuesday morning, March 14, at seven-thirty?'

'I'd have been in work,' Cerith said. 'I start at seven every day. I like the early shift.'

'We can easily check.'

Cerith nodded and looked at his solicitor. 'I was in work.'

'I will make sure that statements are obtained from your employer,' Rees said.

Meadows sat forward. 'Do you like to go to the seaside?'

'Is that relevant?' Rees asked.

'Yes,' Meadows said.

Rees nodded at Cerith.

'I like to go in the summer.'

'Do you go to Tenby?'

'No. Caswell or Ogmore. I've been to Porthcawl.'

'Are you sure you haven't been to Tenby? Perhaps to buy some rock.'

Cerith's brows furrowed in confusion. 'Why would I buy rock?'

'Someone gave rock and seashells to Alys. Left them in her house on her birthday.'

'I didn't give her anything,' Cerith said.

Meadows sat back. They weren't getting anywhere.

'How did you hack Macsen Lloyd's Messenger account?' Valentine asked.

'Who?' Cerith asked.

'Alys' boyfriend.'

Cerith shook his head. 'I don't know him.'

'How did you get Alys to meet you at Llyn y Fan?' Valentine asked.

'I didn't.' Cerith looked from Sue to his solicitor. 'I only met Alys on two date nights.'

The door to the interview room opened and Blackwell beckoned Meadows.

Meadows excused himself and left the room.

'I think you'll want to take a look at this,' Blackwell said. He handed Meadows a sheet of paper.

Meadows read the sheet, which was a printout of Cerith's hours at work. It showed him clocking in at 6.58 a.m. on Tuesday, March 14 and clocking out at 15.02.

'Damn,' Meadows said.

'Yeah,' Blackwell said. 'Although that wasn't the exact word I used.'

'Is there any chance someone could have clocked in for him?'

'No. It's a sophisticated system, it uses fingerprints. According to his manager, he's a good worker but keeps to himself. I don't think he could be working with anyone else. Sounds like he's a loner.'

'Thanks,' Meadows said. He walked back into the interview room and handed the paper to Valentine. He saw the same disappointment on her face that he felt.

'Are you going to share?' Rees asked.

'Cerith, we've just had confirmation that you were in work, Tuesday morning, at the time you told us.'

'I told you I didn't hurt anyone,' Cerith said. 'Can I go home now?'

'You will be charged with stalking. We have evidence. There are a lot of photographs of different women taken over a period of time. This could add up to a lengthy sentence.'

'What do you mean?' The colour drained from Cerith's face. 'You're not going to send me to prison, are you?'

'I will be challenging the scope of culpability and harm,' Rees said. 'I don't think this warrants a custodial sentence.'

'It will be up to the CPS. However, your cooperation will be taken into account. Do you understand, Cerith?'

Cerith shook his head.

'You need to answer all their questions and recognize what you've been doing is wrong,' Sue said.

'I have answered their questions,' Cerith said.

'There are a few more things we need to ask you,' Meadows said. 'If you've been watching Alys for some time then you may have seen something that could help us catch her killer. It's very important you answer us honestly.'

Cerith nodded.

'How often did you watch Alys?'

'Not all the time,' Cerith said. 'I followed her home after the first date night to see where she lived. After that, I went back a few nights just to get to know her. I went different evenings of the week, sometimes on the weekends, just to see what she liked to do. It wasn't every day.'

'You must have got a good idea of her lifestyle. Tell me what she liked to do.'

'Mostly she just came home from work. Sometimes in her own car, or her friend would drop her off – the one with the ginger hair. On the weekends, she would see her friends or all of them would be together. She didn't go out much in the week. Her boyfriend would come over or she went to his house.'

'What did the boyfriend look like?'

'Big, dark hair, good-looking. He drives a jeep. He wasn't the only one.'

'You mean she had another boyfriend?'

Cerith nodded. 'I followed her one evening. She went to the quarry car park up the mountain. There was another car there with a man standing next to it. He was smoking.'

'What did he look like?' Meadows asked.

'Don't know. It was dark and he had his hood up. He was bigger than Alys but not as big as her other boyfriend.'

'How do you know she was meeting him and not just out for a drive?'

'I drove on then turned around. When I passed them again they were both sitting in his car. They had the light on.'

'Do you know what make of car it was?'

Cerith shook his head. 'I was trying to see Alys.'

'Did you see her with this man again?'

'No.'

'Anything else? Did you see someone following her? Someone going into her house late at night?'

'Just her friends. I'd seen them all before at the date nights. The ginger one was friendly but not my type. The one with the long hair didn't talk to me the whole time we were sitting at the table. I had to stop going so often because one of them nearly caught me.'

Meadows sat forward. 'Which one?'

'I don't know. She was dressed in black and had her hood up. I could tell it was a girl. She came around the back. She looked around but I don't think she saw me.'

'What did she do?'

'She just walked up the garden. Then she went back around the front. I think she was trying to catch me. I thought maybe Alys had seen me and got scared. I didn't go back after that.'

'When was this?'

'About two weeks ago.'

Meadows looked at Valentine. She gave a small shake of the head to indicate she had no more questions to ask.

'OK, Cerith. You will be charged with stalking. Detective Valentine will talk you through what happens next. If there is anything else you remember about Alys, you need to let us know.'

'Do I have to stay here?'

'You may be able to go home but there will be conditions. You won't be able to go out at night. There will be no more following women and taking photos.'

Meadows left the interview room and went back to the office. He could tell by the atmosphere that Blackwell had delivered the bad news.

'I really thought we had him,' Paskin said.

'What are the chances of a stalker and a murderer going after the same person?' Harvard asked. 'It has to be connected somehow.'

'Yeah,' Edris said. 'The killer had to know Alys was being stalked and used that as an opportunity to kill her. It has to be one of those lot.' He pointed to the names on the board.

'We're no further along than when we started,' Blackwell said. 'All we've done is waste time chasing that peeping tom downstairs.'

'We do have some new information though,' Harvard said.

'We know Alys was seeing someone else. Cerith saw them in the quarry car park together. Hang on.' Meadows grabbed the sheet of paper that showed the diary entries from Alys' phone. 'QCP. Quarry car park.'

'It's all the places she was meeting her secret lover,' Paskin said.

'We just have to work out what the other abbreviations are,' Meadows said.

'It could still be someone she met at one of the date nights,' Paskin said.

'From what we got out of Cerith Ryan, it doesn't sound like she went anywhere else to meet someone,' Meadows said. 'We've got a list of the attendees. It looks like most of them have attended before. Let's start contacting them and see what information we can get. It's worth a try. Blackwell, Cerith saw a girl at Alys' house late one night. Go and talk to Iona, Christie, and Sammy. Ask them why they were creeping around Alys' garden. See what reaction you get.'

He walked over to the board and looked at the photos taken from Alys' phone and laptop. Harvard had put them into a timeline.

'Alys and Iona are drinking from a fishbowl in this one,' he said. 'Looks like some sort of party.'

'Yeah,' Harvard said. 'It was taken in September 2018, the beginning of their third year at uni. It was one that she had deleted.'

'Why delete them?' Edris asked. 'There's nothing embarrassing in them.'

'Because they remind her of her time there,' Meadows said. 'Brianna didn't find anything in Alys' room at her parents' house. No university books. No trace that she had been there. Question is, what was she trying to forget? She left less than four months after this photo was taken, cut her hair and changed her lifestyle. Her parents didn't really give us an answer and neither did her friends. They've all been evasive. We thought she left because of Macsen but what if it was nothing to do with him?'

He glanced across the board. 'Look at the items left at Sammy's – the fishbowl and card. I'm sure the drawing is of the Clifton Suspension Bridge in Bristol.'

'Sammy didn't go to Bristol University,' Edris said.

'What if they weren't meant for Sammy? What if they were left to send a message to Rhodri?' Meadows said.

'It's over four years ago she was there,' Harvard said.

Meadows nodded. 'There is nothing in Alys' recent history. Maybe we need to go back further. Edris, call the university and set up a meeting with Alys' lecturers. I want to know why she suddenly left.'

Chapter Seventeen

Christie turned the volume up on her car radio as she drove to work. The traffic was moving slowly and she wished she'd taken the back roads. She tried to sing along to the song that was playing but she couldn't remember the words. It didn't matter. She just wanted to distract her wandering mind. It wasn't working. She felt constantly on edge. It was like she had to keep looking over her shoulder. Her eyes felt heavy. She couldn't get off to sleep at night no matter how tired she was. The music was interrupted by an incoming call. She looked at the display. Iona.

She hit accept. 'What's up?'

There was a moment of silence, then a whimper and gulping of air.

'Iona, what's wrong?'

'You have to come. Now.'

Iona's voice was so shrill Christie felt like it would pierce her eardrums. She turned down the volume. 'What's happened?' She heard the quiver in her own voice. Her heartbeat quickened.

'Someone's been in my flat,' Iona screeched. 'I'm scared.'

'I'm on my way. Call the police.'

'No, I can't. Just come as quick as you can.' Iona hung up.

Christie sighed. Why is she calling me? she thought. It would've made more sense to call Macsen or Rhodri. She put in a call to work. Her boss as usual was understanding, nevertheless she asked him to put it down as a holiday. She would make Iona call the police no matter how much persuasion she had to use.

It took another forty minutes until she pulled up outside Iona's block of flats – a red-brick building which had been converted from a factory. Iona had obviously been watching for her because she was standing at the door. Her face was streaked with tears, her hair a mess, and she was still in her pyjamas.

'Thank God you're here,' Iona said and ushered her inside.

'Why do you think someone was in here?' Christie asked.

Iona grabbed her hand and led her to the kitchen. 'In the fridge. I can't look again.'

Christie opened the fridge. Inside she saw a tub of low-fat spread. The lid had been removed and it was standing on its side. The letter *J* had been cut into the pale-yellow fat. On the next shelf was a packet of condoms and on the top, a fishbowl with blue liquid.

'Did you call the police?' Christie asked.

'No.'

'Why not?'

'I can't?'

'What's going on?' Christie asked. 'First Alys, then Sammy's house gets broken into and now this.'

'I can't tell you.'

'Fine,' Christie said. 'If you don't feel you can trust me then at least tell the police. Are you trying to protect someone?'

Iona shook her head and fresh tears ran down her face.

'I'll make us a cup of tea.'

'No,' Iona said. 'What if he comes back, or is still here?'

'Who?'

'I don't know,' Iona said.

'You're not making any sense. You said "he". You must know who it is.'

Iona put her hands to her head. 'I told you I can't tell you.'

'How did he get in?' Christie asked.

'I don't know.'

Christie made two cups of tea and handed one to Iona. 'Stay there, I'm going to take a look around.'

'No. I'm coming with you,' Iona said.

Christie didn't think for a moment that an intruder was hiding but figured it would calm Iona down if she looked. She walked through the flat checking the wardrobe, under the bed, and the shower. Next, she checked all the windows. All the time, Iona stayed close behind. She jumped every time Christie opened a door.

'There's no one here and no way they could have got in,' Christie said. 'Are you sure the front door was locked?'

'Yes. I'm not stupid. I used the keys to let you in.'

'Then how did he get in?'

Iona looked down and fiddled with the hem on her top. 'I went to see Macsen when he got back from the police station. He'd messaged and asked me to come. He said to use the spare keys he'd left outside the backdoor. They were Alys' keys. She had a spare to my flat.'

'What was Macsen doing with Alys' keys?' Christie asked.

'I don't know. He went mad when he saw me, accused me of killing Alys. He said he'd never sent a message and he didn't know anything about the keys.'

'Do you think Macsen has done this?'

'I don't know,' Iona said. 'He hurt me. Knocked me to the floor. I thought he was going to kill me.'

'Why would he do this and why use the initial *J*?'

Iona didn't say anything.

'Iona, you can trust me,' Christie said. 'You know something. Don't you? If Macsen killed Alys then you have to tell the police. Why would you want to protect him?'

'I'm not protecting him. I think he's trying to frighten me.'

'Why?'

'There was this guy we knew. Jake.'

'You think he's doing this?'

'No, it can't be. I think Macsen wants me to think it's him.'

'You're not making any sense.'

'Alys told Macsen things. He must've been putting stuff in her house and then he killed her.'

'Macsen didn't break into Sammy's. He was at the police station.'

'Then it has to be Rhodri. He's doing this.'

'Why would Rhodri do that to Sammy?'

'I don't know,' Iona cried. 'Maybe it's Sammy, or you're doing this.'

Christie knew Iona was just lashing out because she was upset. It still made her feel uneasy. 'Shall I just go?'

'No, I'm sorry. I don't know what to think.'

'OK. Why don't you get dressed? We'll go to the police station and tell them what's happened. You must tell them about Macsen having Alys' keys.'

Iona shook her head.

'You don't have much of a choice,' Christie said. 'Why would Macsen have Alys' keys? If someone put them at his back door then why didn't he hand them in to the police?'

'Maybe because the police would think he had taken them from Alys.'

Christie didn't comment. She watched Iona as a range of emotions flitted across her face. Then realisation struck.

'What if he had them all along? Him and Rhodri. You told the police that Alys found out something about Macsen. What was it?'

'I don't know. She never told me,' Christie said. 'Go and get dressed. The longer you sit here the worse you'll feel.'

'Come with me,' Iona said. 'I don't want to be on my own.'

Christie sat down on the bed while Iona got dressed. Even in this state she fussed about her outfit and insisted on putting on make-up.

'I think you should tell the police everything you know,' Christie said.

'I can't. I did something stupid. Telling the police isn't going to help. We'll tell them about the stuff that's in the fridge and the keys.'

Christie recognized that look. It was shame. 'Whatever it is, can't be that bad. It's not worth your life.'

'I'm scared,' Iona said. 'Even if I told the police everything, I could still end up dead.'

Christie nodded. 'I'd be terrified if someone broke into my house. Pack a bag. We'll go to the police station and then you can come and stay with me. You'll be safe.'

'Thank you.' Iona hugged her.

Christie helped Iona pack and by the time they were finished there was a suitcase and two bags. It looked more like she was moving out than just staying for a few nights.

'Better bring your car,' Christie said. 'You don't want to be stuck asking me for a lift when you need to go somewhere.'

Iona nodded. She picked up one of the bags, grabbed the car keys, and let out a shriek. The keys clattered to the floor.'

'What's wrong?' Christie asked.

Iona pointed. 'The keyring.'

Christie bent down, picked up the keys, and examined them. 'Bristol University,' she said.

Iona looked terrified. 'I never put that on there.'

Chapter Eighteen

It was warm in the dean's office and the scent of polish lingered in the air. Edris was standing looking out of the large Georgian window while Meadows glanced at the books on the shelf. All of them were leather-bound, academic titles.

'Takes me back,' Edris said.

Meadows turned away from the books and moved to the large oak desk. 'Let me guess. You were a regular visitor to the dean's office.'

'No. Well, maybe a few times. I was thinking about the parties and going to lectures with a hangover. Best years of my life. Come on, you must've had some fun at uni.'

'Yeah, I did.' Meadows didn't want to say he'd spent most of his first year stoned. 'It's all fun until you have to cram in the third year.'

'Yeah. I remember that.' Edris moved from the window and looked at the wooden framed pictures and certificates. 'Bit ostentatious.'

Meadows laughed. 'We're in the dean's office, what do you expect? It's just a display of what can be achieved through hard work.'

'Yes but…' The door opened and Edris stopped talking.

A portly man in a dark grey suit entered. He held himself with an air of importance. A woman followed behind. Her hair was pinned loosely and she wore a long flowing skirt with a belted jumper.

'Sorry to have kept you waiting,' the man said. 'I'm Professor Armstrong and this is Professor Talby. Please take a seat.'

Professor Armstrong took the green leather seat behind the desk. Professor Talby chose the armchair. That left two seats. Meadows guessed they were reserved for students.

Professor Armstrong waited until they were all seated. He then folded his hands and placed them on the desk. 'We were all very saddened by the news of Alys' tragic death. It was some time ago she was with us. I'm not sure how much help we can be.'

'We're looking for background information,' Meadows said. 'Particularly the relationships Alys formed when here, that may have continued after she left.'

'I lectured Alys in the second and third year,' Professor Talby said. 'She was a good student, consistently good marks and on course to get an upper second, maybe even a first. From what I recall she was close to Iona Young, whom I also taught.'

'Alys left before she completed her third year. Do you know why?' Meadows asked.

A look passed between the two professors. Meadows saw Professor Talby shift in her seat. Whatever had happened, she was clearly uncomfortable talking about it.

'There was a problem between Alys and another student,' Professor Armstrong said. 'I thought you'd have a record of it.'

'The police were involved?' Meadows asked.

'Yes,' Professor Armstrong said.

'What sort of problem?'

'It was a very unpleasant business. There was an allegation of rape.'

'What was the name of the other student involved?' Edris asked.

'Jake Ellis.'

Meadows sat forward in his chair. He glanced at Edris and saw the excitement in his eyes. Why didn't her parents or Iona mention it? he thought. 'When was this?' he asked.

'The start of the third year,' Professor Armstrong said. 'That would be September 2018. We'd had freshers' week, then the second- and third-year students came back. There had been a party in the student union. Lots of drinking and high spirits. It was reported to me the next morning. I called the police and Jake was arrested.'

'Was Jake Ellis convicted?' Edris asked.

Professor Armstrong shook his head. 'It wasn't straightforward.'

'I also lectured Jake,' Professor Talby said. 'Nice boy. Studied hard. He'd never been in any trouble. He wasn't charged. I wouldn't like to speculate but it was a difficult situation. Drunk students telling different versions of the story. There was a lot of talk among the students and on social media.'

'Were Iona Young and Rhodri Williams involved in any way?' Meadows asked.

Professor Armstrong thought for a moment. 'From what I recall, Rhodri shared accommodation with Jake. I don't think they were friends. There was some sort of confrontation between them after the event. Nothing serious enough to involve the police.' He nodded to Professor Talby.

'Iona was a witness,' she said. 'She gave a statement to the police but didn't leave it there. She posted on social media and was very vocal about safety. Alys withdrew her complaint and Iona continued to fuel the situation. We had to intervene and ask her to stop her campaign against Jake.'

'So Jake came back here,' Meadows said.

'Briefly,' Professor Armstrong said. 'Things were difficult for him, as you can imagine. I'm not saying he was innocent but given that there were no charges, we had no reason to expel him. He took a break and was expected to come back after the Christmas holidays. He took his own life that New Year's Eve. Alys never returned.'

Chapter Nineteen

Rhodri heard his phone ping but ignored it. He had a suspicion it would be Iona again. She'd sent a message earlier threatening to tell the police. He didn't know how she had found out. He grabbed a beer from the fridge as his phone pinged again. I'll just ignore the bitch, he thought.

He took a swig of beer then rolled himself a joint. Sammy was lying on the sofa watching some series he had no interest in. All he wanted to do was get wasted. She'd been with him for four nights and he figured she wouldn't be going home for the weekend. He didn't mind her staying over but he liked his own space. He just wanted his life to get back to normal. There didn't seem to be much chance of that.

He'd just lit the joint when Sammy came into the kitchen. He saw the disapproval on her face.

'I just got a message from Macsen,' she said. 'He wants us all to go over.'

'It's probably someone pissing about again,' Rhodri said.

'No, this was a text message. He said not to use Messenger.'

Rhodri picked up his phone. 'Oh yeah.'

'Are we going to go?'

'Yeah. He's stuck in the house. He was released under special conditions or something. He has a curfew. Are the others going?'

Sammy shrugged.

'Can't see Iona going after Macsen caught her creeping around his house.'

'He'd asked her to go. She wasn't creeping,' Sammy said.

'So she says.' Rhodri huffed. 'Sounds like he wants us all there.' He didn't want to see Iona but it would look strange if he backed out. 'Come on then. You can drive.'

'What if I want a drink?' Sammy asked.

'I'll drive next time.'

When they arrived at Macsen's cottage, Christie and Iona were just getting out of the car.

'I brought all the alcohol from the house,' Christie said. 'There's plenty left over from the–'

'Party,' Iona finished for her.

Rhodri could see Christie was uncomfortable. 'It's OK, Christie. We can't all avoid mentioning anything to do with Alys. Macsen said he wanted to drink so I'm sure he'll be happy with what you brought.'

'I hope he is going to apologise,' Iona said.

'For what?' Rhodri asked. 'From what I understand, you should be the one apologising.'

'I didn't do anything,' Iona said. 'He's the one acting like a dick.'

Rhodri felt anger pulsating through his veins but before he had a chance to react Sammy spoke.

'Haven't you spoken to him since?' she asked.

'No. It's up to him to message me,' Iona said.

'Does he know what happened at your place?' Sammy asked.

Iona shrugged.

Sammy turned to Rhodri. 'Didn't you tell him?'

'I haven't spoken to him,' Rhodri said.

'Are you OK, Rhodri?' Iona asked.

She was smiling at him. He couldn't believe how two-faced she could be. 'What do you think?'

'Shall we go in? It's cold,' Christie said. She knocked the door and tried the handle. 'It's locked.'

'I guess we're all going to be locking the doors from now on,' Sammy said.

They waited a few moments then Rhodri moved to the window. He felt something crunch under his foot and looked down. He yelped and jumped backwards, causing the girls to squeal.

'Oh God, what is it?' Iona screeched. She grabbed Sammy by the arm and pulled her close.

Rhodri could feel his heart thumping in his chest. 'It's just a dead crow.' He started scraping his shoe on the grass.

'Isn't that a bad omen?' Sammy asked.

Rhodri laughed but a coldness had crept over him. He stepped to the side of the dead bird and knocked his knuckles against the glass. 'Oi, let us in.'

The door opened and a dishevelled-looking Macsen stuck his head around the door. 'What are you all doing here?'

'You call, we come,' Rhodri said.

'I didn't call,' Macsen said.

'Text message,' Sammy said.

Macsen shook his head. 'For fuck's sake. I thought it was just Messenger. I'm going to have to get a new phone and number.'

'Well… we're here now,' Rhodri said. 'We've brought booze.'

'I'm not in the mood for a party.'

'You can watch.' Rhodri pushed his way in and the rest of them followed.

'How can someone text from your phone?' Sammy asked.

'Easy enough,' Iona said. 'It's caller-ID spoofing.'

They all looked at her.

'I didn't do it. I'm just saying it's easily done. Don't you ever read posts warning about scams going around? Someone sends you a message pretending to be a relative. I think I saw one that said something like. "Hi, Mum. I'm in trouble. I owe money to these people. Please help." Then it gives an account number.'

'Do people actually fall for that?' Christie asked.

'Yeah,' Iona said.

'Maybe I will have a drink,' Macsen said.

'I'll get one for you,' Iona said. 'Do you want one, Rhodri?'

'I'll get my own,' Rhodri snapped.

'What's your problem?' Iona asked.

'As if you didn't know,' Rhodri said.

Iona put her hands on her hips. 'Actually, I don't. I'm the one who should be upset. Someone broke into my house and Macsen tried to kill me.'

'Oh, piss off,' Macsen said. 'I didn't try to kill you. You were creeping around. You could have shouted out. This isn't all about you. You're not the only one that had a break-in.'

'Has someone been in here?' Rhodri asked.

'Yeah, and left some things behind.'

Rhodri saw the fear on everyone's face.

'Did you call the police?' Sammy asked.

'What's the point? They don't believe anything I say. Now they think I killed Alys and took her keys. Thank you, Iona.'

'It was my idea to tell the police about the keys,' Christie said. 'If the killer had them, he could have made copies. He could be in and out of our homes and we wouldn't know it.'

'No one is going to want to go creeping around your place,' Macsen said.

Christie looked like she had been slapped.

'Don't be an arsehole, Macsen,' Rhodri said. 'The fucker's got us turning on each other.' He walked into the kitchen. 'Where's the booze?' he called out.

'Beer in the fridge,' Macsen shouted.

'I want something stronger than that,' Rhodri said.

Christie came into the kitchen and dumped the bag on the table.

Rhodri pulled out a bottle of vodka. 'That's more like it, thanks. Take no notice of Macsen. He's not in a good place.'

'I know,' Christie said. 'I miss her too.'

Rhodri put his arm around her and gave her a squeeze.

'I've brought some snacks,' Christie said.

'Great,' Rhodri said. 'Put them in a bowl and bring them in.'

Sammy came into the kitchen and flicked on the kettle. 'Are you going to tell me what's going on with you and Iona?'

'Nothing,' Rhodri said. 'She just winds me up.'

'Sounds like more than that,' Sammy said.

Rhodri picked up the bottle of vodka and grabbed two glasses. 'Just leave it.'

'Is this what it's going to be like all night?'

'Just have a drink and chill,' Rhodri said.

'I can't, I'm driving. Remember?'

'If you want a drink I can drop you both home,' Christie offered. She opened the cupboard and pulled out a bowl.

Rhodri thought a drunk Sammy would be less likely to ask questions. She'd pass out and he'd just put her to bed. 'That's great, thanks,' he said. 'Maybe you can leave Iona here. I don't want to listen to her bitching all the way home.'

Christie smiled as she filled the bowl with crisps. 'Count yourselves lucky she isn't staying with you,' she whispered.

Rhodri laughed. 'You poor bugger.' He downed the drink then walked back into the sitting room. He poured Macsen a shot and handed him the glass.

Macsen downed it in one go. 'That one didn't touch the sides.'

'That's the spirit,' Rhodri said. He refilled the glasses.

Christie and Sammy came back in and, after placing the snacks on the table, took a seat on the sofa next to Iona. The atmosphere in the room was tense and the conversation stilted. Iona tried to tell them all about the funeral plans but no one seemed interested. Her voice grated on Rhodri's nerves. He grabbed a bowl from the table and started stuffing crisps in his mouth.

'You're getting crumbs all over the place,' Macsen said.

'Don't be such a pussy,' Rhodri said. 'You've got a hoover.'

'I'll clean up for you,' Iona said.

Sammy laughed. 'Do you even know how to use a hoover?'

They all laughed.

'I can clean,' Iona said.

'Your place is a tip,' Sammy said.

'Why are you being a bitch?' Iona asked. She stood up and refilled the glass then perched on the edge of Macsen's chair. 'You know we are all happy to help out. We could come around and clean. Maybe do a bit of decorating. It would cheer you up.'

'Are you out of your fucking mind?' Macsen said. 'You think a bit of paint is going to make me feel better?'

'I'm only trying to help,' Iona said.

An uncomfortable silence fell on the room. Rhodri refilled his glass and looked around. He had to admit, the place was depressing. Macsen hadn't changed much since his grandparents lived there. The stone walls were whitewashed with old-fashioned pictures hung on nails. Two table lamps lit the room and an open fire crackled in the background. He thought of the dead bird outside and shuddered. He didn't want to think about death but he felt like he couldn't escape it. It hung in the air and swirled around them. He knocked back his drink and pulled a leather pouch from his pocket.

'You're not skinning up in here,' Macsen said.

Rhodri ignored him and rolled a joint. He lit it and inhaled deeply.

'You gonna share?' Iona asked.

Rhodri handed it over. Iona took a few puffs and handed it to Sammy. It was passed around until everyone except Christie had taken a few puffs. Iona took it back and smoked it down to the roach. She started giggling.

'What's so funny?' Rhodri asked.

'You are.' Iona held her stomach in a fit of giggles.

Rhodri glared at her. He hadn't had enough for it to have any effect on him.

Sammy and Christie joined in with the laughter. Macsen didn't crack a smile. Rhodri got up and filled Macsen's glass with vodka and topped up his own. Iona moved further in on the arm of the chair and leaned in until her arm was up against Macsen's. Rhodri shook his head and returned to his chair. He watched the flames dancing in the fire as he tried to block out the chatter and giggles around him. He kept refilling his glass. The more he drank, the more he brooded. Finally he could stand it no longer.

'Are we going to talk about what's going on or just pretend everything is normal?' he asked.

They all turned to look at him.

'What do you mean?' Iona asked. She grabbed a handful of crisps and started stuffing them in her mouth.

'Alys, the rock from Tenby, *J*, and the fishbowls. Do I have to say any more?'

'It's obvious,' Macsen said. 'He came back.'

Iona stopped eating and emptied her hand back into the bowl. 'It can't be him, he's dead.'

'His body was never found,' Rhodri said.

'Who are you talking about?' Sammy asked.

'Jake,' Macsen said.

Sammy looked confused.

'It's someone they used to know from school,' Christie said.

'I don't understand,' Sammy said. 'What do you mean, his body was never found?'

'He went missing,' Iona said.

'I understand the *J* for Jake but what's all the other stuff got to do with it?' Christie asked.

'Why would he want to kill Alys?' Sammy asked.

Rhodri looked at Macsen.

'He was obsessed with her. He made her life hell. I thought we had got rid of him,' Macsen said.

'What did you do?' Sammy asked.

'Nothing,' Rhodri said. He wasn't drunk enough to tell them everything.

'It was our fault,' Macsen said. 'Alys told me that–'

'Don't,' Iona cut in. 'Alys wasn't to blame. None of us were. If you start saying shit like that then the police are going to start asking questions.'

'What are you so afraid of?' Rhodri asked.

'Why aren't any of you going to the police?' Christie asked.

'It's complicated,' Iona said. 'Besides, the police aren't going to believe someone is back from the dead after four years.'

'It can't be him,' Rhodri said.

'You got a better explanation?' Macsen asked.

'Why would this Jake come after me?' Sammy asked.

'To get at me,' Rhodri said. He stood up and filled Macsen's glass.

'I'll get another bottle,' Iona said. She tried to get up and fell back down onto the sofa.

'Maybe I should make some coffee,' Christie said getting up.

'Not for me,' Rhodri said as she left. 'I'm getting wasted.'

'I'll have one,' Macsen shouted.

Silence fell around him and Rhodri started to feel uncomfortable. All this talk about Jake was giving him flashbacks. He downed another drink to try and chase them away.

Christie came back in the room and handed Macsen a mug before sitting down on the sofa.

'We're supposed to be drinking,' Rhodri said. He got up and tipped the vodka into Macsen's coffee.

'Never mind getting pissed,' Sammy said. 'You need to sort out what's been going on.'

Iona looked at Rhodri. 'So, what are you going to do about it?'

'Who? Me?' Rhodri couldn't believe her nerve. He wished at that moment she had been the one in the lake. The thought made him laugh.

'What's so funny?' Sammy asked.

Rhodri hadn't realised he'd laughed out loud. 'It's all bullshit,' he said. 'It's not him. It's got to be one of us.'

'Now who would want to kill Alys and scare the hell out of the rest of us?' Iona asked.

Rhodri noticed the accusing look she gave him.

'You got something to say, Iona? Spit it out. I'm sick of your games.'

'S'nough,' Macsen said. He tried to stand but couldn't get out of the chair.

'I think we should put him to bed,' Christie said.

'He's fine,' Rhodri said.

'He is slurring.'

'I'm 'k,' Macsen said.

Rhodri put his hand in his pocket and pulled out a small clear bag. He opened it and tipped out the tablets. 'Here.' He handed one to Macsen, popped one in his own mouth and offered the others round. Iona, Christie, and Sammy shook their head.

'Gorra be shim,' Macsen slurred.

'Yeah,' Iona said. 'It's Jake.'

'Get real,' Rhodri said. 'It's impossible.'

'No. People have faked their own death before,' Iona said. She looked at Sammy and then Christie. 'It's not a stupid idea.'

'Was he clever?' Christie asked.

'Yeah. He was doing a degree in aerospace or something like that.'

'Sounds like he'd know how to hack phones,' Sammy said.

'Was he rich?' Christie asked. 'You'd have to have money.'

'Don't think so,' Iona said.

'This is ridiculous,' Rhodri said. 'I don't want to talk about it anymore.'

'You're the one who brought it up,' Iona said.

Rhodri felt a sudden urge to pee. Without a word, he headed to the bathroom. The floor felt uneven beneath his feet. He had to use the wall to steady himself. He wanted to go home. Usually the tablets energized him but they weren't working. He emptied his bladder and made his way back to the sitting room. The others were still talking about Jake. Hearing his name made him feel nauseous. He didn't want to keep seeing his face.

'I want to know how I got dragged into this,' Sammy said. 'Why is he leaving things for me?'

'He didn't have any friends at the end,' Iona said. 'He's going to take ours. Make us suffer.'

'I'll make you suffer if you don't shut up,' Rhodri said.

'I saw…' Macsen said, 'saw him–'

'You're pissed,' Rhodri cut in. 'Come on, let's take you to bed.'

'No,' Macsen said. 'Hesh coming for me.'

'No one is coming for you,' Rhodri said.

'You don't know that,' Iona said.

'Stuff in fridge. Been here,' Macsen said.

Rhodri pulled Macsen to his feet. 'Give us a hand,' he said to Sammy. 'I can't hold him up on my own.'

'What the hell did you give him?' Sammy asked.

'Just some beans,' Rhodri said. He turned his back and pulled Macsen's arms over his shoulders. Gripping tight, he led him to the stairs with Sammy pushing from behind.

'If he falls, I've got no chance,' Sammy said.

'I've got him,' Rhodri said.

It was slow progress up the stairs. Between them, they managed to manoeuvre Macsen through the bedroom door and onto the bed.

'Do you think he'll be OK?' Sammy said.

'Yeah, don't fuss.' Rhodri pulled off Macsen's shoes and threw the duvet over him. 'Come on. I wanna go home.'

'We have to wait for Christie,' Sammy said.

'Tell her you're tired.' He followed Sammy downstairs to the sitting room where Christie was plumping the cushions on the sofa.

'Leave that,' Rhodri said.

'You know he likes it tidy,' Iona said. She picked up two glasses. 'You can bring the rest and help me wash up.'

'I'll take a glass of water up to Macsen,' Sammy said. 'He's going to be thirsty when he wakes.'

Rhodri grabbed the rest of the glasses and followed Iona into the kitchen. Sammy filled a glass from the tap and left.

'What's going on with you?' Iona asked as she filled the sink. 'You've been at my throat all evening.'

'I wonder why that is?' Rhodri asked.

Iona scrubbed hard at the glass in her hand. 'It's because I took the keys to the police. I didn't tell them anything about Jake if that's what you think.'

'I don't give a fuck about the keys,' Rhodri said. 'But if you think you can threaten me–'

'Threaten you?'

'Yeah, that message you sent. Alys told you. Didn't she?'

Iona set the glass on the draining board and picked up another one. 'I don't know what you are talking about.'

Rhodri felt anger bubbling in his stomach. It spread through his veins until every muscle tensed. He grabbed hold of Iona and spun her around. 'If you tell Macsen about the baby being mine then I'll kill you.'

Iona pulled away. 'Get off me, you maniac.'

'What's going on?'

Rhodri turned and saw Sammy standing in the doorway.

'Nothing,' he said.

'I heard you,' Sammy said. 'You and Alys! No wonder you've been a dick lately. You were sleeping with her. You… you got her pregnant.'

'Keep your voice down.' Rhodri expected Macsen to come thumping down the stairs at any minute. Sammy was advancing on him. He tried to take a step back but he collided with the kitchen worktop.

'How could you?' Sammy slapped him hard across the face.

Rhodri put his hand up to ward off another slap. He could feel the sharp sting on his cheek. Christie had come into the kitchen and was staring at him. He turned and saw Iona smirking.

'It was you,' Sammy cried. 'You killed Alys.'

'No.' He put his hand out to Sammy.

'Don't touch me,' she shrieked.

All three women were now staring at him, their eyes accusing.

Rhodri felt trapped. He moved to the back door, unlocked it, and left. It was cold outside but it did little to sober him up. He pulled the handle on his car but it was locked. He remembered Sammy had the keys. He walked down the track and onto the main road. He needed to find somewhere to hang out until they left. Then he'd go back and sleep on the sofa. He'd talk to Macsen, convince him that Iona was trying to cause trouble. He nodded to himself. Macsen would believe him over Iona. He walked on, oblivious to the fact that his phone in his back pocket was being tracked.

Chapter Twenty

It was another Saturday morning at the station and Meadows was pleased to see all the team in without one word of complaint. He knew how they all felt. It was another missed weekend. He'd left Daisy at home when they should have been spending some time together. He looked around at the team now. They were all waiting for him to start the briefing. First, he had to address the mistake that had been made. His stomach churned, he hated to start on a negative note.

'How did we miss Alys Pugh's alleged rape case?' he asked.

'I did the background checks,' Harvard said. 'I searched the PNC. I should have looked at the PND to see if she had been a victim or witness to a previous crime.' Colour rose in his cheeks. 'I'm sorry.'

To Meadows' surprise the team didn't comment, not even Blackwell. He guessed they had all messed up at some point in the past. He looked at Harvard. His shoulders were slumped and worry creased his face.

'Don't be too hard on yourself,' Meadows said. 'I'm sure you won't make that mistake again. We now know Alys made an accusation of rape against Jake Ellis in

September 2018. Iona gave a witness statement. Alys then withdrew the allegation. Jake Ellis took his own life on New Year's Eve. He jumped off Tenby harbour. It was his twenty-first birthday. I'm waiting for the full details.'

'I'd say we're looking at revenge,' Blackwell said. 'It was Alys' birthday when she died, plus the references to Tenby and Bristol University. Iona and Christie came in yesterday. Iona's had a night-time visitor and the same sort of gifts were left. It turns out Alys' keys were left at Macsen's or so he says. I picked them up and dropped them into forensics. I told them all to get their locks changed.'

'Now we know how the killer is getting in,' Harvard said.

'Did you talk to any of them about creeping around Alys' garden late at night?' Meadows asked.

'Yeah. It was Christie,' Blackwell said. 'She said Alys was worried she was being watched so Christie went around to check. She didn't see anyone.'

'Do you believe her?'

'Seemed genuine. She couldn't remember what night it was. She said she would check through her messages and let us know.'

'OK. Meanwhile I want all the information we can find on Jake Ellis. If this is revenge then it has to be a relative or someone close.'

'It's over four years ago,' Valentine said. 'Why wait so long?'

'Something triggered them,' Edris suggested.

'The phone hacking and getting access to the houses would take some planning,' Paskin said.

Meadows nodded his agreement. 'Paskin, can you get the files sent from Bristol CID?'

Paskin nodded.

'Edris–' Meadows was cut off by the arrival of Sergeant Folland.

'Thought you should know that Macsen Lloyd was found dead in his home this morning.'

* * *

Hanes was standing at the bottom of the lane to Macsen's cottage when they arrived. Meadows stopped the car and opened the window.

'Forensics are already here,' Hanes said. 'I've only just managed to get his father to leave. One of the farm workers picked him up.'

'He found him?' Meadows asked.

'Yeah. He's been picking him up for work every morning because forensics still had his jeep. He got here at six and tooted the horn. When Macsen didn't come out, he thought he must have slept in. He went in and made a coffee. He found him when he took it upstairs.'

'Poor man,' Meadows said. 'Was the front door locked?'

'No. He said the keys were inside on the doormat. He stepped on them when he went in. He hung them up.'

'OK. Thanks, Hanes.' Meadows drove on and parked behind the forensics van.

Edris pointed to the vehicle parked next to the van. 'I'm sure that's Rhodri's car.'

'If it is, then where is he?' Meadows asked.

They got out of the car and put on protective clothing before entering the cottage. A path had been marked and a forensic officer was dusting the stair banister for prints.

The officer on the stairs turned to the detectives. 'Upstairs bathroom. Mike is up there.'

Meadows nodded his thanks and took the stairs with Edris following. The door to the bathroom was open. Mike was collecting samples as a photographer snapped pictures of the scene.

'We'll give you some space,' Mike said. He beckoned to the photographer and they both stepped outside. 'Interesting one for you.'

Meadows used the metal stepping stones that led to the cast-iron bath in the centre of the room. Macsen was lying fully clothed under the water. His legs dangling over the bottom of the bath.

'What's that in the water?' Edris asked.

'Looks like seaweed,' Meadows said.

'That would be my guess,' Mike called from the door.

Meadows bent over so he could inspect the water. Shells and what looked like sand had settled on his clothing.

'Given the seaside theme I think there is no doubt now this is connected to Jake Ellis' death,' Edris said.

'Can't see any obvious signs of trauma,' Meadows said.

'Could he have done it to himself? Out of remorse?' Edris asked.

'Not judging by his position. His arms are behind his back,' Meadows said. 'The question is how did the killer get him in the bath?' He straightened up and looked around. The floor was wet and there was a bar of soap and a bottle of shampoo on the floor. Yellow markers had been placed next to them. 'Looks like there was a struggle.'

'We're not going to know much more until we get him out,' Mike said.

Meadows moved away from the bath and picked up a leather case from the sink. It was black with what looked like gaming characters printed on the front. 'Last time we were here, everything was tidy. What is this doing here?' He pulled the zipper and opened the case. Inside were several discs.

'Looks like games for a PS4,' Edris said.

'Mike, can you process these for prints as priority, please?' Meadows asked.

'Yeah, no problem,' Mike said. 'I'll get one of the boys to run them in. Can we move him now?'

'Yes,' Meadows said. He didn't like to think about how they were going to manage that. 'We'll let you get on.'

They walked back down the stairs and Meadows stopped at the front door. 'Why would the keys be on the doormat?'

'Someone locked up and posted them through the letter box,' Edris said.

'That's what I was thinking. We know it wasn't the killer as the door was unlocked this morning. Someone else was here before them and locked up. Which means the killer had a key to open the door,' Meadows said.

'Rhodri would likely have a spare key.'

Meadows stepped outside. 'Or the killer made a copy. They had Alys' keys. Let's hope the others took our advice and got the locks changed. Give Blackwell a call. Get him to pick up Rhodri and I want a warrant to search his house.'

'Are we going to see Macsen's parents?'

'No. I doubt they will be able to tell us much. Valentine and Harvard can go. I want to speak to Iona and see what she has to say about Jake Ellis. She is staying with Christie. It's not far from here.'

Meadows drove as Edris made the calls. He couldn't shake the feeling that Macsen would still be alive if they had known about Jake. Even with this information, they still didn't have a suspect. Then there was Rhodri. Opportunity, motive, and he could be using the references to Jake to cause confusion. Then why hasn't one of them mentioned the incident? he wondered.

He had seen both Christie's and Iona's cars parked outside when they arrived but was surprised to find Sammy there. All three women were now sitting on the sofa crying. Edris had made them all a cup of tea and handed them out before settling into a chair.

Meadows waited for the crying to subside. He had only told them Macsen had been found dead at his home, nothing else. So far not one of them had asked how. He wondered who was going to be the first. He looked around. The room wasn't as tidy as it had been on his last visit. He guessed the stuff that was lying around belonged to Iona.

Sammy blew her nose and wiped the tears from her eyes. 'What happened?'

'He was fine when we put him to bed,' Christie added.

Edris sat forward. 'You were there last night?'

'We all were,' Christie said.

'What about Rhodri?' Meadows asked.

'Yeah, he was with us,' Iona said.

'We are treating Macsen's death as suspicious,' Meadows said. 'Why were you all at his house last night?'

'He asked us to come,' Sammy said.

'But he didn't,' Iona said. 'We all had a text message from him. He said he didn't send it. His phone had been hacked again.'

'OK,' Meadows said. 'You all turned up at Macsen's, then what did you do?'

'We had a few drinks,' Sammy said.

'Except me,' Christie said. 'I was driving.' She twisted her hands. 'This doesn't seem real.'

Iona started to sob again.

'Rhodri's car was parked outside Macsen's house,' Edris said.

'I drove it there,' Sammy said. 'Christie offered to drop us home so I drank and left the car there. We drank a lot. Macsen was out of it.'

'Yeah, because Rhodri…' Iona sniffed and looked at Sammy.

'I don't care if he gets in trouble,' Sammy said. 'Macsen is dead.' She wrapped her arms around her body.

'What did Rhodri do?' Meadows asked.

'He gave him something,' Iona said.

'Drugs?'

Sammy nodded. 'I don't know what. He had some pills.'

'He was slurring and couldn't get out of the chair,' Christie said. 'Oh God, we thought he was just drunk. We just left him there.' She put her hand to her mouth.

Meadows glanced at Edris and let the silence fill the room for a few moments.

'OK, so you left him in the chair. Then what happened?' Meadows asked.

'No, we didn't leave him. We put him to bed then came back here,' Iona said.

'All of you?' Meadows asked.

'Not Rhodri,' Sammy said.

Meadows saw Iona give Sammy a warning look. 'Two of your friends are dead. This is not the time for loyalty,' he said. 'If you know something, you need to tell us.'

'We had a fight,' Sammy said. 'I walked into the kitchen and Iona was arguing with him. I heard him say he was the father of Alys' baby.'

Meadows looked at Iona. 'Is this true?'

Iona nodded.

'How long have you known?'

'She told me when she found out she was pregnant. That's what we were arguing about that day outside the café. She didn't know if the father was Macsen or Rhodri. That's why I didn't tell you. I could've got Rhodri in trouble for no reason. He didn't know about the baby. I was so angry with her. She had Macsen and everything she wanted. I told her to get a termination. She wanted to keep it. She said it didn't matter if it wasn't Macsen's, he would never find out.'

Sammy stiffened and she turned on Iona. 'You knew! All this time, and you never told me.'

'I couldn't,' Iona said. 'I promised Alys.'

'Don't give me that shit,' Sammy raged. 'You love all your little secrets and games.'

'Just stop it,' Christie said.

Meadows could see that Sammy was seething but she folded her arms and sat back.

'Iona, is that what you and Rhodri were arguing about last night?' Meadows asked. 'He didn't want Macsen to find out about his affair with Alys?'

'No. He said I'd sent him a message threatening to tell Macsen. I didn't.'

'Is that all?'

'Yes,' Iona said.

Meadows didn't trust her. 'You keep withholding information from us. Obstructing an investigation is a serious offence.'

'I've told you everything,' Iona said.

Meadows could see that both Christie and Sammy looked uncomfortable. Iona flicked her hair over her shoulder and picked up her cup of tea.

'You didn't tell us about your argument with Alys, about her being pregnant, or the alleged rape,' Meadows said.

'What?' Christie turned to Iona with wide eyes. 'Someone attacked you?'

'Not me,' Iona said. 'Alys.'

'Oh God,' Sammy said. 'Poor Alys. She never said.'

'It was a long time ago,' Iona said. She turned to Meadows. 'I didn't say anything because I didn't think it was important.'

Meadows didn't trust himself to speak. It was a rarity for him to lose his patience but Iona was pushing his limits. He looked at Edris. He could tell by his expression he felt the same way.

Edris flicked back the pages in his notebook. 'We asked you if the initial *J* meant anything to you. You answered no. We asked you about the seashells, the fishbowl, Bristol University, and if Alys had any problems. If there was anyone you could think of who would want to harm her. Again, you answered no. Do you honestly expect us to believe that you made no connection between what happened to Alys and the accusation against Jake Ellis?'

Iona's eyes narrowed. 'How could they be connected? He's dead. You would think I was mad if I told you he had killed her.'

'Unbelievable,' Sammy said. 'All you think about is yourself.'

'Did it not cross your mind that someone connected to Jake was seeking revenge?' Edris asked.

'No,' Iona said. 'I thought…' Colour rose in her cheeks.

'You thought he was back from the dead,' Edris said.

'What would you think if someone came into your house and left things without making a sound or leaving a trace. He did the same to Alys and Sammy. He also left stuff at Macsen's and then he killed him. He's going to try and kill me next.' Iona covered her face with her hands and sobbed.

'I think it's clear now both the murder of Alys and Macsen are related to the incident with Jake,' Meadows said. 'We will be looking closely at anyone connected to Jake. For now, you need to tell us everything you know. We will judge what is important. Iona?'

Iona took her hands from her face and nodded. 'Jake went to school with us. He was always strange.'

'In what way?' Meadows asked.

'Didn't mix with the other kids. He hung out with Shaun Jones. Both of them were top of the class. Getting A's and thinking they were better than the rest of us. They took extra classes and worked on science projects. Then they ended up going to the same university as us.'

'Was Alys friendly with Jake?' Meadows asked.

'She was friendly with everyone. She talked to Jake occasionally. That's what she was like. I told her he fancied her and she shouldn't encourage him. She wouldn't listen. She had some problem with her laptop once and she got him to fix it for her. After that, we couldn't get rid of him.' She took a sip of her tea and cradled the cup in her hands.

'Then in third year we had just started back and there was a party. It had been arranged by the student union. We were all drunk and some of us were high. Alys bought Jake a drink. Then he came to our table with his friends. I was pissed off but I stayed around. Alys sent Jake to get a fishbowl. We shared it then we kept drinking. The next thing Alys and Jake are dancing.'

'Would it be fair to say they were both drunk at this stage?' Edris asked.

'Jake was OK. Alys was all over the place. They came back to the table and Alys said she was thirsty. Jake went to get her a drink. I think he must have spiked it.'

Sammy shook her head and Christie kept her eyes down and was rubbing her thumb in the palm of her hand.

'Did you see him put something into her drink?' Meadows asked.

'No, but after that she got up to go to the toilet. I went with her. She couldn't stand on her own. She was sick. I helped clean her up. I was going to take her back to her room but Jake was waiting outside. He said he would take her back; make sure she got to her room OK. I was wasted myself so I let him. He never took her back. Instead, he took her to his flat. I didn't know. The next morning Alys called me. She was in a state. I went to find her. She was sitting on the stairs near his block of flats. She was crying so much I couldn't make out what was wrong at first. I took her back to my room. She didn't want anyone to know. I didn't know what to do so I went to talk to the dean. I had to report it. If I hadn't, he would've got away with it. Probably would've raped another girl.'

'Jake was arrested,' Meadows said.

'Yeah, the dean called the police but he wasn't charged.'

'Alys withdrew her complaint,' Meadows said.

'Do you have any idea what it's like?' Iona asked. 'The endless questions. The implication that because she had danced with him she consented.'

Meadows could see the disgust on Christie's face. 'I do understand how difficult an investigation of that nature is. I assure you, I'm not here to make a judgement. I'm looking at the facts. Did Alys come under any pressure from Jake to drop the charges?'

Iona shrugged. 'I don't think she spoke to him after that night. I suppose he could have got to her somehow.'

'You mentioned Jake was with his friends that night. Can you give me their names?' Edris asked.

'Shaun was one of them. I didn't know the others.'

'Alys left university after Jake took his own life. Was that because she felt responsible?' Edris asked.

'No. She was traumatised by what happened that night. She didn't even tell her parents. Why would she feel guilty? She didn't do anything wrong.'

'It sounds like Alys was a caring person,' Meadows said. 'You had all gone through school together. It must have come as a shock when she heard about Jake. I doubt she would have wished him dead.'

'She was upset, she thought people would be talking about her,' Iona said. 'She wanted to go and see his mother but she was afraid of her reaction.'

'Did any of Jake's friends or family contact Alys after his death?' Meadows asked.

'No.'

'Macsen must have been very angry with Jake,' Meadows said.

'He went nuts. He came up to the university. He was shouting about wanting to kill Jake. Lucky for Jake, he was at the police station. By the time Jake was released, Macsen had gone home.'

'Did Macsen go after Jake when he came home for the Christmas break?'

'No one saw Jake after that. He didn't come back home for Christmas. I think he went to stay with his father.'

'He didn't come back at all? Not even to see his mother for a few days over the Christmas holidays?' Meadows asked.

'If he did, I didn't know about it. Alys didn't say anything. I'm sure Macsen would have said if he'd seen him.'

'What about Rhodri?' Meadows asked.

'What about him?' Iona asked.

'He shared a flat with Jake. Were they friendly?'

'No. Rhodri had words with Jake. Told him to stay away from Alys.'

'Did he threaten him?'

'No. He never touched him. He didn't want to get involved.' Iona picked at her thumbnail.

'What are you not telling us?'

'There's nothing more to tell.'

'Oh come on, Iona,' Sammy said. 'You've lied to us all along.'

'I haven't lied,' Iona said.

A soft patter against the window made Iona turn her head. Fat drops of rain were splashing against the glass and trickling down. The sky outside was brooding and the room in which they sat had darkened while they had been talking.

'This all happened over four years ago,' Meadows said. 'Why would you think Jake killed Alys now?'

Iona shrugged and turned her gaze back to Meadows. 'He could have been hiding away. He was in love with her.'

'If that's the case then why would he want to hurt her?'

'She was with Macsen. He wanted her for himself. I don't know.'

'Why leave stuff in your house?'

'Because I told the police what he had done.'

'Did you know anything about this, Sammy? Christie?' Meadows asked.

'No, I had no idea,' Sammy said. 'Alys didn't say anything about this.'

Christie shook her head. She grabbed a throw from the back of the sofa and put it around her shoulders.

Meadows looked at Iona. 'It doesn't make sense that someone connected to Jake would break into Sammy's house and leave those objects.'

'It's to get to me through my friends,' Iona said. 'Jake lost all his friends after his arrest. He wants to take everything from me. I want to be put in a safe house.'

Meadows could understand her fear although it appeared to be self-centred. There were no concerns for her friends' safety. 'If all you did was give the police a statement, I don't see how that would make you a target,' he said. 'The police would've taken statements from everyone that was at the party.'

'It was me who told them that he was waiting outside the toilets. No one else would have seen him leave with Alys.'

'You started a social media campaign against him,' Meadows said.

Iona folded her arms. 'Yes, because he had gotten away with it. I had to warn others about him. So are you going to give me some protection?'

'As far as we know, there have been no break-ins. It looks as if Alys' keys were used to gain entry into your flat. Probably the same in your house, Sammy,' Meadows said.

'What about Macsen?' Christie asked.

'The door was open,' Edris said. 'Who was the last to leave last night?'

'We were,' Christie said.

'Rhodri left before us,' Sammy said.

'I locked the door and posted the keys through the letter box,' Christie said.

'Does Rhodri have a key?' Edris asked.

'I think so,' Sammy said.

'Did you see Rhodri after you left?' Meadows asked.

'No,' Iona said. 'We drove back here, had a drink and went to bed. If he turned up here, I wouldn't have heard him. I was out for the count. I think we all were. Even Christie couldn't get up this morning.' She looked at Christie. 'You weren't even drinking.'

'I had one when we came back. Must have been a strong one. I don't remember going to bed. I couldn't open my eyes this morning,' Christie said.

'What were you drinking?' Meadows asked.

'The vodka we brought back from Macsen's,' Sammy said.

Meadows saw Edris raise his eyebrows. 'Did Macsen drink vodka last night?'

'Yeah, Rhodri and Macsen drunk most of the bottle,' Sammy said.

'Have any of you heard from Rhodri today?'

They all shook their heads.

'OK. We'll leave it there for now.' Meadows stood up. 'I would advise you all to stay together for now. Have you had the locks changed?'

'I have someone coming later today to change the locks,' Christie said. 'I'll ask if he can change all our locks. You can stay with me until then.'

'Thanks, Christie,' Sammy said.

'I don't think I can go home,' Iona said. 'Just the thought that someone has been in my flat, looking through my things. I feel violated.'

'You can stay as long as you like,' Christie said.

'I'll also ask for officers to check on the property during the night,' Meadows said. 'Meanwhile, if any of you hear from Rhodri, ask him to get in contact with us. We need to speak to him.'

Christie saw them to the door and Meadows heard the lock click once they were outside.

'Iona gives a good account of the night of the alleged rape considering she was wasted,' Edris said.

'Yeah, I thought that too. It's like she had the story memorised. She only told us about Rhodri and Alys because she had no choice. It makes me think she's still not telling us everything.'

'They all seemed on the same page with what happened last night,' Edris said. 'Then there's the vodka. Christie claims she was out of it after one shot. Seems unlikely. What if someone slipped something in the bottle? It would make him more pliable.'

Meadows nodded his agreement. 'Give Blackwell a call to see if he's managed to track down Rhodri. Then we need chase up the warrant to search his house.'

'Do you think he's our man?' Edris asked.

'He was seeing Alys. It sounds like he got her pregnant and Macsen was about to find out.'

'He knew about the incident with Jake,' Edris said. 'He probably put that stuff in the houses to move suspicion away from himself.'

'Could be, but I think there is more to the story than is being told. And if Rhodri is not our killer, then he could be the next target.'

Chapter Twenty-one

Meadows made himself a cup of tea and carried it through to the office. He felt weary. They had been working on the case non-stop. The only time he'd been home was to sleep. No downtime, no relaxation. Still they seemed no closer to catching Alys' killer than they were a week ago.

'Did you find anything in Rhodri's house?' Blackwell asked.

'Nothing of interest,' Meadows said. 'Cannabis, cocaine, and a few suspicious-looking tablets. Personal use. Edris is taking his laptop and gaming computer to tech. I've asked if they can process it as a matter of priority. How was he when you brought him in?'

'He was shocked when I told him about Macsen. I'd say genuinely cut up, but who knows. It could be an act.'

'Has his solicitor arrived yet?'

'No. He didn't want one.'

'It's his right to refuse. I don't like it but we need to talk to him.' Meadows picked up a file.

'No doubt he knows the drill, given his cautions for possession,' Blackwell said.

'I hope he realises this is more serious.'

Rhodri was sitting quietly in the interview room with Hanes. He glanced at Meadows then looked away.

Meadows and Blackwell took their seats and Hanes left the room. As the recording was being set up, Meadows watched Rhodri. His legs jiggled and he drummed his fingers on the table. He couldn't tell if it was nerves or withdrawal symptoms.

'You have been advised that you are entitled to legal representation,' Meadows said. 'You can either appoint a solicitor of your choice or we can contact the duty solicitor.'

'I know the spiel,' Rhodri said. 'You've already fucked up by arresting Macsen. If you'd been looking for Alys' killer then he'd still be alive. Now you've brought me in. You're wasting your time.'

'We've brought you in to help with our enquiries,' Meadows said.

'Just get on with it.' Rhodri sat back and folded his arms.

'You can start by telling us where you were last night,' Blackwell said.

'I was with Macsen. You already know that.'

'What time did you leave?' Blackwell asked.

'I don't know. It was late.'

'Where did you go?'

'I walked around and then slept in a barn. I was wasted. I woke up with a blinding headache so I called a mate to pick me up. I went to bed to try and get a few hours' sleep then you were hammering at my door.'

'You had an argument with Iona last night,' Meadows said.

'Oh, I get it. She's been bumping her gums so you come after me. She's always causing trouble. We had too much to drink and said some stupid stuff. That's all.'

'Like you being the father of Alys' baby?' Meadows asked.

The colour rose in Rhodri's cheeks. 'I didn't even know she was pregnant. She never said anything about me being the father.'

'But you were sleeping with her,' Blackwell said.

'Yeah, it just happened. It didn't mean anything.'

'When did it start?' Meadows asked.

'She'd broken up with Macsen before Christmas. She came to see me. She was in a state. We had a few drinks and one thing led to another.'

'Why did she come to see you?' Meadows asked.

'Because she thought I could talk to Macsen, help them sort things out.'

'But you didn't. You kept on seeing her,' Meadows said.

'Only a few times.'

Meadows took a sheet of paper from the file and slid it across to Rhodri. 'These are dates and locations taken from Alys' phone calendar. Can you confirm that you met up on those dates?'

'I can't remember dates,' Rhodri said.

'What about locations? We know QCP is quarry car park. Did you meet her there?'

'Yeah, we met there a couple of times.'

'What about the other abbreviations? Do they mean anything to you?' Meadows asked.

Rhodri looked at the paper. 'I suppose GS could be Gorslas. She came over to mine. Maybe MP is my place. I went to her house a couple of times.'

'What about Bristol?'

'We never went there together.'

'Why was Alys going to Bristol?'

'I don't know. She never said anything to me about going.'

'Could it have had something to do with Jake Ellis?' Meadows asked.

The colour drained from Rhodri's face and he shifted in the chair.

'We know all about the allegation made against Jake,' Blackwell said. 'Why didn't you mention it?'

'I'd forgotten about it,' Rhodri said.

'Oh, come on. All the reminders that have been left. Do you expect us to believe you never considered the possibility that Alys' murder had something to do with Jake Ellis?' Blackwell said.

'Why would I?' Rhodri asked.

'Were you and Jake friends?' Meadows asked.

Rhodri looked confused. 'What?'

'You shared rooms in university,' Meadows said.

'Yeah. I was allocated a room, I didn't have a choice. We weren't friends.'

'Living together, sharing a kitchen, and probably a few parties. You must have got to know each other.'

'We stayed out of each other's way. We had nothing in common.'

'You had an altercation with Jake when he was released from police custody,' Meadows said.

'I had words with him. He'd attacked my best mate's girlfriend.'

'And a girl you were fond of,' Blackwell said.

'There wasn't anything between us then.'

'You grew up together. You'd been friends for a long time. You must have cared for Alys,' Meadows said.

'Yeah, but as a friend.'

'Did you threaten Jake?' Meadows asked.

'No. I told him to stay away from Alys.'

'Alys and Macsen broke up not long after. Was that because he couldn't get past what had happened?' Meadows asked.

'No. He wasn't a dick.'

'Why did they break up before Christmas?' Blackwell asked.

'I don't know.'

'Really? She came to you with her problems,' Blackwell said. 'Why not go to one of her girlfriends?'

Rhodri shrugged.

'So, she comes crying to you and you persuade her that you are a better option,' Blackwell said.

'No. I told you, it just happened.'

'You kept on seeing her behind Macsen's back.'

'No. We ended it after they got back together.'

'Who ended it?' Meadows asked.

'We both agreed. We only saw each other once after they got back together.'

Meadows found that difficult to believe. 'It wasn't the end though because she was pregnant.'

'I didn't know at the time.'

'Were you worried that Macsen would find out?'

'That's why we ended it. We had been careful so there was no reason for him to find out.'

'But Iona knew,' Blackwell said. 'I think Alys told you she was pregnant. I think she was going to tell Macsen. It would have been easy for you to hack Macsen's phone; you probably knew his passwords. You sent the messages to Alys then made sure Macsen was out of the way. I get it. You just wanted to talk her out of telling him, maybe persuade her to get rid of the baby. Things got out of hand–'

'No!'

'Then Iona tells you she knows about you and Alys. She threatens to tell Macsen. You knew he would work it out. You went back last night–'

'No. No!' Rhodri jumped up sending the chair flying. 'You're trying to fit me up.'

'No one is trying to fit you up,' Meadows said. 'We are trying to get to the truth.'

'You must realise how bad this looks for you,' Blackwell said.

'I didn't kill Macsen,' Rhodri shouted.

'Then sit down and start answering our questions. The more you lie, the bigger hole you are digging yourself,' Blackwell said.

Rhodri moved from foot to foot.

'You're rattling,' Blackwell said. 'You need a hit.'

'No. I'm not a druggie.'

'We found your stash,' Blackwell said.

'Fine then, charge me for possession and let me go.'

'You're not going anywhere,' Blackwell said.

'Sit down, Rhodri,' Meadows said. 'If you didn't kill Macsen then you have nothing to worry about.'

Rhodri picked the chair up and plonked himself down. His legs continued to bounce up and down.

'You were afraid Macsen was going to find out about you and Alys,' Meadows said. 'He was your friend and you went behind his back.'

'Yeah, I was worried that Iona would blab but I could've convinced him she was lying, trying to split me and Sammy up.'

'Why would he have believed that?' Meadows asked.

'Iona's always flirting with me. Tried it on a few times but I wasn't interested.'

'What did you give Macsen last night?' Meadows asked.

'A couple of beans.'

'Ecstasy?'

'Yeah, that's all, I swear. Then he started acting up. He was afraid.'

'Of what?'

'That Jake was going to get him.'

'Jake Ellis is dead. Why would Macsen think that he would come after him? Did Macsen do something to Jake?'

'No. Macsen was pissed at Jake after what he did to Alys but he never touched him. He didn't see him after that. He said Jake had left things in his house. Rock from Tenby and some seashells. There's been stuff left in my house. Someone is messing with us.'

'Why didn't you report it?' Meadows asked.

'I don't know. No one had broken in and… well, I thought it was Iona trying to scare me.'

'Why would Iona want to scare you?' Meadows asked.

'Because of me and Alys.'

'Why didn't you tell us about Jake?'

'There was nothing to tell. It was years ago. This has got nothing to do with Jake.'

'That's not what Macsen thought,' Meadows said.

'He was off his face.'

'Yet he was right to be afraid.' Meadows saw Rhodri's eyes fill with tears and he looked away. 'If you know something that will help us find his killer then you need to tell us.'

'I've told you everything I know. Macsen was like my brother, what I did with Alys was stupid. I wish it never happened. I didn't kill them. I've told you where I was last night. If you're not going to charge me then I'm leaving. You can't stop me.'

He's right, Meadows thought. They had no evidence against him. 'We will be examining your computer, laptop, and phone.'

'Look all you want,' Rhodri said. 'You won't find anything.'

'You will be released under investigation,' Meadows said.

'Meaning you are not in the clear,' Blackwell added. 'You will need to make sure you are available for questioning so don't go taking a holiday.'

Meadows and Blackwell left the interview room and went back upstairs to the office.

'Get a confession?' Edris asked.

'If only it was that easy,' Meadows said.

'He's got motive and had the opportunity,' Blackwell said. 'The DNA results will show if he is the father of Alys' baby. He looked like he shat himself when we mentioned Jake Ellis. There's something going on there.'

'Yeah, I got that impression too. What though? It was the same with Iona, she came up with some excuse for not mentioning Jake. They're afraid of something,' Meadows said.

'Are you sure this kid killed himself?' Blackwell asked.

'The thought had crossed my mind that they had some hand in his death,' Meadows said.

'The coroner ruled it as suicide at the inquest,' Paskin said, 'although he hasn't been legally declared dead. I've requested a transcript of the inquest.'

'Then what's Rhodri not telling us?' Meadows said.

'We know he was seeing Alys and she was pregnant,' Edris said. 'Alys threatens to tell Macsen about them. He tries to scare her by leaving things in her house to remind her of Jake. It could be she felt guilty that Jake took his own life. By reminding her, he hoped she'd think twice before ruining his life and his long friendship with Macsen. When that doesn't work, he kills her. Then he continues to make it look like it has something to do with Jake.'

'What about Macsen?' Valentine asked.

'Iona was going to tell him or maybe she did. Rhodri was afraid he'd guess that he killed Alys.'

'Why not just tell us about Jake?' Blackwell asked.

'He knew we would find out. He left enough clues,' Meadows said.

'Do you think we are dealing with more than one killer?' Harvard asked. 'Macsen was a big guy. It would've taken a lot of strength to drag him into the bath.'

'He was out of it from what Rhodri told us,' Blackwell said.

'And possibly drugged,' Edris added. 'I'm not convinced it was only vodka and ecstasy, after what Christie told us.'

'We'll have to wait for the tox screen,' Meadows said.

'Even if he wasn't drugged, it looks like his hands were bound behind his back,' Edris said.

'Even so, to get him into the bathroom and then into the bath,' Valentine said. 'I'm with Harvard. I don't think one person could have done it alone.'

'What information have we got on Jake Ellis?' Meadows asked.

'He grew up in Llangadog,' Paskin said. 'His mother, Vanessa Evans, still lives there. She divorced Jake's father, David Ellis, when Jake was two years old. I'm still looking for contact details for David. From what I can see so far, neither one of them remarried but Vanessa had three other children with her partner, two sons and a daughter.'

Meadows looked at the board where a photograph of Jake had been added. 'I think this all started four years ago. We need to find everyone who has a connection to Jake. Relatives, friends, girlfriends. I want to look at the alleged rape case as well as the investigation into Jake's death.'

'I'll request the files,' Paskin said and yawned.

Meadows checked the time. 'It's late. Go home. We'll make a start in the morning. I've asked uniform to keep a watch on Christie's house. I'll also ask them to keep an eye on Rhodri. If this is a revenge killing then any one of them could be next.'

Chapter Twenty-two

The church bells were ringing for Sunday morning service as Meadows and Edris got out of the car. Meadows stretched and breathed in the crisp air.

'At least the sun is shining for a change,' Edris said.

'Yeah, makes you feel re-energized.'

Edris laughed. 'I wouldn't go that far. I could have done with a lie-in. I reckon that's what everyone here is doing.'

'It is quiet. They're all probably in church.'

'I doubt it,' Edris said. 'From what I hear most congregations only have a handful of members now.'

Meadows looked at the row of houses in front of them. They were all well-kept. Daffodil-filled window boxes danced in the breeze. No curtains twitched and he guessed Vanessa Evans wasn't patiently waiting for them. He felt a twinge of anxiety. It seemed cruel to be questioning a woman who never got the chance to bury her son. There had been no closure and talking about it would only pick at the wound.

He pushed the gate open, knocked at the door, and waited. He was about to knock again when the door opened. Meadows smiled and introduced himself and Edris.

'You better come in,' Vanessa said.

She led them into a small but neat sitting room, took a seat, and folded her arms. Meadows guessed her to be in her early fifties, she had highlighted shoulder-length hair which surrounded an oval face. She didn't smile. He took a seat on the sofa next to a snoozing black and white cat. Edris remained standing.

'You can move Erol,' Vanessa said.

Meadows picked up the cat and put it on his lap. He stroked it as Edris took a seat.

'We appreciated you taking the time to talk to us,' Meadows said. 'I expect you heard about Alys Pugh's murder on the news.'

'Couldn't have happened to a nicer girl,' Vanessa said. 'Sorry, I should probably keep my thoughts to myself.'

'Do you blame Alys for your son's death?'

Vanessa nodded. 'If you're here to find out if I had anything to do with her death then you'll be disappointed. I can't say I never wished her dead at the time, but Jake wouldn't have wanted any harm to come to her, and I would never inflict the pain of losing a child on another mother.'

'There are certain aspects of the case that lead us to believe Alys' murder and the death of your son are connected,' Meadows said.

'I imagine she pulled the same stunt on some other poor sod,' Vanessa said. 'At least you can clear Jake's name.'

'We don't have the full details of the complaint Alys made against Jake. I would much rather hear about Jake from you than read notes in a file. Can you tell us about him?'

Vanessa stood up and moved to the mantle. She took down a photograph and handed it to Meadows. 'That's Jake.'

Meadows looked at the young man. He had dark blond hair and blue eyes framed by long lashes. 'Handsome young man.'

'Yes, he was.'

'I understand he was very bright,' Meadows said.

Vanessa's face softened. 'He was into everything as a child. Inquisitive. He devoured books and was always studying. He was also kind and funny.'

'Did you know Alys as a child?' Meadows asked.

'Yes. They started school at the same time. She'd come over here sometimes. She struggled with maths and Jake would help her. She was a nice girl. Iona was the problem – spoilt little bitch, always wanting her own way. She teased Alys about being friends with Jake. Then Alys started seeing Macsen and she had no time for Jake. It was like she was embarrassed to talk to him.'

'Did Jake have any close friends growing up?'

Vanessa nodded. 'Shaun Jones. They were always together. Then they went to university and met with Ethan. They were his two closest friends.'

'Do you know Ethan's surname?' Edris asked.

'Steward, I think.'

'Was Jake happy at university?' Meadows asked.

'Yes, he was doing well, he had good grades and was enjoying the course. The first summer, he went to India with Shaun and Ethan. They worked on a project helping disadvantaged children. They planned to go back after their finals. After Alys accused Jake of rape, he became withdrawn. He went to stay with his father because he was too afraid to come home.'

'Was that because of Macsen?' Meadows asked.

'Yeah, and Rhodri. He was also worried about the gossip. You know what it's like in the village. Iona was posting vile things on social media. He thought everyone would hate him. I don't think the rumours spread. No one ever said anything to me. Alys' parents even sent flowers and a card when he died.'

'Did Jake talk to you about what happened that night?' Meadows asked.

'That last Christmas, he came home. He told me he and Alys had become friendly at university; they talked often and even went for coffee together. That night there was a party. They both had a lot to drink. Alys went back to his room and stayed the night. They had sex. He never denied that but he didn't force himself on her. He couldn't understand why she made it up. Lots of people were there that night. There was never any evidence to charge him. I think Alys knew what she had done was wrong. That's why she withdrew the complaint. Jake's father, David, wanted to take it further. He was going to take Alys to court for making a false allegation. He'd taken Jake to a solicitor. He thought he had a good case against Alys. They were also going to pursue Iona for malicious communication and lying to the police.'

'Was Jake worried it would stir things up again?'

'No, he was all for it. He didn't want that hanging over his head for the rest of his life, he said the case would prove he was innocent. He was getting back to normal and looking forward to going back to university. He was happy going with Shaun and Ethan to Tenby. We planned a dinner to celebrate his twenty-first birthday when he came back. Something must've happened that night. I got a call from the police on New Year's Day to say he had jumped off the harbour wall. The coroner ruled it as a suicide but I don't think Jake killed himself.'

'What do you think happened?' Meadows asked.

'I don't know. Maybe he went for a walk and fell in. Some sort of accident. David was convinced there was more to it.'

'We haven't been able to contact David. Do you have an address for him?'

'Don't you know? David took his own life after the inquest. Jake was his only child and he couldn't live with the grief.'

'I'm sorry to hear that,' Meadows said.

'Alys' lies took two lives and destroyed many more,' Vanessa said.

'It must have been hard for you. I understand Jake had two brothers and a sister.'

'Yes, it was a difficult time for them. I'm proud to say they all managed to get on with their lives, make the most of what they have.'

'Do you still keep in contact with Shaun and Ethan?'

Vanessa shook her head. 'They both went away to work as far as I know.'

'Was there anyone else who was close to Jake?'

'You're asking me if I can think of anyone so grief-stricken they went on a killing spree? I heard about Macsen Lloyd. While I'm sorry for the parents, I can't help you.'

Can't or won't, Meadows thought. 'Thank you for your time.' He moved the cat and stood up.

'I'm sorry to have to ask but we need to know your whereabouts at the time of the murders. That would be the early morning on the Tuesday, March 14 and last Friday night, March 24,' Edris said.

Vanessa raised her eyebrows. 'You're seriously asking me?'

'It's just for elimination,' Edris said.

'Fine. Tuesday morning I would have been in work. I'm a receptionist at the doctor's surgery. Friday night I would have been here. Alone.'

'Thank you.' Edris wrote a couple of notes then closed his notebook before standing.

'If I was you,' Vanessa said, 'I'd talk to Iona. That one was always trouble. I doubt if she's changed.'

'We'll bear that in mind,' Meadows said.

They left the house and didn't speak until they were back in the car.

'That's a family with motive,' Edris said.

Meadows nodded. 'Jake's siblings were young at the time. Maybe now they are older they decided it was time to seek revenge. Then there are David's relatives. We're going to have to track them all down.'

'I wouldn't put it past Vanessa to have killed them.'

'She's angry enough but I can't see her killing Alys and Macsen. That doesn't mean she has no idea who did. She wasn't willing to give us any names of people close to Jake, that makes me think there is someone. Best check out her alibis to be sure.' Meadows' phone trilled and he hit answer. 'Hi, Mike.'

'Got something for you,' Mike said.

'Great,' Meadows said. 'We need a break.'

'Yeah, well, this is going to blow your case apart. Erm… you better come in and see for yourself.'

'OK, we're on our way.'

'Mike sounds worried,' Edris said.

'I guess we better go and find out what's got him vexed.'

They were in the forensic offices in just under half an hour. Mike was waiting for them.

'OK, you've got my interest,' Meadows said.

Mike tapped the keyboard of his computer and an image of a fingerprint appeared. Meadows and Edris leaned in closer.

'This is one of the prints we took off the discs we found in Macsen's bathroom.' Another click and an identical print appeared next to the first. 'This is one we matched on the system.'

Meadows felt a fizzle of excitement. 'You got a name for us?'

'That's where the problem lies. I've doubled-checked and checked again. The print belongs to Jake Ellis.'

Chapter Twenty-three

Meadows pinned copies of the fingerprints to the incident board and called the team around for the morning briefing.

'How is that even possible?' Blackwell asked.

'Mike was in no doubt,' Meadows said. 'There were no prints on the case. It looks like it's been wiped clean. The game discs did at one point belong to Jake. The prints could've been on the discs for years. Especially if the case hadn't been opened.'

'Is there any way of determining the age of the prints?' Harvard asked.

'No,' Meadows said. 'So, we are looking for someone who was close enough to Jake to have his possessions.'

'Or he's not dead,' Edris said.

'I'm still waiting on the transcript of the inquest,' Paskin said. 'Now the weekend is over, things should move quicker.'

'Edris and I will be meeting with DI Tom Allen this afternoon. He dealt with Jake's case. I want to get his personal opinion. We won't get that from case notes. Maybe he had a suspicion something wasn't right about what happened in Tenby that night.'

'I've tracked down Ethan Steward,' Harvard said. 'He's living in London. He said he is going to Bristol for a meeting tomorrow and can come and see us after. He was keen to help.'

'Have we had the details of Alys' rape case?'

'Yes,' Valentine said. 'Arrived this morning from DS Sita Khan.'

'OK, I'll leave you to go through them. Harvard, call Ethan back and tell him we'll meet him in Bristol and arrange to meet with DS Khan,' Meadows said.

Harvard nodded and picked up the phone.

'Blackwell, can I leave you to track down Shaun Jones?'

'Yeah,' Blackwell said. 'It is worth looking at the possibility Jake is alive. Look at his finances and phone records before he died. See if he had the means to disappear. His body was never recovered. Now the fingerprints. What are the odds of finding his prints at a crime scene?'

'I can't see he would let his parents believe he was dead,' Meadows said. 'His father killed himself because of the grief.'

'Six months later,' Valentine said. 'Maybe Jake intended to let them know he was alive when things calmed down. He wouldn't have expected his father to react in that way. It adds to the motive for wanting Alys and Macsen dead.'

'You're right,' Meadows said. 'We need to rule it out. It won't be the first time someone has faked their own death. He was a bright kid; he'd know his way around a computer. Who knows what records he could have changed.'

'Or documents he could have faked,' Blackwell said.

'I'll leave that with you. Edris and I will go to the hospital for Macsen's post-mortem results. Hopefully they will give us some answers rather than more questions. This whole case feels off,' Meadows said.

'Yeah,' Blackwell said. 'Fingerprints from a dead guy will do that. Add in the seaweed, shells, and rock, two dead and no suspects.'

'It's more than that,' Meadows said. 'We're being played. There is so much going on, I keep thinking it's hiding the obvious.'

'What would be the obvious?' Harvard asked.

'That one of these four is responsible.' Meadows pointed to the names on the board. 'Rhodri and Iona are withholding information. The only reason to do so would be guilt. Then there's Sammy and Christie. Where do they fit in? I'm not sure either of them is trustworthy.' He grabbed his coat and turned to Edris. 'Come on, let's go.'

* * *

The hospital car park was full and Meadows had to drive around several times before a spot became available.

'It's getting worse here,' Edris said. 'Maybe we should ask for priority parking.'

'What for? We're not in a hurry. Why would you want to take the space from someone who has an appointment? They've probably waited months.'

'When you put it like that,' Edris said. 'It's just a pain parking each time we come. It wastes so much time.'

Meadows smiled. 'You need to chill out. You could always utilise the time by thinking.'

'I've done enough of that over the last two weeks. I can't wait for a day off.'

'Never mind, a nice trip to the seaside will do you good.'

'In this weather?'

'The sun is out.'

'Yeah, and it's still freezing.'

'You need to get yourself a bobble hat like Harvard. I'm sure if you ask him, his mum will knit one for you.'

Edris laughed. 'Yeah, that would do a lot for my reputation. I am known for my style.'

The basement of the hospital was quiet as usual. When they entered the office, Daisy was typing away at her computer.

'Morning,' Edris said.

She saved the document and turned to face them. 'I was just finishing the report,' she said. 'I'll take you through.' She grabbed an overall and put it on as she was walking.

Meadows pushed open the heavy double door and stepped into the morgue. Macsen was laid out on a steel gurney. A green sheet covered his body and reached just under his chin. It had been less than two weeks ago they had viewed Alys laying in the same spot, he thought. He had interviewed Macsen and treated him as a suspect. Now his life had been taken. Two young people that had plans for the future. He felt the weight of the investigation and the sadness of the families involved shrouding him.

Daisy stepped up to the gurney and pulled the sheet back. 'His hands were secured behind his back with a large cable tie.' She indicated his wrist. 'You can see the breaks in the skin.'

'Meaning he struggled,' Meadows said.

'Yes. Bruising to the shoulders and hips.' Daisy moved to Macsen's feet and pulled up the sheeting. 'Also bruising to the ankles.'

'He was probably dragged,' Edris said.

'There are no marks to his back or chest,' Daisy said. 'You would expect to see some friction if he'd been dragged.'

'Then he's likely to have got the bruising from the bath,' Meadows said. 'It's an old cast-iron type. If he was thrashing around, he would have knocked against the side.' He looked closely at the ankles. 'Could the bruising here have been made by someone gripping his ankles?'

'Yes,' Daisy said. 'If he was being held firmly by his ankles and he was pulling back.'

'He was found with his legs over the back of the bath,' Meadows said. 'His head was submerged. So the killer binds his hands, gets him into the bath, then pulls at his ankles to get him under the water. He struggled but couldn't pull himself up. I take it the cause of death was drowning.'

'Yes,' Daisy said.

'How the hell did they get him in the bath?' Edris asked.

'He had large quantities of alcohol in his system as well as ecstasy and morphine.'

'Morphine? Enough to knock him out?' Meadows asked.

'I would say he would have been groggy, maybe he lost consciousness for a while, especially given the amount of alcohol,' Daisy said. 'Not a sufficient amount to completely knock him out.'

'Maybe just enough to make him compliant,' Meadows said. 'Open to suggestion.'

'Someone injected him?' Edris asked.

'No, there are no needle marks. This was liquid morphine.'

'Easy to slip into his drink,' Edris said.

'Yes, but which one of them did it?' Meadows asked.

'Perhaps none of them. If he was already drunk and in bed, then it would have been easy enough to creep in the house and squirt the morphine into his mouth before he had a chance to realise what was happening.'

'Big risk, and they would have had to know he was drunk and asleep,' Meadows said.

'Could have been watching. The message said to bring alcohol. It would have been obvious they were going to have a skinful,' Edris said.

'Once they were inside they had all night to carry out the murder,' Meadows said. 'Rhodri said Macsen was afraid. He knew someone was coming for him. The question is who?'

Chapter Twenty-four

There were plenty of people walking around Tenby as Meadows and Edris made their way to the harbour. The sun was shining and the pink, yellow, green, and blue painted houses gave the town a holiday feel. They reached peer hill where a wooden shed advertised tickets to Caldey Island.

'I haven't been there for years,' Meadows said.

'I've only been once. The boat ride made me sick,' Edris said.

Meadows laughed. 'Yeah, it can be a bit rough.'

Overhead seagulls squawked and boats bobbed in the water below. Meadows breathed in the salty air and let out a contented sigh. They continued down onto the jetty. It was wide enough to drive a car with a few parking spaces to the right against the harbour wall. On the left there was a drop over the side. Ladders embedded into the concrete gave access to the boats below. Meadows imagined it would be dangerous to walk the jetty in the dark, especially as there were no barriers to the left or at the end to prevent you from falling.

'Don't remember that sign being there?' Edris pointed.

Meadows read the sign aloud. '"Incident blackspot. No jumping in the water." I had heard they've had some problems with tombstoning.'

'Nutters,' Edris said. 'They're just asking for trouble jumping off cliffs and harbours.'

'I'm guessing you weren't an adventurous teenager.'

'Adventurous, yes. Stupid, no.' Edris walked to the edge and peered over. 'It's a long way down and I wouldn't like to guess how deep it is. Gives me the willies.'

Meadows joined him and looked down at the greyish green water. Even though it was a calm day, the moored fishing boats were rocking furiously.

'It's not the depth that I'd worry about. Look at those chains.' He pointed to the enormous metal links that were attached to a ring on the wall and disappeared under the water before emerging to anchor the boats. 'Imagine jumping in and hitting one of those things.'

'You'd think they'd put railings up,' Edris said.

'People wouldn't be able to get to the boats,' Meadows said.

They walked past the harbour master's office to the benches on the right. A man was sitting with a folder held in his hand. He was in his fifties with receding grey hair. Dressed in a pair of jeans and a wax jacket, he looked like any other person out enjoying the sea air. To Meadows, he was unmistakably a police officer. He had an awareness about him and was on his feet as they approached.

'DI Allen?' Meadows asked.

Allen nodded and held out his hand as Meadows made the introductions.

'I thought this would be a good place to meet,' Allen said. 'I visit often and think of the lad.'

'I guess some cases never leave you,' Meadows said.

They took a seat on the bench and Meadows looked over the harbour. 'I can see how this would be a dangerous place at night-time.'

'There have been a few tragedies here,' Allen said.

'I haven't had a chance to read the transcript from the inquest. I understand it was ruled as a suicide.'

'Yes, there was no evidence to suggest otherwise, although I always felt something was amiss. I spent a lot of time with his family. The picture I built gave no indication he intended to take his own life. I would have been happier with a ruling of death by misadventure or an open verdict. Honestly, I had nothing to suggest the contrary.'

'You think it was an accident?' Meadows asked.

'All I can do is talk you through the case, I'll let you draw your own conclusions. It was New Year's Eve and the town was buzzing. It is every year. Uniform was stretched, there had been a stabbing on Christmas Eve so we were keeping a presence around the pubs and clubs.' He opened a folder and took out a photo. 'This is a still of the CCTV taken in Tudor Square.' He handed it to Meadows.

Meadows looked at the crowds. It would be impossible to identify everyone in the shot. 'You can't get a hair between them.'

Allen pointed. 'There's Jake. That was taken at eleven-thirty. He was out with his friends Shaun and Ethan.' He pointed to the two young men standing next to Jake.

'They look like they are having a good time,' Edris said.

Allen took another photo out and passed it to Meadows. 'Five to midnight. Ethan and Shaun are texting their families. You can see Jake moving out of the shot. We don't know why he moved away from the others.'

'Difficult to see the expression on his face from this angle,' Meadows said.

'He remains in the shot for a few more seconds, moving through the crowd. He is next picked up on camera heading down the high street. They were staying at a flat on The Croft, it looked like he was heading in that direction. The next sighting is on Upper Frog Street, he's moving fast in the opposite direction. Last sighting of him is on St Julian's Street; if he was heading straight to the harbour, then that's not the route he would have taken.'

'Maybe he was lost,' Edris suggested.

'The streets were crowded. He could have asked directions to the harbour if he was determined to get there. The last sighting was six minutes after midnight. He would have had to be running to get to this position at that time.

'Shaun and Ethan stayed in Tudor Square for another hour then they made their way back to the flat. They thought Jake had gone back. When they discovered he wasn't at the flat, they went out to look for him, calling his phone several times. They returned later and fell asleep for a few hours.

'A 999 call was made from the train station at ten to one in the morning. The caller claimed he had seen a man jump off the jetty. He didn't give his name. The lifeboat was launched shortly after. It was high tide and a rough night. Despite their best efforts, after a few hours, the coxswain made the decision to call off the search for the safety of the crew. The search resumed as soon as the wind died down. Jake's mobile phone and glasses were found at the end of the jetty.' Allen handed Meadows another photo and pointed. 'The screen of the phone was smashed. At just after seven, Shaun reported Jake missing.'

'Had Jake been drinking a lot that night?' Meadows asked.

'Not according to his friends. They said he'd only drank lemonade. He looked steady on his feet on the CCTV footage. There were too many out that night for any bar staff to remember serving him alcohol.'

'Could he have tripped, lost his glasses, and accidently gone over?' Edris asked.

'That seemed more likely than him jumping in of his own accord,' Allen said.

'What makes you think it wasn't suicide?'

'I can't see why he'd take off his glasses and throw down his mobile phone,' Allen said. 'You'd jump with them on, and why did he have his phone out? He would've had it in his pocket. There was no history of depression, drug, or alcohol abuse. I was made aware of the allegation of rape. According to his father they were making a complaint of a false allegation. They were confident they had a good case against Alys Pugh and Iona Young. Jake wanted to clear his name. It was thought the allegation was the reason he took his own life. Who knows? Maybe that was the case. The kid may have taken things too far that night. It could've been his father pushing the complaint against the girls. Perhaps Jake thought it would make things worse, prove his guilt.'

'Did you talk to Alys Pugh?' Meadows asked.

'Yes, and to Macsen Lloyd. David Ellis was convinced something sinister had happened to Jake. Alys said she went to a local pub and saw the New Year in with her parents. Macsen was with a friend.'

'Would that have been Rhodri Williams?'

Allen checked the file. 'Yes, and Macsen's brother, Iwan, stated he had been drinking with them that evening. Neither Shaun nor Ethan saw anyone they recognized that evening. Jake was alone on the CCTV footage. There was no other explanation than he went to the harbour alone that night.'

'Is there any possibility Jake didn't go into the water that night?' Edris asked.

'You mean he chose to disappear?' Allen shook his head. 'His family and friends were devastated. I saw them all, day after day, searching the coastline. From what I learned about him, I can't see how he would do that to his own family. I expect you know what happened to David Ellis.'

Meadows nodded. 'I take it there is no CCTV coverage close to this area,' Meadows said.

'No, so there is no way of telling if others were in the vicinity, other than the person who made the phone call. They claimed they saw him jump. That call always troubled me; why use a public phone? It makes more sense to use a mobile, everyone carries one now.'

'Maybe they had run out of battery,' Edris suggested.

'There were so many people out that night. Wouldn't you grab the first person you ran into and ask them to make a call?'

'Yeah, I guess that is odd,' Edris said.

'We put out an appeal but no one came forward. Maybe the caller had been drinking underage, taking drugs, or for some reason shouldn't have been here.'

'Or they had something to do with Jake going into the water that night,' Meadows said.

'That's what I was afraid of,' Allen said. 'If that's the case someone has found out and it's payback time.'

Chapter Twenty-five

Meadows was sitting in a café watching people walk by outside the window. Harvard set down a cup of tea in front of him and took a seat.

'Nice city,' Harvard said.

Meadows didn't like city life but he had to admit Bristol had a certain charm. 'I'm not sure I would like to work here. You get so used to the countryside this feels alien.'

'I heard you grew up on a remote erm… farm,' Harvard said.

Meadows laughed. 'Is that your polite way of asking about the commune?'

Harvard reddened. 'Sorry, I was just interested.'

'It's OK. It's not a secret. I was raised on a commune. I left when I was a teenager as my brother was ill. We needed a stable environment.' Meadows had got so used to saying that version, it didn't seem like an untruth. It was partly true. The real reason was far too complicated and only a few people knew about it.

'It must have been a difficult adjustment,' Harvard said.

'It wasn't easy. After I graduated, I worked in London. I don't know how I managed it; I could never go back.'

'I don't blame you,' Harvard said. 'I'd jump at the opportunity to move permanently to Wales.'

'You don't think you'll get bored?'

'Nah. Perfect place to raise a family.'

Meadows laughed. 'Got plans, have you?'

'Yep, as soon as I find my soulmate, I'm getting married. What's the point of waiting? I want a nice house down a quiet country lane and a big garden for the kids to play. I didn't have any of that.'

'I can't make any promises but I'll see what I can do. You already feel like part of the team.'

The café door opened and a tall, slim man entered. He was dressed in a suit and had a mop of dark hair. He looked around at the people seated at tables.

'This must be him,' Meadows said. He stood up. 'Ethan?'

Ethan nodded.

Meadows introduced himself and Harvard. 'Thank you for coming to see us. I find it's always better to meet in person. Can I get you a drink?'

'Americano, please,' Ethan said.

'I'll get it,' Harvard said.

'Thanks,' Ethan said. He took a seat at the table.

Meadows sat down opposite him. 'I expect this has brought up a lot of bad memories for you.'

'Yes, it's not something I talk about.'

'I understand you and Jake met at university,' Meadows said.

'I knew him before that. We met at geek camp.' Ethan smiled. 'It was a summer school run by Nottingham University. You got a chance to study chemistry, engineering – that sort of thing. We stayed in touch. Then we both applied to Bristol and got in. We shared rooms along with Shaun.'

Harvard returned to the table and handed Ethan a cup of coffee.

'Thanks.' Ethan took a sip from the cup.

'Other than that one occasion, were there problems with other students? Bullying?'

'No, nothing like that. It wasn't like school. You were with like-minded people; you could be yourself.'

'What about Rhodri Williams? He shared rooms with you. Did he cause any problems?' Meadows asked.

'He was loud, boisterous, and mostly off his face. I didn't have a lot to do with him.'

'Was there any friction between Jake and Rhodri?'

'Not really. They were on different courses so they didn't move in the same circles. They seemed to get on OK.'

'What about Iona and Alys? Did they have much to do with Jake before the accusation?'

'They were friends. Alys and Jake more than Iona – she avoided any contact with him if she could. Alys always had a smile for Jake. She'd stop and talk. He fixed her computer for her a few times. They even went out for coffee. Alys could be a little cold when Iona was around. It was as if she was embarrassed by their friendship.'

'Do you think Jake wanted more from their friendship?'

'Yeah, and I got the impression the feeling was mutual.'

'But she was dating Macsen,' Meadows said.

'I saw him a few times. He came to visit Alys. I don't think she was that happy with him.'

'What makes you think that?'

'She was popular. Always surrounded by people. She was also kind and funny. When she was with Macsen she was a different person. She'd go off with him and not get involved in anything to do with uni. It's hard to explain. I'll give you an example. Halloween was always a big celebration on campus. Everyone dressed up and partied. The second year we were all dressing up as characters from *The Rocky Horror Show*. Alys came to show her outfit to Jake. She was excited for the party. Then Macsen turned up for the weekend. She never came to the party. She could have brought Macsen along; he wouldn't have been the only one there that didn't go to Bristol Uni. It was like she wanted to keep that part of herself separate, didn't want to show him she was having fun.'

'Did Jake date any girls while he was there?' Meadows asked.

'A few but nothing serious. He spent most of his time with me and Shaun.'

'As far as you know, were there any problems with the girls he dated?'

Ethan's eyes darkened. 'If you are asking if he was some sort of pervert, then no. There was never any talk of inappropriate behaviour.'

'What do you remember about the night of the alleged rape?' Meadows asked.

'It was a party for the start of the third year. Just an ordinary night at the student union bar. Shaun, Jake, and I had a few drinks. We sat at a table watching the rest of the students make idiots of themselves dancing.

'Alys bought Jake a drink. He'd helped her out setting up a new laptop or something like that. She joined us at our table. Shaun bought a fishbowl and we all shared it. Then I think Alys got one.'

'Who was there altogether?' Harvard asked.

'Me, Shaun, and Jake. Will – another one from our course – Iona and Alys.'

Harvard wrote the names down. 'Sorry, go on.'

'We had a few more rounds of drinks. Alys and Jake got up to dance, it showed how drunk Jake was because he never danced. Iona was pissed off so she went off with some guy. I saw them leave together a little while later. Alys and Jake came back to the table. They drank some more. They were sitting close together and holding hands. Then they left together.'

It's a very different story to the one Iona told, Meadows thought. 'Are you sure Iona wasn't around at this stage?'

'Yes, I think she would have kicked up a fuss about Alys leaving with Jake if she was there.'

'Because Alys was drunk?' Meadows asked.

'No, because she didn't have any time for Jake. It was like she was better than him. Shaun and I carried on drinking. The next morning Jake came into the kitchen. He was hungover but really happy. Then the police turned up and arrested him.

'There were all sorts of rumours around campus. I didn't believe them. I still don't. Shaun called Jake's dad to let him know what had happened. Jake didn't come back until the next day. It was just as well because Macsen came to the flat looking for him. If Macsen had found him, he would have killed him. He was kicking off; Jake wouldn't have stood a chance against him. When Jake came back, Rhodri had a go at him in the kitchen. He told him to stay away from Alys.

'Jake was terrified. Not just of Macsen but that he would be charged. He thought his life was over. He told me Alys had come back to his room willingly. They had slept together but he never forced her. She had left before he woke up. Jake adored Alys. He would never have done something to upset her, let alone take advantage.

'Things on campus got out of hand. Students shouting "rapist" every time he left the flat. He became withdrawn; stayed in. Shaun and I were the only ones to talk to him. The dean came to see him, told him he had to suspend him while the investigation was ongoing, so Jake went to stay with his father.'

'Did you see Jake during that time?' Meadows asked.

'Not face to face. I talked to him on Skype and text, tried to keep him up to date on coursework.'

'Whose idea was it to go to Tenby for New Year's Eve?' Meadows asked.

'Shaun's. By that time, Alys had withdrawn her allegation. Jake was talking about coming back to uni after the Christmas break. He did tell me he was working on clearing his name. The dean had put things in place for his return. An email was sent out, warning of repercussions for anyone posting about the incident on social media or approaching Jake. Shaun thought a night out would do Jake good, get him used to being out and around people. It was also Jake's twenty-first birthday.

'Jake's dad had a holiday flat near the beach. We had the place to ourselves and were going to stay a couple of nights. He wanted Jake to have a good time. We had a meal then went out for the night. Jake was enjoying himself but he didn't drink any alcohol. I think after what happened with Alys he was afraid of letting his guard down.'

'What went wrong?'

Ethan shook his head. 'I don't know. We went to the square to see in the new year. It was crowded. Shaun went to get some drinks and I stayed outside with Jake. I sent some texts to my family, I wanted to do it before midnight. When I looked up Jake was gone. He didn't tell me he was leaving, or if he did, I didn't hear him. It was loud with the crowd shouting and music playing. We looked for him but it was hard to move. We saw the new year in. We thought Jake had gone back to the flat. When we got back, he wasn't there. We went out again and looked around. We kept calling his phone, but after a while we gave up and went back to the flat. We fell asleep. When we couldn't find him the next morning, we called the police.'

'Did you have any reason to believe he was depressed and considering taking his own life?' Meadows asked.

'No, absolutely not. He was fine. We were talking about taking a gap year after uni. We had a list of places to visit. Jake's dad was giving him money for his birthday. He was going to use it to travel. He wanted me and Shaun to go with him. He said he had enough to pay for our accommodation. I remember saying it wasn't fair for him to pay but he insisted. He said it would be more fun if the three of us went. We were all excited.'

'Did you or Shaun see anyone that night whom you recognized? Someone from university?' Meadows asked.

'No. We talked to people but not anyone we knew.'

'When was the last time you saw Shaun?'

'Erm… about two years ago. He's been travelling and working abroad since uni. He used to come home every New Year's Eve. We'd go to Tenby harbour and take flowers. Shaun always went to see Jake's mum and siblings when he was back.'

'When was the last time you had any contact with him?'

'I think around November last year. He was in South Korea. He was supposed to come back for Christmas, we were going to meet up but he didn't come home.'

'Is it usual for you not to hear from him for months?' Meadows asked.

'Yeah. The time difference makes it difficult and we've both been busy with work.'

'What about Iona, Alys, and Rhodri? Did you see them after Jake died?'

'No. I didn't go back to uni. I retook the third year. To be honest, I had a breakdown after we lost Jake. It took me a while to get my head together.'

'That's understandable,' Meadows said. 'Did Shaun go back to university?'

'Yes. He finished his course that year. As far as I know, he had no contact with Alys. He saw Iona and Rhodri around campus but kept his distance. There really isn't anything else I can tell you about that time. The days after Jake went missing seemed to drag out. There was this constant dark cloud that hung over us. Sometimes we wished his body would wash up. I know that sounds awful but it was better than the not knowing. The baseless hope that fades slowly is excruciating. If Alys and Macsen's death had anything to do with what happened to Jake then I can understand why.'

Meadows nodded. 'I appreciate you being so frank with us. Can you think of anyone who would seek revenge for Jake?'

'I haven't had contact with anyone, other than Shaun, from that time for years. I never met Jake's family.'

'OK, thanks. If there is anything else you remember that you think might be relevant, please get in touch.'

Ethan nodded and drank down the remainder of his coffee before standing up.

'Thank you for meeting us,' Meadows said.

'No problem, I had a meeting with a client.'

'What's your line of work?' Meadows asked.

'I'm an IT consultant. I build and implement systems. Good luck with your case,' Ethan said then left.

'Interesting,' Meadows said. 'I bet he'd have no problem hacking phones.'

'He doesn't look like a cold-blooded killer,' Harvard said.

'Who does? He admitted to struggling with Jake's death. He's got the capability and motive.'

'What about opportunity?'

'We'll need to check that out. Jake could have left those gaming discs with him. Then there's Shaun, supposedly abroad. What if he came back? They could be working together.'

'Or Shaun is working alone. He could've come back Christmas time, watched Alys and Macsen, then killed them. He could already have left the country.'

'I have a feeling whoever is doing this still has unfinished business.' Meadows checked the time. 'We need to get going. Give Edris a call on the way and ask him if he can find out if Shaun is in the country.'

* * *

DI Sita Khan showed them to the corner of the office where they took a seat around a desk. Around them was the usual hubbub of noise; officers on phones, tapping away at keyboards, or discussing cases. It was a larger department than Meadows' and a very busy one.

'I didn't expect this case to reappear,' DI Khan said. 'I'm not sure how much help I can be. What exactly are you looking for?'

Good question, Meadows thought. 'I'm fairly certain the case is connected to the murder of Alys Pugh and Macsen Lloyd.' He outlined the case to date. 'I wanted to get your view of the case and those involved. More importantly, I wanted to hear your impression of Jake and Alys.'

'You're thinking this is a revenge killing? That wouldn't surprise me if it happened at the time. There was a lot of unpleasantness. If I'm honest, it wasn't straightforward. I took the initial statement from Alys. She was clearly distressed. It was her friend, Iona, who did most of the talking. Alys claimed she didn't remember much between dancing with Jake and waking up in his bed the next morning.

'Iona claimed Alys had been sick. When they left the bathroom, Jake was waiting for them. He then offered to take Alys back to her room. I took the girls' statements and escorted Alys to hospital. She was examined and had swabs taken.'

'Were there any physical injuries?' Meadows asked.

'No. No bruising or tearing. There were traces of lubricant indicating a condom was used. We arrested Jake. He appeared shocked but he came willingly to the station and gave samples. He admitted to having intercourse with Alys but claimed it was consensual. We held him overnight and he was bailed the next morning pending further enquiries.'

'We understand Jake's father was notified.'

'Yes, he arranged for a solicitor to be present when we interviewed Jake. We took statements from the other students that were at the party that night. We interviewed the night staff in the accommodation and spoke to Jake's lecturers. Iona's statement was inconsistent with the others we took: according to more than one witness, she left the party with another student before Alys. We spoke to the student who confirmed Iona went back to his room and stayed the night. When I spoke to Iona, she claimed he was mistaken about the time they left.'

'We spoke to Ethan Steward. He told us Jake and Alys left the party together,' Meadows said. 'He said Iona had left by then. I take it he was one of the witnesses.'

'Yes, but he wasn't the only one. Several of the students gave the same account.'

'Did you think at the time Alys was telling the truth?'

'Honestly, I had my doubts. There was CCTV in the accommodation building. When Alys and Jake entered the building, it was Jake that appeared unsteady on his feet. Alys was laughing. Then in the lift she seemed to be the one in control of the situation. At one point she tried to pull the zipper down on Jake's trousers. He pulled her hands away. She continued to kiss and grope him. These cases are always difficult when alcohol is involved. Proving consent is even harder. We have no way of knowing what really went on when they reached Jake's room. I could only go on what I had and put it to the CPS. I explained to Alys that the lack of evidence and the witness statements was going to make the case difficult to prove. I assured her that she would be supported throughout.'

'How did she react to that?' Meadows asked.

'I expected tears or anger; instead she appeared relieved. A few days later, she contacted me to say she wanted to withdraw her complaint. I informed her the CPS were happy to proceed with the case but she said she wanted to put it behind her.'

'I understand Jake wanted to pursue a case of false allegation.'

'Yes, he made a formal complaint. We were also looking at charging Iona with providing a false statement, there was plenty of evidence she lied. CCTV showed her entering the accommodation with the other student some time before CCTV picked up Alys and Jake going back to Jake's room. I'm not sure Jake would have been able to prove Alys lied. But in Jake's favour, he had no previous complaints against him. Also, two students were in the kitchen the morning after the alleged incident. Both claimed Alys didn't appear distressed. That and the footage would have made a good case.'

'Was one of the students in the kitchen that morning Rhodri Williams?'

'Yes, why?'

'He was a friend of Macsen, Alys' boyfriend. I wonder if being caught leaving Jake's room panicked her. She knew Rhodri would tell Macsen.'

'I guess it's possible. She'd had too much to drink and did something she regretted. I found it odd at the time that she didn't appear angry or to hold any animosity towards Jake. It was Iona that was vocal.'

'When were Alys and Iona made aware charges may be brought against them?'

DI Khan flicked through the file. 'We interviewed Iona again in December.'

'Do you think Jake would have gone through with the case?'

'I'm not sure but we would have pursued it. There are so many women that are victims of sexual assault and never report it – you know the stats. Those who do, face a lengthy and traumatising process. Every false allegation makes it all the more difficult for the true victims. But without Jake, we couldn't continue with the case. I've sent everything we've got over to you.'

'Thank you,' Meadows said. 'We won't keep you any longer.'

'No problem,' DI Khan said. 'I hope you catch your killer soon.'

'So do I,' Meadows said.

'That was interesting,' Harvard said as they made their way out of the building.

Meadows nodded his agreement. 'If Alys lied, that would be motive to kill her. It marks Iona as a target as well. There's also something else to consider. Alys and Iona were about to be charged. That would give them good reason to get rid of Jake.'

'Yeah, but it doesn't explain who killed Alys and Macsen,' Harvard said.

'If Jake was killed and Alys and Macsen knew who did it, then the killer would want to make sure they didn't tell anyone. Problem is if anybody else knows what happened that night in Tenby, they are in a lot of danger.'

Chapter Twenty-six

Christie was the first to wake up. Iona was sleeping in the double room and Sammy in the single. They hadn't left the house since the news of Macsen's death and Christie wanted to get away from Iona for a few hours.

She moved quietly to the bathroom. She needed to get into the shower first. Iona always took a long time and left a mess. Christie didn't want to be late. If necessary she would leave before the other two. After a quick shower, she dressed and roughly dried her hair before weaving two braids.

'Shower is free,' she called out as she left the bedroom.

'What time is it?' Sammy asked.

'Just after seven. I want to get in early today,' Christie said.

Sammy came padding out of the bedroom. She smiled at Christie as she tried to flatten her hair with her hand.

'I think I'll stay in bed,' Iona called out.

'Come on,' Sammy said. 'It will do you good to get dressed and go to work.'

'I don't feel like going in. I have to answer the phone all day and speak to stupid people. It's not like I can take myself off for a few minutes' break.'

'You said you'd try,' Sammy said. 'Even if you only manage half a day, it'll be a start.'

'Maybe it will help take your mind off things for a while,' Christie added.

'It's OK for you to say but it's not that easy. I've lost two of my closest friends,' Iona said.

'We all cared about them,' Sammy said. 'You're not the only one who's hurting.'

'Oh, all right. I'm getting up.'

'Better get in the shower before she does,' Christie whispered.

'Yeah,' Sammy said.

'I'll make us some coffee,' Christie said as she made her way down the stairs.

In the sitting room, Christie pulled back the curtains which threw light on more of Iona's mess. She was fed up with seeing bottles of nail varnish, make-up, and clothes left lying around. She moved towards the kitchen but only took two steps into the room before she stopped.

The kitchen worktops were covered in white and red rose petals. Some had fallen on the floor and curled. Her eyes moved to the kitchen table where a box and envelope were sitting in the centre.

For a moment, she didn't move. The scent of roses filled the air, it should have been pleasant but it made her feel nauseous.

'Sammy! Iona!' She shrieked.

She stepped back into the sitting room and called out again. She heard thudding down the stairs then Sammy was next to her.

'What is it?' Sammy asked.

'In the kitchen,' Christie said.

Iona joined them. 'What's in the kitchen?'

Sammy moved forward.

'Don't,' Iona said.

Sammy ignored her and kept moving. Christie followed with Iona close to her side.

'Oh my God,' Sammy said.

'He's coming for me,' Iona cried.

'The envelope is addressed to Christie,' Sammy said. 'It's not you who should be panicking.'

Christie moved to the table and picked up the card.

'I don't think you should open it,' Iona said.

'I'm not waiting for the police to take it away,' Christie said. 'We'll never know what it says.'

'She's right,' Sammy said.

Christie tore the envelope and took out a card. On one side was a picture of an aeroplane. She flipped it over and read.

'What does it say?' Sammy asked.

Nearly time to say goodbye.

Christie read out loud. She felt her eyes sting with tears and turned her back. She didn't want the other two to see her upset. She picked up the box and took off the lid. Inside was a smooth grey pebble.

'I'm calling the police,' Sammy said.

Christie took a deep breath and turned around. 'I'll make some coffee.'

'I don't think we should touch anything else until the police come,' Iona said.

'It's my house,' Christie said. 'I'm not going to sit around waiting for permission to have a coffee. Just because some low life scumbag…' She stopped. Iona was staring at her. 'What?' she asked.

'I don't think I've ever seen you angry,' Iona said.

'What do you expect?' Sammy asked. She pressed the numbers on her phone.

Christie moved to the sink and saw the bowl filled with water. Petals floated on top. She couldn't resist putting her finger in the water and swirling it around. She watched the petals twirl in the water.

'Police are on their way,' Sammy said. 'We better get dressed.'

Christie made the coffee and carried the three mugs into the sitting room. She settled into a chair and waited.

Sammy was the first one down. 'Are you OK?'

'Yes,' Christie said. 'I better ring work.' She called her boss and explained she would be in late.

'You're still going to go in then,' Sammy said.

'Yeah, once the police have been. There is no point in hanging around here worrying.'

'Yeah, I guess you're right.'

Iona came down the stairs. It didn't surprise Christie that she wore a flattering outfit and her make-up was flawless.

'How do you suppose they got in?' Iona asked.

'Maybe we should look around,' Sammy said.

A knock at the door made them all jump. 'I'll get it,' Christie said.

She opened the door and was surprised to see Meadows and Edris. She had been expecting uniformed officers.

'You reported a break-in,' Meadows said.

'Yes. Stuff has been left in the kitchen; I'll take you through.'

Christie led them into the kitchen and pointed out the box. 'I opened it,' she said.

'Anyone else touch the envelope or box?' Edris asked.

'No, just me.'

Christie watched Meadows snap on a pair of gloves and pick up the envelope. His eyes scanned the words and his face grew serious. He handed the card to Edris. Sammy and Iona came to stand next to her.

'Are you going to give me some protection now?' Iona asked.

'It appears that Christie is the target this time,' Meadows said.

'He's just trying to get to me,' Iona said.

Christie wished Iona didn't use that whiny voice. It grated on her nerves.

'Do you know how the intruder got in?' Meadows asked.

'No,' Christie said.

'We were about to look around when you came,' Sammy said.

'I did get all the locks changed,' Christie added. 'The house was locked up before we went to bed.'

'I'll take a look around,' Edris said.

Christie didn't like the idea of Edris wandering around the house but she didn't object.

'Shall we go into the sitting room?' Meadows asked.

Christie nodded and they all moved out of the kitchen. She sat down on the sofa and Iona and Sammy joined her. Meadows took the armchair.

'Who has keys to the house?' Meadows asked.

'Me,' Christie said.

'Do you two have spares?'

Iona and Sammy shook their heads.

'I didn't get any cut,' Christie said. 'I have the only set. We agreed to go to work and come home together. I didn't want to risk someone getting hold of a spare set.'

Meadows nodded. 'Christie, does the pebble and the aeroplane on the card mean anything to you?'

'No,' Christie said.

'Sammy? Iona?'

Sammy shook her head.

'Jake was studying something to do with aeroplanes,' Iona said.

Meadows looked at Christie. 'Have you ever been to Tenby?'

'Years ago,' Christie said. 'I went to Caldey Island with my mum.'

'I've been once or twice,' Sammy said. 'Not recently.'

'What about you, Iona? When was the last time you were in Tenby?'

'I went for the New Year's Eve celebrations the last year of school.'

'What year was that?'

Iona shrugged. '2015 or 2016.'

'What about New Year's Eve 2018. Did you and Alys go?'

Christie felt Iona stiffen next to her.

'No. That was the year Jake killed himself. Why are you asking me? Do you think I had something to do with it? That I deserve all this happening to me?' Iona asked with a rising voice.

Christie put her hand on Iona's arms. 'He's just trying to find out what's going on. No one is blaming you.'

Edris came into the sitting room. 'The back door is unlocked. Did any of you open it this morning?'

'It should be locked,' Christie said. 'I was the first one down this morning. No one has been out the back.'

'Do you usually leave it open during the day?' Meadows asked.

'No,' Christie said. 'I only open it to take out the bins or hang up washing.'

'When was the last time you used the back door?' Meadows asked.

'The bins went out last night.' She looked at Iona. 'You took them out.'

'I locked the door when I came back in,' Iona said.

'Are you sure?' Edris asked.

'Yes.'

'You can't have,' Sammy said. 'How else did someone get in here?'

'The keys were in the lock,' Edris said. 'It wouldn't have been possible to open the door from the outside with a key.'

Iona looked from Christie to Sammy. 'How stupid do you think I am? After everything that's happened, I made sure the door was locked.'

'You obviously didn't,' Sammy said. 'No one else went outside last night.'

'It's done now,' Christie said. 'We'll just have to be more careful from now on.'

'I'm not staying here after someone has been creeping around,' Sammy said.

'You think your place is safer?' Iona said. 'You haven't had the locks changed yet.'

'I think you should all stay together for now,' Meadows said.

Christie wished he hadn't said that. The stress of the other two staying was starting to get to her. One would be easier to manage.

'Think about it,' Iona said. 'You're probably still alive because I was here last night. If either of you had been alone, you'd be dead.'

The statement made no sense to Christie. Iona was the cause of all their problems. She wondered if she was deliberately trying to scare her and Sammy for her own safety. She was the one who didn't want to be left alone.

'Do you think you'll catch him soon?' Christie asked.

'We are doing all we can. In the meantime, I can arrange for a patrol car to drive by at intervals during the night. I'll also arrange for a panic alarm to be installed.'

'Thank you,' Christie said.

'Iona,' – Meadows turned to look at her – 'I'm going to have to ask you a few more questions. We can do it here or you can come with us to the station.'

'I'll stay here. I've got nothing to hide, I've already told you everything I know.'

'We've now reviewed the allegation Alys made against Jake,' Meadows said. 'There were several conflicting witness reports. In your statement you claim Jake was waiting outside the toilets and offered to take Alys back to her room.'

'Yeah, that's the same as I told you.'

'That's not what happened, is it?'

'Yeah, it is.'

'We know you left the party earlier with another student. We have his statement as well as CCTV footage. Alys and Jake stayed longer then left together.'

'No,' Iona said. 'Everyone was drunk so they don't remember.'

'You were also drinking that night. You told us you were drunk.'

'Not that drunk.'

'Don't you think enough people have died? How much longer are you going to keep up this lie?' Meadows asked. 'Is it worth your life?'

Iona's eyes filled with tears. Then she started to sob. Christie knew she could cry on command. She'd seen her do it so many times for attention. Doesn't look like it's working this time, she thought. The expression on both detectives' faces told her they were unmoved.

'I don't remember what happened most of that night,' Iona said between sobs. 'I said those things for Alys.'

'You lied about something like that?' Sammy said.

'Alys asked me to. What would you have done?'

Christie felt anger bubbling in her stomach. She could see from the expression on Sammy's face she felt the same. She clenched her fists and concentrated on keeping quiet. She didn't want to say something she would regret.

'Jake didn't take advantage of Alys that night, did he?' Meadows asked.

Iona shook her head. 'Alys was always flirting with Jake. She liked him even when we were in school. I don't know what she saw in him. He was weird. If he'd asked her out then she probably would have ended up with him. I told her she was wasting her time and could do better. All the boys liked Alys; she could have had anyone. She started dating Macsen. No one else had a chance with him. Then she gets drunk and sleeps with Jake. Rhodri saw her that morning and she knew he would tell Macsen. She thought she would lose him.'

'You persuaded her to go to the police,' Meadows said.

'No, I told the dean. I thought it would look better for Alys. The dean called the police. It all got out of hand.'

'You knew all along why Alys was murdered and you let Macsen die,' Sammy said. 'Because of your lies that poor guy killed himself.'

'It was Alys' lie,' Iona said.

'You could have told the police what really happened,' Sammy said.

'Jake was going to take you to court,' Meadows said. 'You lied in your witness statement. You would have been charged with obstruction of justice. You could have faced a prison sentence.'

Iona looked at Christie then turned to Sammy. 'That's why I couldn't say anything. I didn't know Macsen would be murdered. It wasn't my fault. None of it is.'

'Who else knew about the lie?' Meadows asked.

'No one else knew,' Iona said. 'Well, Alys told Macsen.'

'I'm guessing Macsen told Rhodri,' Meadows said.

'I don't know,' Iona said.

'Jake also knew you both lied,' Meadows said. 'You and Alys were in a lot of trouble. With Jake gone, you got away with it. You must have been relieved.'

'Yeah, I guess.'

'What happened in Tenby that night?' Meadows asked.

'How would I know?' Iona stiffened as realisation dawned. 'Wait, you don't think I had anything to do with Jake dying?'

'Were you and Alys in Tenby that night?' Meadows asked.

'No. You can check back through my photos. We went out to some boring pub for a couple of hours then Alys wanted to go home.'

'We will be checking your whereabouts at that time. Who do you think is doing this?'

'I told you. Jake.'

'That's not possible,' Meadows said. 'Who else?'

'I don't know. Shaun and that other friend of Jake's believed him. Maybe one of them. You should be talking to them.'

'We have,' Meadows said.

'What's going to happen now?' Iona asked.

'I'll pass on the information to DI Khan. She'll be making the decision on pursuing charges of making a false statement.'

Iona put her hands to her face and sobbed.

There were a few moments' silence then Sammy spoke. 'If this is all about Iona and Alys lying, why is this person coming after me and Christie?'

'We don't know,' Meadows said. 'It could be just because of your association with Iona and Alys. Unless you can think of any other connection.'

'No,' Sammy said.

Christie shook her head. She saw Meadows give a nod to Edris.

'We now know Macsen was given morphine in liquid form before he was murdered,' Edris said. 'Can you tell me what you were all drinking that night?'

'Macsen and Rhodri were drinking vodka and rum I think,' Sammy said. 'I drank wine and had a few shots of vodka.'

'I was drinking coffee,' Christie said. 'Until I came home. Then I had a shot of vodka.'

'Iona?' Edris asked.

Iona wiped away her tears. 'Same as Sammy.'

'Who brought the alcohol?'

'I did,' Christie said. 'It was left over from the party we were going to have for Alys. There were some bottles at Macsen's.'

'Who poured the drinks?' Edris asked.

'Rhodri had the bottle and was pouring for Macsen. He topped up my glass,' Iona said.

'I opened the wine,' Sammy said. 'I had the vodka from Rhodri.'

'Did Macsen drink anything else other than the vodka and rum?'

'I made him a coffee,' Christie said.

'Yeah, but Rhodri poured vodka in it,' Iona said. She turned to Sammy. 'You took him up a glass of water after we had taken him to bed.'

'Yes,' Sammy said, 'because Rhodri asked me to take it to him.'

'Did Rhodri hand you the glass of water?' Edris asked.

'No, I filled a glass from the tap.'

'Who was the last one upstairs after Macsen had gone to bed?'

'You were, Sammy,' Iona said. 'You and Rhodri argued after you came back down and he left.'

'Then I guess it was me,' Sammy said.

'Who washed up the glasses?' Edris asked.

'I did,' Iona said. 'Macsen was fussy so we all cleaned up.'

Christie watched Edris scribble notes in his book. She would have loved to know what he was thinking. Her own mind was racing.

'What did you do with the bottles?' Meadows asked.

'We put the empty ones in the recycle bin and brought home the rest of the vodka,' Christie said.

'And you all drank from that bottle?' Meadows asked.

They all nodded.

'How did you feel after drinking the vodka? We're any of you ill or feel out of it?'

'I was fine,' Iona said. 'Slept well and didn't even have a hangover. Christie was the one who staggered to bed after only two drinks.'

'I couldn't get up the next morning,' Christie said. 'Do you think the bottle was spiked?'

'It's possible,' Meadows said. 'What about you, Sammy?'

'I suddenly felt very tired,' she said. 'I was upset about Rhodri so I kept knocking back the shots. I was OK the next morning.'

'Who poured the drinks when you got back?'

'Erm… I think I poured the first one,' Sammy said. 'Then you had the bottle.' She looked at Iona.

Iona nodded.

'OK. That will be all for now,' Meadows said. 'An officer will be in touch about the panic button. In the meantime, keep all the doors locked in the evening and if you are at all worried, call.'

Christie saw the detectives out and returned to the sitting room.

Sammy stood up. 'I'm going to pack.'

'Don't go,' Iona said. 'They said we should stay together.'

'You lied to all of us,' Sammy said. 'You and Alys ruined a boy's life.'

'I didn't know he was going to kill himself.'

'I don't care what you thought. I don't feel safe here with you. You left the door open. How do I know it's not you who killed Alys? You were jealous of her. You're always flirting with Rhodri. You probably let the killer in to get me out of the way.'

Iona leaped up from the sofa. 'You were the one who took a glass of water up to Macsen. You were the last one to see him alive. It was you. You drugged him then went back.'

Christie put her hands to her head as the two women screamed at each other. 'Just stop it. Both of you,' she shouted.

'I'm not staying here with her,' Sammy said and walked off.

Christie heard her stomping up the stairs.

'I can't go home,' Iona said. 'Please. I didn't mean to lie, I did it for Alys. I'm sorry, I was trying to help her.'

Christie found it hard to believe Iona would help anyone if it she didn't get something out of it.

'Fine,' she said. 'I'm going to work.'

'You're going to leave me here alone?' Iona said.

'The forensic officers will be here soon. You can let them in. Keep the door locked after they leave. I'll make sure all the doors are locked before we go to bed tonight. When this is over, you can go home.'

'Thank you,' Iona said.

Christie didn't say anything. She grabbed her car keys and left. She couldn't bear to look at Iona a minute longer.

Chapter Twenty-seven

Meadows called for the team's attention. Phone calls were ended and document saved. Edris quickly filled them in on what had been found at Christie's house.

'Could one of them have left the door open deliberately?' Valentine asked.

'It's possible, but which one?' Meadows said.

'Iona is scared but she could be putting on an act,' Edris said. 'Maybe she's working with Rhodri.'

'Or Shaun Jones,' Paskin said.

'Any news on him?' Meadows asked.

'Nothing yet. It's not so easy to check if he's back in the country when we don't have a firm date. He still has an active visa for South Korea. I'm waiting for immigration to get back to me,' Paskin said.

'What about Sammy?' Harvard asked. 'Her boyfriend was sleeping with her friend. She had motive to kill Alys.'

'Then why Macsen?' Meadows asked.

'Maybe he found something out or she just wants to set up Rhodri to get back at him.'

'Well, she's not doing a good job,' Blackwell said. 'We have nothing on Rhodri. He couldn't have got in unaided last night. It's looking less likely that he's our man.'

'That leaves Christie,' Meadows said. 'She's the quieter of the three women. She's smart with good qualifications so what's she doing working in a plumber's?'

'I'm sure I asked her about that.' Blackwell grabbed his notebook and started flicking through the pages. 'She wanted to take some time to work and save money before doing her master's. She saw the job advertised for Rhodri's start-up company. Thought it would be a good opportunity. She worked on his books and forecasts. Then when the business went under, she took the job she has now. She's planning on doing her master's in September.'

Meadows nodded. 'Seems like a reasonable explanation. It also sounds like she was drugged the night Macsen was murdered. The only ones who have any connection to Jake are Iona and Rhodri.'

'That we know of,' Valentine said. 'Four years have passed. What if Sammy or Christie hooked up with Shaun or Ethan? They could have helped plan revenge for Jake's death.'

'What do we know about Christie and Sammy's background?' Meadows asked.

'Christie's parents are divorced. The mother still lives in Bridgend, her father lives in Essex. Sammy's parents live in Llanelli. Neither of them has a connection to Bristol University. Christie's not big on social media. Sammy uses Facebook, Instagram and Twitter. I've checked for friendships with Jake, Ethan, and Shaun – nothing, no mutual friends other than the group,' Paskin said.

'I'm still not convinced he is dead,' Blackwell said. 'His glasses and mobile phone were conveniently left behind.'

'There's the phone call,' Meadows said. 'Someone saw him go in.'

'Yeah, someone who wouldn't give their name. If he set the whole thing up, he would need a witness to report it.'

'Ethan?' Paskin suggested.

'Checked out,' Edris said. 'He has a solid alibi for both murders.'

'Then we are back to Shaun Jones,' Valentine said.

Meadows looked at the incident board. 'We don't have one shred of physical evidence from the killer. We can explain the lack of fingerprints by gloves but there should be fibre, a hair, something. The only anomaly we have is the discs with Jake's prints on them.'

'It's like chasing a ghost,' Blackwell said. 'Everything points to Jake or Shaun Jones.'

'We haven't even got a shoeprint to go on,' Meadows said.

'Forensics still have to eliminate a few from Macsen's house. The problem is he had friends and family in and out of the place. It is carpeted throughout, apart from the kitchen and bathroom.'

'You would have expected something in the bathroom,' Edris said.

'There's so many documentaries on crime scenes now,' Harvard said. 'Criminals have got savvy. Pair of gloves, a hairnet, and covers for the shoes is all it takes.'

'Even better if your prints are expected to be there,' Meadows said.

'Then Iona, Christie, Sammy, or Rhodri,' Paskin said. 'We just don't have a clear motive for Macsen's murder.'

'I've been reading through the statements and notes sent from Tenby,' Valentine said. 'DI Allen noted Shaun had a black eye and cut lip. These injuries happened a few days after Jake disappeared. When asked about it, Shaun said he had fallen. Allen put a note in the margins. He said it looked more like he had been in a fight than accidental.'

'Perhaps he had a go at Macsen,' Edris suggested.

'Why?' Harvard asked.

'Because Jake was afraid Macsen would go after him. Shaun could have seen it as a contributing factor to Jake taking his own life.'

'Given the size of Macsen, I doubt anyone would go out of their way to antagonise him,' Harvard said.

'Perhaps it was Macsen who went after Shaun. What if Macsen was in Tenby that night and Shaun saw him? Macsen would want to make sure Shaun kept quiet.'

'Both Rhodri and Macsen were drinking at Macsen's house that night,' Paskin said.

'The only one to confirm that is Macsen's bother, Iwan,' Meadows said. 'Blackwell, have a word with Iwan. He may have been covering for his brother. Edris, how are you getting on with the CCTV from New Year's Eve?'

'Slow-going,' Edris said. 'Crowds of people and the quality is poor. Trying to pick out Macsen, Rhodri, Iona, or Alys is a nightmare.'

'OK, I'll leave that with you,' Meadows said. 'Valentine and Harvard, can you speak to Shaun Jones' parents. They must have a contact number for him. We need to find him. Then go and see Jake's mother. She told us she had not had contact with Shaun. Ethan said Shaun was visiting her each time he was home. If she lied about that, then she must have her reasons. Perhaps to steer us away from someone else. If that's the case, who is she protecting?

'There has to be something we're missing. I think we should move these women to a safe house or put a watch on Christie's house.'

'Do you think the killer will make a move?' Harvard asked. 'If they are watching, they would see the police activity there today. Nothing happened after items were left in Iona's flat and Sammy's house.'

'Sammy went to stay with Rhodri,' Valentine said. 'Iona went straight to Christie's. They haven't been alone.'

'Yet someone went into Christie's last night with three of them there. Paskin, can you check it out? See what options are available. Unless we catch this killer soon, one of them could be the next target.'

Edris' phone tinged and he looked at the screen. 'Chris from tech has something for us. He asked if we could see him ASAP.'

'Hasn't he been working on Rhodri's computer?' Blackwell asked.

'Yes,' Meadows said. 'Let's hope this is the breakthrough we need.'

* * *

Chris still looked tired when Meadows and Edris arrived but his whole body radiated excitement. Meadows couldn't help smiling. This usually timid man was practically bouncing towards his workstation.

'I take it you've solved the case for us,' Edris said.

Chris grinned. 'I think I might have. I've looked at all the devices that were brought in from Rhodri's house, the most interesting one being his laptop. He's your hacker.'

'Are you sure?' Meadows asked.

'Yep. Emails, phones, social media, the lot. He has a list of accounts and passwords. Not just Iona, Christie, Sammy, Macsen, and Alys, but others. Notably Shaun Jones, Ethan Steward, and Jake Ellis.'

'Why would he need to hack Jake Ellis' accounts?' Edris asked.

'Jake's social media accounts haven't been accessed since his death but messages have been sent to all his contacts.' Chris hit the keyboard and the screen displayed a series of messages.

'That's creepy,' Edris said. 'His old friends would think he was trying to contact them.'

'Rhodri also has advanced software for cracking passwords,' Chris said. 'And he's using a spoofing service.'

'What's that?' Edris asked.

'Simply put, you pay for an account, log in, give a destination phone number, provide the caller ID you wish to be displayed, and the call is bridged. The person receiving the call or text is none the wiser. They think the call or text is from someone they know.'

'That's got to be illegal,' Edris said.

Chris shook his head. 'There are loads of providers out there. The one Rhodri is using is Mischiefstixx. He's also been tracking phone activity and locations for Christie, Sammy, Macsen, Iona, and Alys. There's also some other complex software which I won't try and explain. Basically, this guy is smart. He can code and develop programs. Most of the messages sent to Alys and Macsen came from this laptop. I'm guessing he also used a burner phone.'

'Is there any way this laptop could have been tampered with?' Meadows asked. 'Could a hacker have somehow set it up to make it look like this was the device used?'

Chris shook his head. 'No, it's not the same as what we saw with Macsen's phone. That was a social media account that had been hacked. This is the source of the hacking. Programs have been downloaded onto the computer. Not the sort of thing you buy in a store or online. It could be done remotely but I checked the connection history to see if someone tunnelled in. There would have been a different ID.'

'What about if someone had access to the laptop?'

'Not impossible but it would take a lot of time. Not something you could do in a few minutes. There's more. He's been surfing the dark and deep web. As well as a VPN, he used TOR. It's a browser–'

'That I have heard of,' Meadows said. 'Masks your identity.'

'It encrypts the data transmitting through the browser. The VPN encrypts all data coming from the device.'

'Right,' Meadows said. 'Can you see his browsing history?'

Chris nodded. 'What I have seen is that he has a keen interest in forensics. I've saved the best till last.' He opened a file.

'Morphine,' Meadows said.

'Yes, he placed an order, paid for it, and it was delivered to his address.'

'We've got him,' Edris said.

'If he's that clever, why keep the laptop?' Meadows said.

'He's cocky,' Edris said. 'Thinks he's covered his tracks. It's all there. You said yourself it had to be one of them. His fingerprints were all over Alys' house as well as Sammy's and Macsen's home. Yeah, he had reason to be there and that's what he was counting on.'

It all makes sense, Meadows thought. Yet it seems too simple. 'Let's bring him in.'

Chapter Twenty-eight

Meadows stepped through the doors of the station. Sergeant Folland was sitting behind the custody desk so he stopped for a chat.

'Quiet night?'

'Yeah, not too bad,' Folland said. 'Rhodri was kicking off after you brought him in. Went on until late. I cuffed him and took him outside for a comfort break. Once he'd smoked a couple of cigs, he calmed down. Put him back in the cell and he went to sleep. Happy days.'

Meadows laughed. 'Maybe you should take him out for a smoke before the interview. We'll get more sense out of him when he's calm.'

'I can do that,' Folland said.

'Did uniform report any activity at Christie's house last night?'

'No, all quiet. They drove by every hour until five this morning. Hanes is going to call in on them in about an hour. The panic alarm is being fitted as well as alarms to the doors as you requested. He's going to talk them through it.'

'I'm hoping they won't need it after today. What time is Rhodri's solicitor due in?'

'About quarter past eight.'

'Just enough time for a quick cuppa,' Meadows said. 'See you later.'

Upstairs Meadows switched on the kettle in the small kitchen. He tried to conjure up the feeling that usually came with solving a case. Nothing. It must be an anti-climax, he thought. They'd already had Rhodri in for questioning. He was a suspect. There hadn't been that moment of discovery when everything slots together. Could this have really only been about cheating on his friend and the fear of being found out?

He made his tea and carried it into the office. He immediately felt the same vibe from the team.

'Do you think we've missed something?' he asked.

'I just don't see the point of him using Jake's death to disguise murdering his lover and her boyfriend,' Blackwell said.

'Were you hoping for something supernatural?' Valentine asked.

'No but we've been chasing our tail for two weeks and the little bastard has been right in front of us.'

'What about the PS4 discs found in Macsen's house? How did Rhodri get them from Jake?' Meadows asked.

'They shared a flat in uni,' Paskin said. 'Maybe he took them after Jake left.'

'If that's the case his fingerprints would be all over them,' Meadows said.

'They could've got mixed up with his things when he moved out. He was hardly going to pitch up at Jake's mother's house to give them back,' Paskin said. 'He probably wiped the outer case.'

'Why keep them?' Harvard asked. 'It's not as if he thought they would come in handy in case he wanted to murder someone.'

'Good question,' Meadows said. 'Maybe he thought more of Jake than he let on.'

'It's the only anomaly,' Valentine said. 'Motive, opportunity, and now evidence.'

Meadows nodded. 'OK, let's go and see what he has to say for himself.'

Edris picked up a file. 'I don't think he can explain his way out of this.'

'Don't be too sure,' Meadows said as they left the office. 'He's had all night in the cell to think about it.'

When they entered the interview room, they found Rhodri sitting next to his solicitor. This time Rhodri didn't look so sure of himself. He was still in the same clothes and his hair was unkempt. Dark circles shadowed his eyes and he fidgeted in his seat.

The solicitor, a delicate-looking man, introduced himself as Rob Lewis for the recording.

Edris read out the charges.

Rhodri paled.

'I'd like to start by asking about your time in Bristol University,' Meadows said. 'I understand you shared accommodation with Jake Ellis.'

Rhodri gave Meadows a suspicious look. 'What do you want to know?'

'Jake liked to play video games. More specifically PS4 games.'

Rhodri shifted in his seat. 'Yeah.'

'You play the same sort of games. We found a PS4 console in your house.'

'Yeah, so what?'

'Did you play those types of games in university?' Meadows asked.

'Sometimes.'

'Did you and your housemates share games?'

Rhodri looked at his solicitor. 'What is this?'

'I was wondering myself,' Lewis said. 'Is there a point to this?'

'Yes,' Meadows said.

Lewis nodded at Rhodri indicating he should answer.

'Yeah, we played against each other. Sometimes we used each other's games.'

'Did you ever play Jake's games?'

Rhodri shrugged. 'I suppose. It depended on what disc was in the console. We all shared the same one.'

'Whose console was it?'

'Jake's.'

'He didn't mind you using it?'

'No. We weren't buddies but we got on OK.'

'What happened to Jake's games when he left?'

'I suppose he took them with him.'

'Is it possible they could have got mixed up in your belongings?' Meadows asked.

'No.'

Rhodri seemed oblivious of the significance of the discs. It troubled Meadows. He would have expected to see some reaction, even a small one. He took out a picture of the case and discs and slid it over to Rhodri. 'Have you seen the case or discs before?'

Rhodri looked at the photo. 'I've got a couple of those games at home but the case isn't mine.'

'We found the case and discs in Macsen's house.'

'Macsen is a gamer,' Rhodri said.

'They were in his bathroom,' Edris said. 'Interesting thing about these discs is they have Jake's fingerprints on them.'

Rhodri shook his head. 'That's not possible.'

'Why?' Meadows asked.

'He's dead,' Rhodri said.

'Are you certain about that?' Edris asked.

Rhodri's legs jiggled so much his body shook. 'How would I know? If you think he's alive then you should be asking him what his discs are doing in Macsen's house.'

'We don't think he's alive,' Meadows said. 'We think someone had those discs in their possession. They then left them in Macsen's house to make us believe Jake is still alive and that he killed Macsen.'

'This is fucked up,' Rhodri said. 'I didn't take any stuff that Jake left behind.'

'Tell me about your degree,' Meadows said.

Rhodri looked relieved by the change of direction in questioning. 'I got a third.'

'In business studies?'

'Yeah.'

'You must have taken a computer module.'

'You have to be able to use spreadsheets, databases, and Word.'

'Do you know what a VPN is?' Edris asked.

'Yes, you use them to protect your data.'

'And to disguise your IP address,' Edris said. 'You use one on your laptop.'

'No, I don't.'

'We have a digital forensic report that shows you do.'

'Well, it's wrong.'

'Tell us about Mischiefstixx.'

Rhodri looked blank.

'It's a spoofing service provider,' Edris said.

'Never heard of it,' Rhodri said.

'Funny that,' Edris said. 'That's also on your laptop.'

'You must have heard of TOR. The dark web? The deep web?' Meadows asked.

Rhodri looked panicked. He turned to Lewis. 'Are you going to say something?'

'My client has told me about Macsen's phone being hacked. The confusing messages,' Lewis said. 'Clearly his laptop has been compromised.'

'Not this time,' Meadows said. 'Your client's laptop was used to hack the social media accounts of Macsen, Iona, Christie, Sammy, and Alys. All their passwords and personal information are on there. Phone tracking and software for message spoofing. I could go on.'

Rhodri slammed his fist down on the desk. 'I didn't do any of that. You're setting me up.'

Meadows ignored the outburst. 'Who else had access to your laptop?'

'Sammy stays over.'

'Are you saying Sammy used your laptop at various times to send messages to your friends, track their phones, and surf the dark web?'

'No,' Rhodri said.

'Your laptop is password-protected.'

'Yeah.'

'Then it's unlikely someone else has been using it,' Meadows said.

'They've all been in my house.'

'They being…?'

'Iona, Macsen, Alys, Christie, and Sammy.'

'Have any of them been in your house alone? Spent hours there? On more than one occasion?'

Rhodri shook his head. 'Oh, hang on. I told you someone had been in my house. They left stuff.'

'That's not going to work,' Edris said. 'We have the timings of when the messages were sent. The intruder would have been in and out of your house at all hours. Are you going to tell us someone was on your laptop when you were sitting eating your dinner and you didn't notice?'

'I don't bloody know,' Rhodri said.

'The only fingerprints found on the laptop are yours,' Meadows said. 'We also found an order for morphine. Paid for by you and delivered to your address. Macsen was given morphine before he was murdered. Probably put into his drink that night.'

Rhodri looked like he was going to be sick.

Meadows took a sheet of paper from the file and handed it to Rhodri. 'Can you confirm that is your bank account?'

Rhodri picked up the sheet of paper which shook in his hands. 'Looks like it.'

'Look at the highlighted amount.'

'I don't know what that's for,' Rhodri said.

'Payment for the morphine,' Meadows said.

'I never made that payment. Someone must have got hold of my card.'

'Can you see any other transactions you didn't make?' Meadows asked.

Rhodri ran his finger down the sheet. 'No.'

'Odd someone would steal your bank details and only buy one item,' Meadows said. 'Did anyone have access to you bank card?'

Rhodri shook his head.

'As you are aware, fraudulent transactions are found on people's accounts all the time,' Lewis said.

'Not often for morphine,' Meadows said. 'It was delivered to your client's address.'

'My client also informed you he had an intruder,' Lewis said.

'Which he didn't report at the time,' Edris said.

'Because nothing was taken,' Rhodri said. He turned to Lewis. 'Can't you do something? They're fitting me up.'

'You have no alibi for the time Alys was murdered,' Meadows said. 'You were in a relationship with her. You were the father of her unborn child. She was the long-term girlfriend of your best friend. By your own admission, you gave Macsen ecstasy the night he was murdered. You also plied him with alcohol. These are facts.'

'We were all drinking that night,' Rhodri said.

'Did anyone else pour Macsen a drink?'

'I don't know, I can't remember.'

'You don't have an alibi for the time of Macsen's murder,' Meadows said. 'You have motive and opportunity. We have the evidence on your laptop, your fingerprints are all over Alys and Macsen's homes. Sammy and Iona had an intruder. Your fingerprints were also found in their homes.'

'Because I've been to all their places. They're my friends.'

'I'll be honest with you. It's not looking good,' Meadows said. 'Unless you can give us an alternative explanation for the evidence then you will be tried for the murder of Macsen Lloyd and Alys Pugh.'

Rhodri's eyes filled with tears. 'I didn't kill them. I wasn't the one who lied.'

'Lied about what?' Meadows asked.

'This is because of what happened to Jake. It's why Alys and Macsen are dead. Because of what they did. It's got to be Jake. He must have grabbed one of the ladders.'

Meadows sat forward. 'What ladder?'

Rhodri looked scared. 'I'm not saying any more.'

'You were there the night Jake died,' Meadows said. 'How else would you know about the ladders?'

'I've been to Tenby. I know what the harbour looks like. All harbours have ladders going down to the boats.'

'How do you know he went off that side? The other side doesn't have ladders. Jake didn't kill himself, did he?' Meadows asked.

'I'd like a few moments alone with my client,' Lewis said.

'OK, we'll take a break,' Meadows said. He suspended the interview and left the room with Edris.

'Do you think he killed Jake?' Edris asked.

'I think he was there that night and I'm guessing he wasn't alone. Now that's something Rhodri wouldn't want anyone to know.'

'If Macsen was with him then he could have told Alys,' Edris said.

'Maybe Macsen and Alys wanted to come clean. We know Alys planned on going to Bristol. I'm betting she was going to tell the police.'

They were quiet for a few moments. Different scenarios played out in Meadows' mind. 'Right, he's had enough time. Let's go back in.'

Back in the interview room, Meadows restarted the recording. He noticed Rhodri was sweating and Lewis didn't look so happy.

'You've had time to confer with your solicitor?' Meadows asked.

Rhodri nodded.

'My client is willing to divulge certain information that may assist you in your enquiry,' Lewis said.

'If you're thinking of making a deal, forget it,' Edris said. 'We have enough evidence against your client.'

'We will listen to what he has to say and his cooperation will be noted,' Meadows said.

Lewis nodded.

'Alys lied about that night with Jake,' Rhodri said. 'She got drunk and slept with him. I saw her coming out of his room. It was Iona who persuaded her to lie. She said Macsen would never forgive her for what she did. Alys didn't want to involve the police. She just wanted Macsen to think Jake took advantage of her. It was Iona who told the dean. She was the one who posted all over social media that Jake was a rapist. It got out of hand. That's why Alys withdrew her allegation.'

'We knew that already,' Edris said.

'I didn't know at the time,' Rhodri said. 'You can read my statement. I never said Alys looked upset when she left his room.'

That much is true, Meadows thought. 'You had a go at Jake.'

'Yeah. I told him to stay away from Alys. I never touched him.'

'Did you follow him to Tenby?'

'No. We didn't know he was going to be there. Me and Macsen went to Tenby for New Year's Eve. Alys and Iona didn't come with us. We were out having a good time and then we spotted Jake in the crowd. Jake saw us and moved away. Macsen went after him so I followed. It was so crowded, we lost him for a while. I said to Macsen to forget it. We should just go back to the square and party. Macsen wanted to keep looking. Then we saw him again, just a glimpse. He must have doubled back to get away from us. He kept going up and down backstreets. Eventually we caught up with him. Macsen chased him to the jetty.' Rhodri put his hand to his head and gripped a handful of hair.

'Take your time,' Lewis said.

'Macsen was wound up. He'd taken some tabs. He shouted at Jake, called him a rapist, told him he was going to teach him a lesson. Jake got his phone out. I think he was going to call for help but Macsen knocked it out of his hand. Jake kept saying he didn't do anything. I tried to tell Macsen both Jake and Alys were drunk. I grabbed his arm to pull him back but he pushed me away. The waves were crashing over the top of the wall and we were all soaking. Jake kept saying sorry, telling Macsen to ask Alys the truth. That's when Macsen hit him. Jake's glasses went flying, he staggered back, then he sort of teetered on the edge. I saw the fear in his eyes. He knew he was going to go over. Knew he was going to die. Then he was gone.'

'Did you try to help him?' Meadows asked.

'Yeah. I switched on the torch on my phone. I tried to look over but I couldn't see anything. Just waves crashing against the wall and blackness. I shouted. Called his name. There was nothing we could do.'

'You could have called for help,' Meadows said.

'I wanted to but Macsen stopped me. He said we'd both be in the shit. We ran. I couldn't just leave Jake in the water without anyone knowing. I went to the train station. It was heaving with people trying to get home. They'd put on extra trains. I put my hood up and used the payphone.'

'What did you do after you made the call?' Meadows asked.

'We sobered up and drove home. We were supposed to stay the night but we didn't want to be seen the next day.'

'Shaun and Ethan were there that night,' Edris said. 'Do you think they saw you?'

'We saw them with Jake but we didn't know if they'd seen us or if Jake said something before he left. We kept watching the news and checking Facebook for updates. We knew the police and search and rescue were searching for Jake. Macsen was in a state. He expected the police to knock on his door at any moment. When Shaun came home, Macsen was waiting for him. He made sure he kept his mouth shut.'

'You mean he threatened him, knocked him about?' Edris said.

'Yeah,' Rhodri said. 'I never touched him.'

'So Shaun knew Macsen had a hand in Jake's death even if he didn't witness it,' Meadows said.

'He swore he didn't see us but it was too late by then.'

'Did Alys find out?'

'Not then. Just before Christmas, last year – that's why they broke up. I couldn't believe he'd told her. Alys had fessed up about lying. She couldn't live with the guilt. With the anniversary coming up she decided to go to the police and tell them what she had done. Macsen told her what happened at the harbour. He begged her not to tell the police; in the end, she persuaded him to go with her. I thought he had changed his mind and killed her. When the stuff was left in our homes, I thought it was Macsen trying to scare us so we would keep quiet.'

'Did you ask him about it?'

'Yeah, he said he didn't kill Alys. He was so cut up I believed him.'

'You had a lot to lose if Alys went to the police,' Meadows said. 'If Macsen told them what happen then you'd be questioned, maybe charged. That's motive to kill them both.'

'No. I didn't kill them,' Rhodri said.

A knock at the door interrupted the interview. Harvard peeked in and gestured to Meadows.

Meadows suspended the interview and joined Harvard outside the door. He could see by the look on his face that something bad had happened. His thought turned to the three women. 'Who?' he asked.

'Iona and Christie,' Harvard said.

Chapter Twenty-nine

Hanes was standing outside Christie's front door when Meadows arrived. He could see forensic officers on their hands and knees scouring the driveway. Iona's car was parked halfway up. There was no sign of Christie's car.

'I should have had them moved last night,' Meadows said.

'We thought we had him,' Edris said. 'Besides, Paskin didn't have enough time to organise a safe house. We wouldn't have been moving them until this morning. You had patrol checking on them all night.'

Harvard nodded. 'You organised a panic alarm to be fitted. You didn't know this was going to happen. They should've been safe together.'

The words didn't make Meadows feel any better. 'Iona kept asking for protection. She knew the danger she was in. Christie had become a target. We put our faith in technology.'

'Rhodri could still be involved,' Edris said.

'Even if that's the case we should have considered the possibility he wasn't working alone.'

'He wouldn't have been working with Shaun or Ethan,' Harvard said. 'They would've held him accountable, as well as Macsen, for Jake's death.'

'Then that would leave Sammy,' Meadows said. 'I can't see her taking on the two girls alone. We better see if we can find out what happened here last night.' He beckoned to Hanes.

Hanes joined them on the pavement.

'What went wrong?' Meadows asked.

'Nothing,' Hanes said. 'I called in at ten last night. Christie and Iona were getting ready for bed.'

'Had Sammy already left?'

'Yeah. She didn't tell them where she was going. We haven't been able to get hold of her.'

'Edris, take the car and try to track down Sammy. Start with her parents but try not to alarm them. We have no reason at this stage to think any harm has come to her. Hanes can give you a lift.'

'OK, I'll see you back at the station,' Edris said and left.

Meadows turned back to Hanes. 'Did you check the property?'

'Yes,' Hanes said. 'I waited for them to lock up. I checked the doors and windows, it was secure. I told them I would be back around eight-thirty to talk them through the panic alarm that was being fitted. Then patrol took over, they came by every hour until five this morning. They didn't report anything unusual during the night. I called back just after eight-thirty. When I couldn't get an answer, I went around the back. That's when I noticed the blood on the driveway. The back door was locked but I could see blood on the floor through the window. I called it in and broke the door down. There was no sign of them. Just loads of blood. There was no evidence of a break-in. They must have opened the door, so it has to be someone they trusted.'

'Was Christie's car here last night?' Meadows asked.

'Yeah, it was on the driveway parked in front of Iona's.'

'Did patrol notice what time the car moved?'

Hanes looked uncomfortable. 'Iona's car was moved forward. It would be difficult in the dark to spot one of the cars missing from driving past. I've put out an alert on Christie's car.'

Meadows was tempted to ask who was on duty but there was no point. Attributing blame wouldn't change the situation. He turned to Harvard. 'Let's get suited up and take a look.'

Once they were dressed in protective clothing, they followed the path laid out by the forensic team. Yellow markers denoted the blood on the driveway. There was more blood near the back door and inside on the floor. As they moved further into the house, blood could be seen on the walls. The sight made Meadows feel nauseous. He couldn't help imagining the fear the two women would have felt. Clearly, by the bloody handprints smeared on the wall, at least one of them put up a fight.

The trail led to a bedroom where Mike was taking samples from a bed. Meadows walked towards the dressing table and picked up a brush. He held it to the light and saw long red hairs caught between the bristles.

'Looks like this is Christie's room,' he said.

He approached the empty bed and looked at the white pillowcases that were stained crimson.'

'Looks like she was attacked as she slept,' Harvard said.

'The scene is similar in the other room,' Mike said.

'It's a lot of blood loss,' Harvard said. 'I guess the chances of them being alive are slim.'

'It depends,' Mike said. 'There would be significant bleeding from a head wound. Given the majority of the blood is on the pillow then I would think that is the case. What's interesting is there is a blood splatter pattern in the other room but not in this room.'

'You think it was less frenzied?' Meadows asked. 'It would make sense. Iona would have been the main target.

Perhaps they just used enough force to knock out or stun Christie.'

'Not that, necessarily. If you hit someone over the head' – Mike swung his arm up and down – 'on impact the weapon would force the blood to spread outwards. As the assailant pulled back the weapon, blood would be flicked, which is what we can see in Iona's room. This, however, looks more like an injury from a cut.'

Meadows looked more closely. 'Interesting. You wouldn't expect the assailant to use two different weapons.'

'Could the splatter be covered up by all this blood?' Harvard said.

Mike shook his head.

'They wouldn't have had long to carry out the attack,' Meadows said. 'A scream from one would have woken the other. Perhaps Iona was first and didn't get a chance to react. Then they threaten Christie with a knife. She fights, tries to grab her phone.' He pointed to the mobile phone that was hanging over the bedside table from the power cord. 'She gets injured in the struggle.' He shook his head. 'Still doesn't fit. She wouldn't then lie back down.'

'Maybe the attacker didn't hit her as hard as Iona,' Harvard said.

'You can see the trail of blood dragging downwards,' Mike said. 'She was pulled off the bed. Then there's very little until you get to the stairs. I would say she was on her feet by then. Different again in the other room: Iona was dragged from the bed, down the stairs and to the back door.'

'That would fit,' Meadows said. 'There's blood smeared on the wall going down the stairs. If Christie was forced down then she may have put her hand out to steady herself.'

'Why take both of them?' Harvard asked. 'Christie didn't have anything to do with what happened to Jake.'

'She'd be able to identify the killer,' Meadows said. 'It was too risky to act with the three women in the house. Once Sammy left, they took their chance. The question is why take them from the house? Why not just kill them here?' Another thought struck him. 'By today it would've been too late to act. They would've been moved to a safe house.'

'Yeah, but the killer wouldn't have known that,' Harvard said.

'No, but for some reason they thought they had to act now, and risk taking two of them from the house. They probably knew Rhodri was in custody. Why not wait for him to be charged? Iona would have gone home and been alone.'

'Maybe they just wanted to finish the job,' Harvard said. 'Gone beyond caring if they get caught.'

'Everything else has been carefully planned,' Meadows said. 'OK, let's have a look around.'

Meadows checked the bathroom then moved into the spare room. Iona's clothes were piled in a heap on the floor. There was a faint smell of perfume mixed with the metallic scent of blood. He could see the splatter pattern that Mike had mentioned.

'Definitely looks more of a frenzied attack in here,' he said.

Harvard nodded. 'If she was alive when she left here, I doubt she'll live much longer without medical attention.'

They moved downstairs and checked the kitchen and sitting room before stepping outside.

'No gifts left this time,' Meadows said.

'Maybe they ran out or thought they'd made their point. Each one of them had already been left something,' Harvard said.

Meadows looked around. On this side of the house, a garage and driveway stood between the neighbours.

'They must have been gagged and bound,' Meadows said. 'Put in the car one at a time. Then Iona's car had to be moved forward.'

'All while the neighbours were asleep,' Harvard said.

'Has the garage been opened?' Meadows asked one of the forensic officers.

'It was checked to see if the women were in there but we haven't processed it. It's unlocked.'

'Thanks,' Meadows said.

He pulled at the garage door. It slid up easily. Inside looked like a home gym. There were various items of exercise equipment including a running machine, bench, and weights.

'She doesn't look like someone who works out,' Harvard said. 'Maybe she had someone staying here.'

'We'd have seen signs of another occupant,' Meadows said. 'Christie is always dressed in baggy clothes with long sleeves. She could be fit and muscular.'

'Probably stronger than the killer anticipated,' Harvard said. 'Hence the bloodstains on the wall. She put up a fight and pushed against the wall as she tried to pull back.'

Meadows nodded and made his way to the back of the garage. A metal cabinet with four doors ran the length of the wall. He pulled open the doors. It was empty apart from three browning rose petals.

'Do you think the killer was hiding out in here?' Harvard asked.

'I think they've been hiding in plain sight,' Meadows said.

* * *

The office was a hive of activity and Meadows could feel the tension. He read through the statements that had been gathered then moved quickly to the forensic reports.

'Still no sighting of Christie's car,' Paskin said as Edris came back into the office.

Meadows put down the reports. 'What did you get from Sammy?'

'She claims she slept at a friend's house last night. Had a few to drink and her phone was on silent. She did look a bit rough and was distressed when I told her the news.'

'She could be tired because she was up all night moving Iona and Christie,' Blackwell said.

'They would have let her in,' Valentine said.

'They were in bed when they were attacked,' Harvard said.

'So she let herself in,' Blackwell said.

Meadows shook his head as a thought came to him. 'Keys were used to get into the other houses.'

'Yeah,' Blackwell said.

'Not Christie's. She had the locks changed and there were no spares made. I don't buy that the back door was left open accidently.' He stepped over to the incident board. 'The women had keys to each other's houses. Alys had a key to Macsen's cottage. Sammy's got a key to Rhodri's house. Either one of the women let the killer into Christie's house so they could leave the roses or–'

'One of them is the killer,' Edris said.

'There were rose petals found in a cupboard in the garage. Easier to buy them and hide them until the others were asleep,' Meadows said. 'Then you've got the absence of fingerprints and other forensic evidence. We eliminated any hair, fibre, and prints because we expected to find it from this group. These six were in and out of each other's houses.' He pointed to the names on the board. 'Two dead, one in the cell overnight. That leaves one of these three.'

'Iona, Alys, Rhodri, and Macsen all had a hand in Jake's death,' Valentine said. 'That leaves Christie or Sammy. Given Christie is missing, then we're looking at Sammy.'

'There was something off about the scene in Christie's house,' Meadows said.

'You think it was set up?' Valentine asked.

'Possibly, but we have to wait for the forensic analysis and we don't have time.'

'Neither Sammy nor Christie have a connection to Jake,' Edris said.

'We need to find one,' Meadows said.

'Might not be a connection to Jake,' Harvard said. 'What if one of them is involved with Shaun Jones? It wouldn't be the first time someone killed for love.'

'Good point,' Meadows said.

'Why take both women?' Paskin asked. 'If they were after Iona then they could have knocked out Christie or drugged her.'

'From what Christie told us, it sounds as if she was drugged the night Macsen died. Maybe she was careful about what she ate and drank. No chance of drugging her again. This time she would be able to identify the assailant. They don't want to kill her so they take her with them to buy some time. If that's the case then I doubt she'll stay alive.'

'It could be Iona,' Paskin said. 'She made a big thing about disliking Jake. It could have been to disguise the fact she was in love with him. She finds out Macsen killed him, and she knew Alys lied.'

'Then why bother to take Christie?' Meadows said. 'She could have just left Rhodri to take the blame.'

'Christie is a smart girl,' Harvard said. 'She could have worked it out and confronted Iona.'

Meadows could feel the frustration of the team. They just couldn't pin it down to one of the three women. Even if they could, they still had to locate them. The team looked at him expectantly.

'Harvard and Valentine, stay on Shaun Jones. Speak to all his family members and anyone associated with him. Blackwell, can you talk to Iona's parents? They've already been notified she is missing. See what information you can find out about her relationship with Jake and Shaun. Paskin, go through their social media accounts again, and check all mutual friends. See if Sammy or Christie have any connection to Shaun, Ethan, or Jake. Edris and I will speak to Christie's mother. Uniform will be keeping a watch for Christie's car and checking traffic footage from last night. Without knowing the direction the car went, they have a big job. It may be that the killer used the back roads to avoid the cameras. We need to move fast. If these women are still alive then time is running out.'

Chapter Thirty

Driving on the M4 to Bridgend was the last thing Meadows wanted to be doing but he had no choice. It was where Christie's mother lived. This was something that couldn't be done by a phone call. If Christie was involved and her mother had an inkling, she would lie to protect her daughter. He needed to coax as much information from her without throwing suspicion on Christie. He also didn't want to alert her to the fact that her daughter may be in danger. The last thing he wanted was Rhian Whitley to shut down.

Meadows parked outside Rhian's house and she came running out as soon as he stepped out of the car.

'Have you found her?' Rhian asked.

'We don't have any news yet,' Meadows said. 'We do need to ask you some questions.'

'I already told the police I haven't heard from her. It's not like Christie to go off and worry people. All they said was they needed to speak with her and were concerned about her safety. What's going on? Does this have something to do with what happened to her friend?'

'It appears it could be linked,' Meadows said. 'Right now we need information about Christie. It may help us locate her. Let's go inside.'

Rhian nodded and turned to walk back indoors. She led Meadows and Edris into a sitting room and offered them a seat. As Meadows took the armchair, he looked at Rhian. She had the same flame-coloured hair as Christie. She wore it loose and it frizzed around her oval face.

'I understand how anxious you must be feeling,' Meadows said. 'I assure you we are doing everything we can to find Christie. We know she is friends with Sammy and Iona but we need to speak with anyone else she is close to.'

'I don't think there is anyone. She may have kept in touch with some friends from school and university but she hasn't mentioned anyone in particular.'

'Do you know if Christie has a boyfriend?' Edris asked.

Rhian shook her head. 'I'm sure she does date but there is no one special. She was always more interested in studying than boys.'

'We understand she is very bright,' Meadows said.

'Yes. She got a first at university. Mathematics. She did some other studies while she was there. Something to do with computers. I can find her certificates if that will help.'

'Did she ever mention doing coding on this course?' Edris asked.

'It sounds familiar. To be honest, a lot of it went over my head. She doesn't get her intelligence from me.' Rhian gave a nervous laugh.

'She was going to do her master's but delayed it, why was that?' Meadows asked.

'She struggled after her father died. It was too much for her so she took a break.'

Rhian started pulling at the collar of her jumper. Meadows could see how much she was struggling to hold it together.

'I'm sorry. I didn't know her father had died,' Meadows said.

'Oh, not Steven,' Rhian said. 'He was never a father to her. David was the only dad she knew.'

'David Ellis?' Meadows asked.

'Yes, how do you know about David? What's he got to do with this?' She looked from Meadows to Edris.

Meadows' stomach flipped. I left Iona with her, he thought. 'You and David were together?' he asked.

Rhian turned her attention back to Meadows but she looked guarded. 'For a while. We got together when Christie was three. It lasted five years. David had a son, Jake, he came every weekend. There was only a year between Jake and Christie, so they were like brother and sister. When David and I split up, he stayed in Christie's life. She spent every weekend with him and Jake. He treated her as his own daughter.'

'It must've been hard for Christie when Jake died.'

Rhian jumped up from the chair. 'What's going on? You think she's killed herself, don't you? You think she was depressed about Jake?'

Meadows could see the panic in Rhian's eyes. Her whole body was tense. He didn't want to put her through this anguish but he needed answers. The only thing he could do was to be honest.

'No, we don't think that Christie has or intends to take her own life. However, it is possible that the death of David and Jake is connected to Christie's disappearance and the murder of two of her friends.'

'I don't understand,' Rhian said.

'Please, sit down,' Meadows said gently. 'If you can talk us through what happened after Jake went missing, it might help us find her.'

Rhian nodded and perched on the edge of the sofa next to Edris. 'She was in a state. I don't think she ate or slept for days. When she wasn't searching, she spent her time trying to work out the tide and current. If anyone could have worked it out, it would have been her. She couldn't stand the thought of him being washed up on some rocks, injured and alone. She would work out some location and go off searching. Then she'd come back and start again.'

'How long did it go on for?'

'I don't know. It seemed endless. The days just ran into one another. Then there was the inquest. She didn't go – I don't think she wanted to face the fact he was gone. After that, David took his own life. I was angry with him for a long time for doing that, for leaving Christie. I guess he couldn't live with the grief of losing his son. I thought it would drive Christie over the edge. She was distraught at first then it was like she became numb, switched off all her feelings. She'd always been a happy, strong, and confident girl. But then it was like she was just going through the motions. She went back to university and finished her degree. It gave her a purpose. Slowly she came back. Now this. She's already been through enough.'

'Is there somewhere Christie would go if she needed to get away?' Meadows asked.

'You mean if she was hiding from someone? Do you think that's what happened?'

At some point, Meadows knew he would have to tell Rhian that her daughter had killed two people. Possibly a third.

'We need to cover all possibilities.'

'David was a property manager. He started by flipping one house and making a profit. He ended up with a lot of property. Before he died, he changed his will. He left them all to Christie as well as a substantial amount of money.'

'Are any of these properties near the sea or a large body of water?' Edris asked.

'I don't know. He had houses all over the place.'

'Is there anywhere that was special to Christie? Maybe somewhere she spent time with David and Jake?' Meadows asked.

Rhian shook her head. 'The two of them planned to travel before doing their master's. I'm sure she mentioned India. Jake had been and loved it.'

Meadows stood up. 'Thank you. We'll keep you updated.'

'Please find her,' Rhian said. 'I can't bear to think of her alone and frightened. It's her birthday today.' Her hand flew to her mouth. 'It was Jake's birthday when he died.'

Meadows felt bad having to leave her with those thoughts but they had to hurry.

'We have our answer,' Edris said when they'd got back in the car. 'I don't understand how we didn't pick up on it. Christie would have been in contact with Jake on social media.'

'Four years ago,' Meadows said. 'All she had to do is set up a new social media account. That would be the one we looked at. The one connected to Alys and the others. David and Jake Ellis are not related to Christie. If we hadn't talked to Rhian we would never have known.'

Meadows's phone rang and he hit answer. Harvard's voice filled the car.

'I've found Shaun Jones. He's still in South Korea but I've spoken to him. You'll never guess what he told me.'

'Christie,' Edris said.

'Oh, you know.' Harvard sounded disappointed.

'We've just spoken to Christie's mother, but good work,' Meadows said. 'At least we can rule out Shaun. We'll meet you back at the station.'

While Meadows drove, Edris called the rest of the team and by the time they reached the station they were all waiting.

'Paskin, have you got anything on those properties?' Meadows asked.

Paskin shook her head. 'David Ellis ran his properties under a company name, that company was transferred to Christie. It's managed by Get Away. Offices are closed for the evening.'

'I can't see how she acted alone,' Blackwell said.

'Plenty of time to plan,' Meadows said. 'Which means she knew what she was doing.'

'Iona could already be dead and Christie on her way out of the country,' Valentine said.

Meadows nodded. 'Alert the airports and all ports. Get a description out.' He looked at the incident board. 'She's not going to hurry this. Macsen and Alys were killed by drowning. She's going to take her to water.'

'That could be anywhere,' Valentine said.

'She can't risk the beach. Too many people,' Edris said.

'Somewhere remote,' Blackwell said. 'It'd have to be accessible by car. She's not going to be able to carry or drag Iona any distance.'

'It's her birthday,' Meadows said. 'It was Jake's birthday when he died. She's going to end her life as it is now and start over, possibly with a new identity. She has the resources to do it. I think she'll wait until it's dark.'

'The light is already fading,' Harvard said.

'It has to be Tenby,' Meadows said. 'That's where this started.'

'It started in Bristol,' Blackwell said. 'She could be planning on throwing Iona off Clifton Bridge.'

'That's too much of a risk,' Paskin said. 'Someone would stop her.'

'Would they?' Blackwell asked. 'By the time someone notices what she's doing and stops the car it would be too late. She's beyond caring.'

'We'll have to cover both,' Harvard said.

'Hold on,' Meadows said. 'Harvard, what did Ethan say about staying in Tenby?'

Harvard looked at his notes. 'Jake's dad gave them a holiday home to stay in.'

'She's gone there. She's waiting for it to get dark and she's going to take Iona to the harbour.'

Chapter Thirty-one

Night had fallen as Meadows drove past the holiday property and stopped the car.

'Lights are on,' Edris said. 'If you're sure that's the house, we should just break the door down.'

'It's the address DI Allen noted down in the files. Problem is it could be rented out. We can't go charging in and scaring the hell out of some holidaymakers.'

'Christie's car was picked up on camera coming in this direction,' Edris said. 'She's got to be here. Where else would she be hiding out?'

A car pulled up behind them and Meadows could see Blackwell in his rear-view mirror. Valentine was sitting next to him and Harvard in the back. He knew they were all awaiting his instructions. As soon as they made their presence known, there would be little time. If inside, Christie would seize her chance to kill Iona before they got to her. Another car pulled up behind Blackwell.

'Back-up is here,' Edris said.

'OK, let's go and talk to the others.' Meadows opened the door and felt the full force of the wind. It pushed against him as he made his way to Blackwell's car.

Blackwell stuck his head out of the window. 'What's the plan?'

'You and Valentine go around the back,' Meadows said. 'We'll go to the front and knock. If there are holidaymakers inside, they should respond. If there's no answer, we break the door down.'

Blackwell grinned. 'It could be a honeymoon couple. Poor bastards will have a night to remember if we all go crashing in.'

'We've got no choice,' Meadows said. 'Christie's car isn't here but there's a garage. Harvard, check it out. Be careful, she could be in there waiting to make her move.'

'OK.' Harvard got out of the car and the wind whipped his hair around. 'It's bloody freezing.'

'Where's your hat?' Valentine asked as she came to stand next to him.

'I left it on my desk.'

'Idiot,' Valentine said. 'I'm not giving you mine.' She took a hat from her pocket and pulled it down over her ears.

'OK, let's go.' Meadows signalled to the uniformed officers that were parked behind.

They moved quietly toward the house. When Meadows was sure Valentine and Blackwell were in position, he gave the door a loud knock. He waited a few seconds and peered through the letter box.

'Nothing. Break it down.' He moved aside and two officers used a ram. Two swings and the door gave.

'Police,' Meadows shouted as he moved in.

They spread out and quickly checked all the rooms. Meadows ran upstairs and flung open a door. He flipped the light switch and saw the unmade bed in the centre of the room. He stepped closer. There were bloodstains on the pillowcase.

'They were here,' Meadows said.

He ran back down the stairs where Valentine, Blackwell, and Harvard were waiting.

'Garage is empty,' Harvard said.

'The harbour,' Meadows said.

They raced to the harbour and had just enough room to park the three cars on the jetty. Meadows jumped out and grabbed a torch from the boot. He walked toward the end of the jetty sweeping his torch in all directions. The wind here was fierce and the waves crashed over the wall.

'No one here,' Edris called.

'Keep looking,' Meadows shouted above the wind.

He moved past the harbour master's office to the far end of the jetty. On the left, construction machinery was parked along with pallets of bricks and wood which reached the end of the harbour. With no barriers, there was a dangerous drop into the sea. He checked in between the pallets then made his way back to join the others.

'She could already be in the water,' Blackwell said.

Meadows shook his head. 'The tide hasn't turned yet. If she's going to throw Iona in then she'll wait until she'll be dragged out.'

'Then we just wait here,' Valentine said.

'It could force her to change her plans,' Meadows said. 'Edris, contact the coast guard and put them on stand-by.'

'If she tries to drag her into the sea off the beach we'll have a better chance of stopping her,' Blackwell said.

'Then we need to cover the beaches,' Harvard said.

Meadows called over the uniformed officer who had followed them to the harbour. 'Can you organise getting a car at each exit road? We need to stop her from leaving the area. We also need to have the beaches further upcoast checked.'

'No problem,' the officer said.

'We'll take it in turns to cover the harbour. If we move up and down the jetty with the flashlights then it should deter her,' Meadows said. 'The rest of us will check the North and South beaches.'

'Harvard and I will take the first turn here,' Valentine said.

'We'll get soaked,' Harvard said.

'Yeah, but we get to warm up once they've checked the beaches. They'll get a double soaking.'

'I like your thinking,' Harvard said.

'I'll go to the South Beach,' Blackwell said.

'Edris and I will cover the North Beach. We'll meet back here. Keep in touch.' Another wave crashed over the wall. 'Are you two going to be OK?'

'Yeah,' Valentine said. 'We'll stay away from the edge.'

'We've got this,' Harvard said.

'As soon as Edris and I have cleared the beach we'll swap,' Meadows said.

Meadows jumped in the car and waited for Edris to shut the door. It was a relief to be out of the wind and spray. They didn't have far to drive. He parked midway and they both jumped out. Edris went to the right and Meadows to the left. He could feel his boots sinking in the sand. The wind was against him and he gave up trying to keep his hood up. He swept his torch back and forth going as close to the sea as possible. Each step was a battle. Doubt began to creep in. Christie could easily drown Iona in a bath. She had succeeded with Macsen. He shook that thought away. She'd had her chance to do that. He walked until he could go no further then turned and headed back, and met with Edris somewhere in the middle. They switched sides and carried on searching. In the distance, Meadows could see the flashlights moving up and down the jetty.

'No sign of her,' Edris said when they met up again. 'Nothing from Blackwell or uniform. They're watching for the car.'

'She must be lying low somewhere. The tide has turned. Let's go and swap with Harvard and Valentine. I can barely feel my hands. Those two must be soaked through and frozen.'

Edris turned the heaters up as soon as they jumped in the car. 'How long are we going to keep this up?'

'Until she makes a move,' Meadows said.

'That could be all night.'

'I'm hoping uniform will pick her up by then. There's only so many places you can hide in a car.' A large drop of rain splashed on the windscreen followed by a couple more. 'Looks like we're all going to get a soaking.'

By the time Meadows parked at the harbour, the rain was lashing the windscreen.

Edris opened the door. 'Here we go.'

Meadows could see Harvard and Valentine at the far end of the jetty. He looked down to switch on his torch then headlights were upon him. At first he thought it was Blackwell and he put his hands up to shield his eyes from the glare of the lights. He could just about make out the number plate.

'Christie!' Meadows shouted but his voice was lost on the wind.

He turned his head and saw Harvard and Valentine move towards him at the same time Christie moved the car forward so it was almost touching his legs. The engine revved. He held up his hands, palms outwards in both directions. Harvard and Valentine stopped moving. Christie stopped revving.

'Edris, move away slowly and call for back-up. We need to block her in. Tell them to keep their distance.'

Edris nodded and backed away slowly.

Meadows could see Iona in the passenger seat. She was gagged, her eyes wide with terror. She wasn't moving and he guessed she was bound. He indicated to Christie to open her window. She shook her head. He held up his hands and moved slowly until he was standing directly in front of Christie. He kept plenty of distance between himself and the car; he didn't want her to think he was going to make a move for the door.

Christie opened the window an inch.

Meadows could hear Edris talking. Blackwell wasn't far away. If he could keep Christie talking and distracted, it would give them a chance to get the cars in position. The last thing he wanted was a high-speed chase.

'Christie, I know what happened,' he shouted.

'They killed him. They killed both of them.'

'Yes,' Meadows said. 'We have a statement from Rhodri. He told us he and Macsen were there that night. Iona wasn't. She was at home.'

'It was all because of her lies,' Christie shouted.

'Do you think Jake would have wanted this?'

'I'll never know,' Christie said. 'He didn't want to die.'

'No. What happened to him was unforgivable but this is not the way. Both Rhodri and Iona will be charged for the part they played in Jake's death. You can–'

Meadows was cut off by the sound of a siren and a blue flashing light speeding towards the harbour. He didn't have time to react. The car sprung forward smashing into his leg and sending him backward. He watched in horror as the car sped towards the end of the jetty. It was upon Valentine and Harvard before they had a chance to move. With the pallets blocking one side and a sheer drop over the other side, they had nowhere to go.

Time seemed to slow. Edris shouted out. Meadows tried to get to his feet. There was nothing he could do. He saw Valentine and Harvard illuminated in the headlights. Harvard pushed Valentine out of the path of the car. Then the car went over the edge, taking Harvard with it.

Meadows ignored the searing pain in his leg and took off behind Edris. He could hear shouts but Valentine was nowhere to be seen. By the time he reached the end of the jetty, Edris was on his knees. Valentine was hanging by her fingertips on the edge of the harbour wall. Meadows dropped down next to Edris and together they pulled her up.

'Harvard!' Valentine screamed.

Meadows ran back to the harbour master's office and pulled the life ring off the wall. Blackwell was running towards him.

'No!'

Meadows didn't stop to think. He leapt off the edge.

Chapter Thirty-two

There was a heavy silence in the office. The air was thick with grief. A darkness that spread within. It felt almost tangible. Everything looked, smelled, and tasted different.

Valentine was sitting at her desk, silent tears tracked down her cheeks. Edris was standing by the window, a faraway look on his face. Blackwell had placed his hand on Paskin's shoulder, she leaned her head against him.

Meadows looked over at Harvard's desk. His bobble hat was sat next to his cup. It probably has strands of his hair in the wool, he thought. He tried to chase away the memories of the previous night. The icy cold water. Plunging into the darkness. Battling his way to the surface. Wave after wave battering him. The shouts. The lifeboat. The searchlight. He couldn't save Harvard. He felt the weight of the tears in his eyes and turned away to let them fall.

The phone ringing cut the silence; Blackwell picked it up. Meadows wiped his eyes and turned to listen.

'She's ready for questioning,' Blackwell said. 'Unbelievable. She should have…' Blackwell huffed and shook his head.

Meadows knew what he was thinking. Both Iona and Christie had been pulled from the car. Iona was still in hospital but expected to make a full recovery. Christie had been released with just a bruise on her shoulder.

'Harvard took the full impact,' Valentine said. 'There wasn't enough room for the two of us. He put himself before me. If I'd moved faster…'

'Don't go there,' Meadows said. 'Christie was the one driving the car. You almost went over yourself. She will be charged with Harvard's murder. Edris, are you OK to do the interview?'

Edris nodded.

'The rest of us have work to do,' Blackwell said. 'We need to put together a solid case against Rhodri and Iona. Starting with perverting the course of justice and any other charges we can bring against them. We make sure they are all held accountable. Right, Valentine? Paskin?'

'Yeah,' Valentine said.

'I'll make us some coffee,' Paskin said.

Meadows nodded his thanks to Blackwell. He knew the team needed all the distraction they could handle to prevent them drowning in grief.

Christie looked very different to the woman Meadows had spoken to on previous occasions. She was sitting up straight with an air of confidence. Her hair was loose and hung in soft waves over her shoulders. Her eyes were what caught his attention; they were hard. Any softness he'd seen before had long gone.

He took a seat next to Edris and tried not to wince from the pain in his leg. Edris started the recording. Christie's solicitor, Anna Humphrey, was the first to speak.

'My client is willing to give her full cooperation and will answer any questions you have.'

Christie sat back and folded her arms. The black sleeveless top revealed the thickness of her biceps. 'I didn't mean for that policeman to die,' she said. 'You might want to have a word with your colleagues about their attitude.'

'You of all people should appreciate what grief feels like. Detective Harvard was a kind, caring, hardworking member of our team. He was also well liked and will be missed,' Meadows said. 'You are welcome to make a complaint if you feel you have been unfairly treated.'

'Yeah right,' Christie said. 'They all want to see me locked up. I can see it on their faces. They can barely look at me.'

'All they want is justice for their friend and colleague,' Meadows said. 'Nothing more.'

'Jake never got justice,' Christie said.

'No,' Meadows agreed. 'But he died over four years ago. Why now? Why throw your own life away? Did someone put pressure on you?'

'It wasn't meant to end like this,' Christie said. 'I had it all planned out. No one persuaded me. I acted alone. I knew Alys had lied. Jake told me what happened that last Christmas we were together. We always told each other everything – he was my brother. We played together as kids. Even after our parents split, he treated me as his sister and David was the only father I had. I knew Jake was telling the truth about that night with Alys, I never doubted him. Dad was sorting things out; Jake was getting his confidence back. He was going to return to uni then take a gap year before doing his master's. We were going to travel together; me, Jake, Shaun, and Ethan. I knew he wouldn't have taken his own life.' Christie took a sip of water then sat back.

'I searched and searched for him. Each day that passed it felt like a piece of me was dying. Then after the inquest Dad left me. It was like a tide of grief washing over me; it kept pulling me away, I couldn't fight it. Some days I wished it would just take me.'

'What changed?' Meadows asked.

'Shaun came home for the holidays. He came to see me and we got drunk. He told me Macsen had hit him after Jake went missing, told him to keep his mouth shut about him and Rhodri being in Tenby that night. I knew then Macsen had killed Jake. Two years had passed and I had no evidence to take to the police. Who would believe me? I was so angry. No, it was more than that, I felt pure rage. It burned inside me. I used that rage against the tide. It pushed back the grief so I could see clearly; I knew what I had to do.'

'You befriended them all,' Meadows said, 'spent time with them. You must have got to know them all well, particularly Alys. Are you telling me you harboured all that hate and never once let it show, in almost two years?'

'It wasn't easy,' Christie said. 'I played the part well, don't you think? Dull, quiet, nice, and weak Christie. It was a mask. I used to go to the garage at night and work off all the frustration. It just made me stronger.'

'Did you plan to make friends with them or was it a coincidence you got the job with Rhodri?'

'It was always my plan. It wasn't difficult to hack their social media accounts. I learned everything about them, especially Iona. She posts what she has for breakfast. I was looking for a way in when Rhodri advertised the job. I think it was fate. I was overqualified. I told him it was a stopgap to save for travel. He introduced me to the others. All I had to do was gain their trust, make myself invaluable. Then I got copies of their keys cut so I could come and go as I pleased.

'I enjoyed tormenting Alys. Leaving those little reminders. I knew Macsen was going to propose. I even knew when he bought the ring. I used that information to get her to Llyn y Fan. I'd turned off Iona's alarm; sent out messages to Rhodri, Macsen, and Sammy.' She smiled. 'One to myself. It wasn't a problem getting them out of the way. I met Alys in the car park, told her Macsen had asked me to walk her to the top for the surprise. I waited until she was close to the water then I picked up a rock and hit her. I held her under the water and let her take a breath now and again, just so I could let her know why she had to die. She told me it was Iona who persuaded her to lie. She said she loved Jake. After that I held her under until she stopped moving. I changed into dry clothes in the bothy then ran back to my car. All I had to do was play the concerned friend when she didn't show up for the party.'

'And Macsen?' Meadows asked.

Christie grinned. 'He got a taste of what it's like to be a suspect. Then I played them off against each other. Sent messages. Left gifts. It was fun listening to them argue. They thought Jake had come back for them. That night I put morphine into Macsen's coffee. They all thought he was drunk. What was even better was Rhodri gave him some tablets. I knew Iona and Sammy would suspect him after that. Once we got home, I put the rest of the morphine in the vodka. They didn't notice I didn't drink from my glass. I tipped it down the sink. Once they were asleep, I went back to Macsen's cottage. I had a tracker on Rhodri's phone so I knew he hadn't gone back.'

'How did you get Macsen in the bath?' Edris asked.

'He was out of it. I tied his hands behind his back. Then I woke him. I told him he was ill. He kept saying he couldn't move his arms.' Christie laughed. 'I told him he needed to get into a cool bath to get his temperature down. I said an ambulance was on the way. He was so out of it he didn't know what postcode he was in. He got into the bath with no problem. I'd already filled it. Then I pulled his legs over the top. I used his hair to pull his head up enough for him to confess. He did put up a fight after that. Had me worried.'

'How did you manage to use Rhodri's laptop for the messages?' Meadows asked. 'They were sent at different times of the day and night. There were also the searches, the tracking software, and other stuff. That must have taken time.'

'Easy enough,' Christie said. 'I got an identical laptop. Copied all his stuff from his laptop. Set the new one up to look like his. He didn't notice any difference. I switched them back before you searched his house.'

'Then you set it up so it would look like you and Iona had been taken,' Meadows said.

'That was always the plan but I had to move faster. I was worried we'd be put in a safe house. I should have dumped her in the sea as soon as we got there but I had to wait until the tide was turning. I slept for a few hours then put her in the car. I had to keep moving in case you came looking. I had no intention of going in the sea myself. That was your fault. I had set up everything. I was going to start a new life. You never would have found Iona's body. Or mine.'

'You let Rhodri live,' Meadows said.

'Yeah. Suspicion would have followed him for the rest of his life. You had evidence on the laptop. You would've figured he was working with someone else. Maybe Iona, she was in love with him. I only needed a little more time and I could have set it up properly. I did a good job though.'

'Your mother and Shaun told us about you,' Edris said. 'You would never have got away with it.'

'It wouldn't have mattered. I'd be far away. Somewhere you'd never find me.' Christie stretched, sat back in the chair, and folded her arms. 'Is that it? I'm tired now. I want to go back to my cell.'

There was nothing more Meadows wanted to know. He would have liked to see some remorse, but there was none. He nodded, stood up, and left the room.

Chapter Thirty-three

Meadows looked out over the valley as daylight faded. It was a clear night; the moon was full and the stars were beginning to sparkle. He inhaled the crisp air that was tinged with the scent of burning wood and incense. He exhaled slowly allowing the peace of his surrounding to wash over him.

His brother, Rain, came to stand next to him. 'It's all ready.'

'Thanks,' Meadows said.

'Are you doing OK?'

'Better,' Meadows said. 'The sadness is still there but I guess it will be for a while.'

Rain nodded. 'I'm sure Harvard would have wanted you to be happy. It sounds like he was that type of guy.'

'The last conversation I had with him was in a coffee shop in Bristol. He told me his plans. As soon as he met the right woman, he was going to get married. He didn't want to waste any time.'

'Well, you've waited long enough,' Rain said. 'Talking of which, where is Daisy?'

'I left her talking to Mina. She doesn't suspect a thing.'

'Then what are you waiting for? Once you've gone, we'll set up the pagoda.'

'What if–'

'Are you kidding me? Chill, everything is going to be perfect. Good luck.' Rain threw his arms around Meadows and hugged him tight. 'See you later.'

Meadows walked through the commune, passing the yurts and tepees, until he came to Iggy's caravan. Mina and Daisy were sitting in front of a small fire.

'You two look cosy,' Meadows said.

'We've been having a nice chat,' Mina said.

'Did you have a good walk?' Daisy asked.

'Yeah, thanks,' Meadows said.

'Are you sure you shouldn't be resting that leg?' Mina asked.

'It's fine,' Meadows said.

Iggy came to join them. 'There you are. Rain has been looking for you. He asked me to tell you to meet him in the woods.'

Meadows acted surprised. 'What's he doing in there?'

'He been working on some project. Wants the two of you to see it,' Iggy said.

Meadows smiled. 'OK, lead the way.'

'We've already seen it,' Iggy said.

Daisy stood up. 'Come on. I'm excited to see what he's been up to. You seem a lot better,' she said as they walked.

Meadows took her hand. 'I am. It's been good to get away.'

'Yeah, it feels like the rest of the world doesn't exist when we're here.'

'We could always give it all up and stay.'

Daisy laughed. 'Tempting.'

They reached the edge of the woods and saw a path of solar lights had been laid out.

'He knows how to build suspense,' Daisy said. 'Or maybe the path is the surprise. It's so pretty. I know, he's built himself a tree house.'

Meadows laughed. 'That's something he would do. I guess we just follow.'

The path led to a clearing and in the centre was a bamboo star dome. Fairy lights twinkled around the entrance.

'Wow, it's beautiful,' Daisy said.

'Shall we go in?' Meadows asked.

'They entered the dome and Meadows moved Daisy to the centre. 'Look up at the stars and you'll see my wish,' he said.

Daisy looked up. A diamond ring was hanging down from a silver chain.

Her face lit up. 'Consider your wish granted.'

List of characters

Police:

DI Winter Meadows
DS Tristan Edris
DS Stefan Blackwell
DC Reena Valentine
DC Ben Harvard – trainee investigator
DS Rowena Paskin
PC Abbey Taylor
PC Matt Hanes
DS Sita Khan – Bristol CID
DI Tom Allen – Pembrokeshire CID

Others:

Daisy Moore – pathologist
Mike Fielding – forensics
Chris Harley – forensic tech
Alys Pugh – victim
Liz Pugh – Alys' mother
Gareth Pugh – Alys' father
Iola Young – Alys' friend

Macsen Lloyd – Alys' boyfriend
Sammy Miller – Alys' friend
Christie Bailey – Alys' friend
Rhodri Williams – Alys' friend
Jake Ellis – Alys' friend
David Ellis – Jake's father
Vanessa Evans – Jake's mother
Ethan Steward – Jake's friend
Shaun Jones – Jake's friend
Cerith Ryan – speed dater

If you enjoyed this book, please let others know by leaving a quick review on Amazon. Also, if you spot anything untoward in the paperback, get in touch. We strive for the best quality and appreciate reader feedback.

editor@thebookfolks.com

Also in this series:

THE SILENT QUARRY (Book 1)

Following a fall and a bang to the head, a woman's memories come flooding back about an incident that occurred twenty years ago in which her friend was murdered. As she pieces together the events and tells the police, she begins to fear repercussions. DI Winter Meadows must work out the identity of the killer before they strike again.

FROZEN MINDS (Book 2)

When the boss of a care home for mentally challenged adults is murdered, the residents are not the most reliable of witnesses. DI Winter Meadows draws on his soft nature to gain the trust of an individual he believes saw the crime. But without unravelling the mystery and finding the evidence, the case will freeze over.

SUFFER THE CHILDREN (Book 3)

When a toddler goes missing from the family home, the police and community come out in force to find her. However, with few traces found after an extensive search, DI Winter Meadows fears the child has been abducted. But someone knows something, and when a man is found dead, the race is on to solve the puzzle.

A KNOT OF SPARROWS (Book 4)

When local teenage troublemaker and ne'er-do-well Stacey Evans is found dead, locals in a small Welsh village couldn't give a monkey's. That gives nice guy cop DI Winter Meadows a headache. Can he win over their trust and catch a killer in their midst?

LIES OF MINE (Book 5)

A body is found in an old mine in a secluded spot in the Welsh hills. There are no signs of struggle so DI Winter Meadows suspects that the victim, youth worker David Harris, knew his killer. But when the detective discovers it is not the first murder in the area, he must dig deep to join up the dots.

RISE TO THE FLY (Book 6)

When the bodies of a retired couple are found by a reservoir, the police are concerned to discover fishing flies have been impaled on their tongues. After they find nothing in the couple's past to indicate a reason for the murder, they begin to look local. What will they turn up in this dark and secluded corner of Wales?

WINTER'S CRY (Book 7)

When a farmer clears some trees from a field, he unearths a corpse. Suspicion immediately falls upon the neighbouring commune, a collection of makeshift huts and tents which house a reclusive group of people. Having grown up there, DI Winter Meadows goes to talk to its members, who are wary of the police. But what he finds will have him questioning everything he knows about his past.

All available FREE *with Kindle Unlimited and in paperback.*

More fiction by the author:

BLUE HOLLOW

When a family friend is murdered, a journalist begins to probe into his past. What she finds there makes her question everything about her life. Should she bury his secrets with him, or become the next victim of Blue Hollow?

Printed in Great Britain
by Amazon

28050512R00171